THE BLESSED ISLE

Also by Michael Simms

Poetry Collections

Strange Meadowlark
Nightjar
American Ash
Black Stone
The Happiness of Animals
The Fire-eater
Migration
Notes on Continuing Light

Novels

Bicycles of the Gods: A Divine Comedy
The Talon Trilogy:
The Green Mage, the First Chronicle
Windkeep, the Second Chronicle
The Blessed Isle, the Third Chronicle

Nonfiction

Longman Dictionary of Poetic Terms (Jack Myers)
Longman Dictionary and Handbook of Poetry, (with Jack Myers)

Anthologies Edited

The Autumn House Anthology of Contemporary American Poetry
O. Henry's Texas Stories

THE BLESSED ISLE

Being the Third Chronicle of Tessia Dragonqueen
as recorded by Norbert Oldfoot, the Green Mage
later known as Norbert Dragonheart the Merciful

Michael Simms

MADVILLE
PUBLISHING

Lake Dallas, Texas

Printed in the United States of America

FIRST EDITION

The Blessed Isle: The Third Chronicle of Tessia Dragonqueen is a work of fiction. Names, characters, places, and incidents are entirely products of the author's imagination. Any resemblance to actual events, locales, businesses, companies, or persons, living or dead, is entirely coincidental.

Permissions
Madville Publishing
P.O. Box 358
Lake Dallas, TX 75065

Author Photograph: Eva-Maria Simms
Cover Design: Andrew Dunn
Cover Art: Andrew Dunn
Maps: Jacqueline Davis

ISBN: 978-1-963695-09-0 paperback, 978-1-963695-10-6 ebook
Library of Congress Control Number: 2024941181

for Eva

Prologue

Mnuurluth walked through the battlefield, not bothering to step over bodies and not worrying that blood was splattering on his immaculate, human-hide boots. He could not be seen, only sensed, by the dying men. They felt him as a gust of cold air on their faces, ice in their guts, a feeling of immense loneliness, a fear worse than the pain of their wounds. Some of them called for their mothers, others felt regret over lost love or ruined friendships. All of them wished for a few more days to say what they had always needed to say to the people they loved. Lord Death reveled in the pain and fear. Only here, in the midst of mass slaughter, was he truly happy, truly himself.

He leaned down and touched the blood on a man's face, lifted a drop to his lips and tasted its metallic undertone. He looked up at the dozens of dragons flying overhead, breathing fire and swooping down to rake their claws over the scattered men who still stood, trying to aim their giant crossbows, the ballistas, but the bolts flew in wild arcs and did little damage. And he noticed one dragon, Tyrmiss, who carried two riders, the woman known as Queen Tessia, the archer, and the man known as Norbert the Green Mage, who was throwing fireballs at the soldiers below. These two Lord Death knew well. He had been following their careers for twenty years. They were currently his best suppliers of the dead, vendors to Lord Death, sending scores into the underworld covered in slashes and puncture wounds with scorched and charred skin from the fire of battle. These two, who fancied themselves warriors for the good and true, had become two of his favorites. They would be visiting him soon, and he would welcome them as honored guests.

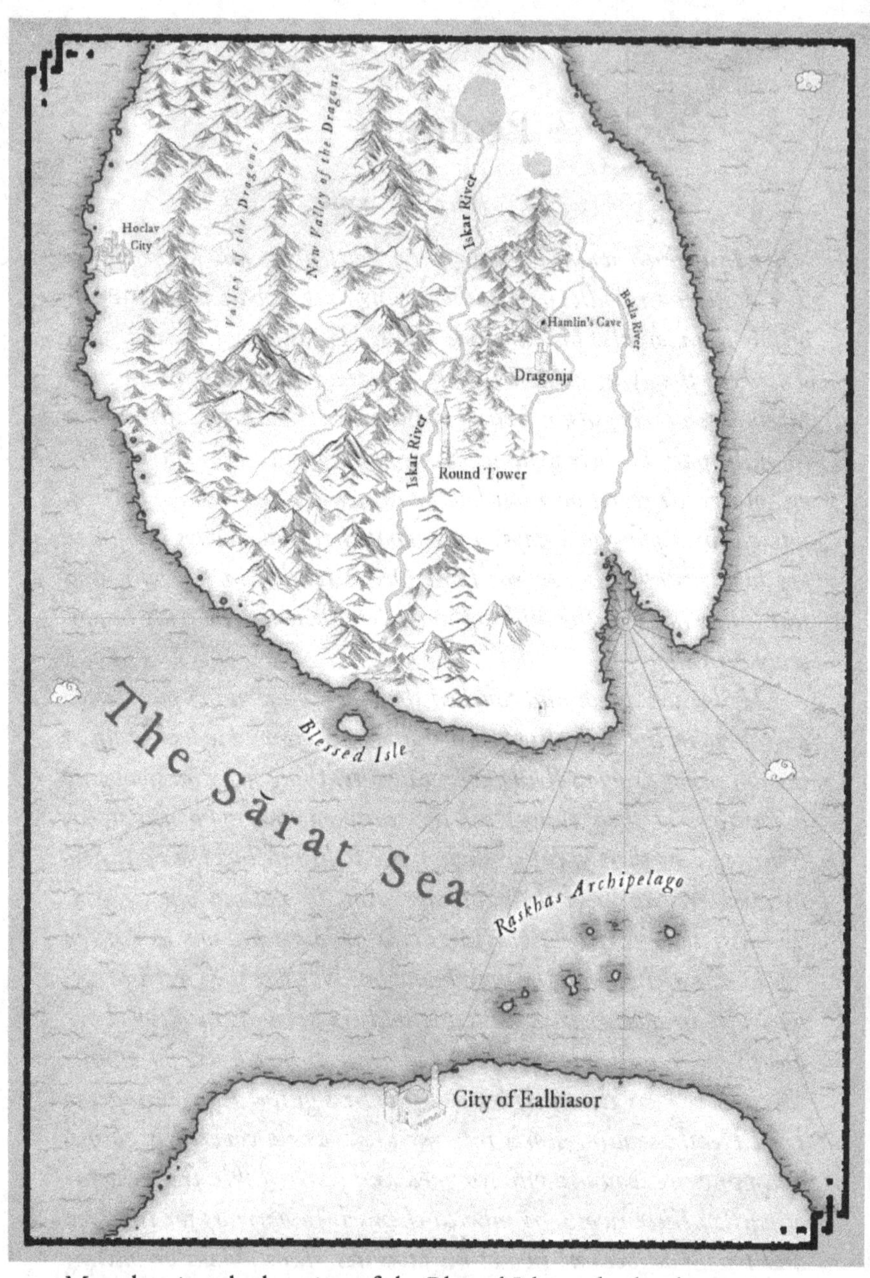

Map showing the location of the Blessed Isle, and other key points.

Part One: The School for Mages

Chapter One

After dismissing my students, I sat on a windowsill of the old stone tower where the School for Mages was housed. My perch looked out on a lovely summer day beyond the curtain wall surrounding Windkeep, and beyond that, I could survey the town of Dragonja—the market square where I'd first met my wife Idella selling her loaves, the Silver Pony Inn where I had played my songs in the tavern while Tessia, now Queen Tessia, worked as a serving wench, and the alleys where my stepson Alaric had spent months living by his wits among the ruffians and thieves during the war against the wizard Ludek.

Bringing my gaze back to Windkeep Castle, I could see the High Tower where the queen held court and where she and her wife Princess Kana had their quarters. The dragon lair she'd built for Tyrmiss had been empty for a dozen years, but Tessia kept the lair exactly as the dragon had left it. I never asked whether Tessia preserved the lair as a memorial to the dragon and all she'd done for us, or whether she expected Tyrmiss to return someday. I knew that some questions were better left unasked.

"Is this the way you spend your time now, Mage?" a familiar voice behind me asked. "Looking out the window and thinking about the old days?"

I turned and saw the queen. She wore a purple blouse embroidered with yellow blossoms and black leggings that showed off her long legs and slim hips. Black leather boots covered her ankles, and she wore a simple gold necklace and a silver diadem around her braided black hair. The crown and jewelry were a conciliatory gesture to her ministers who insisted she display her rank. The people, they said, want their queen to look like a queen. If it were up to her, she would wear a man's tunic, riding breeches and dung-covered boots at all times, including at court.

Since two heavily armed Drekavac members of the Queen's Guard stood behind her, I bowed my head and greeted her formally, "Your Majesty."

She dismissed the guards with a wave of her hand, and after they'd gone, she came over and hugged me fiercely. "Norbert, it's been months since I've seen you. Where have you been?"

I felt my face flush, as the magic of long-held friendship brought a smile to my face. I said, "I've been here teaching and writing, and I've been working in my orchard at home. I often think of you sitting at court, listening to petitions and meeting foreign dignitaries, but that's not my place anymore."

She rolled her eyes. "I miss seeing you, though." She played at stamping her foot and smiled back at me. "But I understand. You feel ill-suited to be a retainer in the queen's court." Her smile twisted to one of chagrin, then she abruptly changed the subject and said, "How's Idella?"

"Idella is well. The bakery is busy."

"How many ovens does she have now?"

"Twenty-five! Can you believe it? She needs seven assistants to keep them all going."

"The bread and pastries are as delicious as always. Please thank her for sending fresh bread to the High Tower every day."

"I'll tell her, Tessia."

"I see Alaric often, but I suppose you know that." My stepson had become her chief advisor on defense and also served as head of the Queen's Guard. "He's been marvelous in overseeing the rebuilding of the North Gate," Tessia said. She gazed distractedly out the window.

"Yes, he told us. We're very proud of him." I wondered why Tessia had come. She had never been one for small talk.

"And Ena?" Tessia asked, as if working her way down a list of social niceties.

"She's still studying here in the Mage's School." Tessia knew all this. I waited for her to get to the point.

"She always had a gift for magic. Obviously, she takes after her father," Tessia said, then caught herself, and an awkward silence rose between us. In fact, my brother Ludek, whom I had killed before Ena was born, was her natural father. Tessia had always known, but Ena had been told only recently. Ludek, as I had been reminded many times when I was a child, was a much more talented wizard than I would ever be, and Ena had inherited Ludek's talent.

"She learns new spells very quickly. She was born for this kind of work," I said, pushing aside the thoughts of my brother.

"How old is she now?" Tessia asked.

"Eighteen summers," I said, growing impatient, but in the spirit of polite conversation, I asked, "And how is Princess Kana?"

"She's well." Tessia nodded. "She wants to renovate our living quarters, but I'm not comfortable spending the people's money on our personal needs. Besides, the expenditure would have to be approved by the Citizens Council, and you know they hate to spend money on us."

"Not like the old days, eh?"

"No, it isn't."

We were both silent as we recalled how the queen's first wife, Taja, and her former finance minister, Caz, had merrily spent gold from the treasury to satisfy her expensive tastes. We laughed, but there was a bitter edge to our laughter. The two traitors had absconded with gold from the royal treasury and fled to another country. And that was one of the reasons a new constitution had been instated, giving control of the kingdom's finances to the Council.

Tessia and I stood face to face, smiling awkwardly. A silence stretched between us. I let the awkwardness grow.

"I heard a rumor that Tyrmiss has been spotted in the Nordtoppen," she finally blurted out.

It was news to me. We hadn't heard anything about Tyrmiss for twelve years. Tessia and I had watched her fly off into the mists over the Nordtoppen Mountains, her dragonlings, Rozae and Banos, trailing close behind.

"Were Rozae and Banos with her?" I asked, once I'd recovered from the initial surprise.

Tessia raised her shoulders, but looked at her hands. "I don't know."

"Who saw them?"

"A hunter crossing the pass between the Two Thumbs of the Giant."

"He must have been close to Hamlin's cave," I said.

"Have you seen Hamlin lately?" Tessia asked.

I nodded. "A few months ago. Alaric and I visited him. He still seems happy living as a bear—probably happier than he ever was as a man."

Tessia turned toward the window, her eyes welling up. Hamlin had been her childhood friend, but during the war, Ludek's soldiers had tortured him for a month. He was never himself afterwards. Then, in a magical mishap in which I turned several of our friends into beasts, Hamlin had become a bear. When he was given the chance to be transformed back to his original human form, he refused.

"Do you think that Tyrmiss has truly returned?" I asked.

"I think so, Norbert."

I had to ask the question: "Have you felt her in your dreams yet, Tessia?"

Tessia held my gaze and nodded slowly. "Yes. Have you?"

"Not yet," I said. "But your connection with Tyrmiss was always stronger than mine."

"I love Tyrmiss," Tessia said. "So, I don't know why I feel so disturbed at the idea that she's returned. I hope nothing has happened to Rozae and Banos."

Again, I looked out the window at the town and the towers, but everything seemed different now—less solid, more vulnerable. Tyrmiss had left the world of humans because she wanted to raise her dragonlings in a world less violent, less corrupt than ours. If she had come back to the world of men, something must have gone terribly wrong. There was only one reason Tyrmiss would come back here. She needed our help.

As I often did, I stopped by the Silver Pony on my way home. The tavern was empty except for Heikum who stood behind the bar, washing tankards from the noon rush.

He looked at me as I entered and without so much as a greeting, he said, "Is it true the dragon has returned?"

"Well, that's a fine way to greet an old friend," I said. "And a fare thee well to you too."

Heikum was in no mood for banter. He stared silently at me from beneath his bushy brow and lifted his hand to stroke his salt-and-pepper beard. It was clear he wasn't going to pour me an ale until I told him what I knew.

"It's just a rumor, Heikum," I said at last, worried I was breaking a confidence with Tessia. But, I rationalized, it couldn't be a secret if people were already talking about it in the inn.

"What did you hear?" The stocky landlord asked, holding a tankard under the spigot and letting it fill slowly with a minimum of froth, the way he knew I liked it.

"I heard that a hunter saw Tyrmiss flying over the Iskar Valley," I said, taking the tankard from his hand and draining half of it in one draught.

Femke, Heikum's wife, came out of the kitchen and stood beside me. She'd been listening to our conversation.

"Why would the dragon return to Dragonja after all this time?" she asked.

"I have no idea," I said, finishing off the tankard of ale and putting a copper coin on the bar. "But I'm sure we'll find out."

At home, Idella was waking from her nap. As a baker, she rose early in the morning to oversee her assistants, and then spent the morning in town with them delivering bread and pastries to the High Tower and the inns. Whatever was left they sold in the market square. By noon, Idella was exhausted, so she came home to sleep before Ena and I got home from school.

Walking into the kitchen, the first thing she asked was, "Is it true that Tyrmiss is back?"

By the Holy Hem, I thought, *has everyone heard this rumor?*

"I know as much about it as you do, my darling," I said, kissing her on the cheek. For a moment I closed my eyes and breathed her in, her ebony skin, the ringlets of her hair, her long fingers—strong from kneading bread—her tall regal posture. I wondered, as I did every day, how I deserved such a woman in my life.

Idella laid out thick slabs of bread, a small pot of honey, and some slices of apple for me then sat down beside me. "There's something we need to discuss," she said to me in her most serious tone.

I thought, *uh oh, what have I done now.*

"I'm sorry," I blurted out pre-emptively.

Idella's eyes narrowed suspiciously, "Why, what have you done?"

"Nothing," I said quickly. "I thought you were going to tell me what I'd done wrong, and I just wanted to apologize before things got out of hand."

Idella waved her hand dismissively. "You haven't done anything wrong, Norbert. We need to talk about Ena."

Panic rose in me. "Is she pregnant?"

"No, no." My wife was starting to sound exasperated. "She wants to move out."

"She wants to move out?" I repeated. "Why? Isn't she happy here? We provide her with a very comfortable life."

Her brow furrowed, and she looked hard into my eyes. "Yes, maybe too comfortable. Norbert, she's eighteen summers now. Her best friend got married last year, and Ena feels it's time to start her own life."

"Where does she want to go?"

"At first, she'll take a room at the Silver Pony. Heikum has offered her a job."

"As a serving wench?" I felt anger rising in me. "I just came from the Silver Pony and Heikum never mentioned he'd hired Ena."

"Well, maybe he thought Ena should talk to you first."

"No daughter of mine is going to work as a serving wench!"

"Stop yelling, Norbert. She's old enough to make her own decisions, and there's really nothing you can do to stop her. She wants to discuss it with you as a sign of respect for her father. You need to give her your blessing on this decision because otherwise, it will become a serious problem between you."

I knew she was right. I had no authority over my daughter. She was a grown woman who could do as she pleased. Still, I puzzled over the way things could change so quickly in a man's life. That morning, I began as a contented scholar and teacher, and this evening, my daughter was planning to be a serving wench and live above a tavern.

And Tyrmiss had returned. But why?

"Here's the thing about magic, the great secret which is actually not a secret except that most people don't believe it. It's a secret hiding in plain sight," I said, looking at the eager faces of my first-year students.

"Everything in the world works perfectly well by itself. The Goddess has created a world where trees and fish and animals thrive without our help. It's only in the world of humans that what we call *magic* plays a role. The Goddess doesn't need our help, but sometimes men and women do, or at least we think they do.

"If we let a field grow by itself, the Goddess will produce a variety of herbs and grasses that thrive on that plot. It's only when we remove what she has planted and replace it with, say, barley corn that we need to bless the field. And blessing the field is really nothing more than asking the Goddess to allow our efforts to thrive. So, a magical incantation, in this case a blessing, is a form of prayer. You must never forget that as mages we serve the Goddess. We do *not* serve kings or queens."

A boy in the front row with a face full of freckles raised his hand, "What about the time you tried to kill your brother, the evil wizard Ludek, by dropping a wooden beam on his head? Were you serving the Goddess then?"

"How did you know about that?" I asked, more sharply than I intended.

He looked sheepishly at the floor. "Some of the second-years were talking the other day."

I've never understood why innocent boys fresh from their mothers' homes are fascinated by war. People who have actually been to war, such as Tessia and I, are haunted by memories. More than once, I'd been called in the middle of the night to the Queen's chambers by servants terrified by her rants and hallucinations. In her dreams, she saw the men she'd killed lined up at the Shore of Reckoning, calling her name, just as the old scrolls describe. War, despite what boys think, is not a game of heroics, but a vile poison we should recoil from. More than once, I'd held poor Tessia, my dear friend, in my arms as she relived the horrors of war. A sleeping potion helped her get through the night, but nothing would ever salve her conscience. As for me,

I often woke in the middle of the night seeing my brother's face in the moment he realized he was about to die.

Coming back to the present, I realized that I had been staring at one of my students in anger, and the rest of the class was silently waiting for me to lash out at him. I took a steadying breath and said, "Never mind, son. We'll talk about war and violence later in the year. Tomorrow we will continue to talk about the *proper* uses of magic."

A girl in the front row with buck teeth that made her surprisingly beautiful raised her hand. "When do we start learning spells?" she asked.

"You'll start learning spells after you learn what spells are for," I countered.

She looked at me with a thousand questions on her face, but she was a long way from being a mage, and probably few, if any, of these first-years would ever be able to practice magic beyond the most basic spells. But the truth is that it wasn't my job to teach these youngsters how to cast spells—although that was usually why their families had apprenticed them to me. Instead, it was my responsibility to teach them how to be enlightened men and women. The only magic worth learning is the magic the Goddess creates every day for every living thing. This was the principle these new students needed to learn before they ever picked up a wand.

I normally went to the Silver Pony for a bowl of Femke's soup at midday, but today I would have to skip my accustomed meal because there was a Citizens Council meeting in the tall tower. As a Council member who represented the small but growing Guild of Mages, I needed to attend the meeting, rumbling stomach and all.

A guard opened the heavy oaken door for me, and I entered the wide hall where Queen Tessia presided over one hundred council members, half men, half women. Resolutions and laws were passed by a simple majority with the queen voting only to break a tie. When there were disagreements between members, it tended to be over economic issues. For example, farmers and herdsmen wanted their animals to have access to the river, while fishermen wanted the river to be clean and free of manure, so agreements needed to be hammered out about when and where animals could drink. Then there were the copper miners in the mountains who wanted protection from bandits, but the soldiers disliked being assigned to the mining camps, so duty rosters had to be rotated, extra leave time being given to soldiers who volunteered to guard the mines, and the expense had to be covered by taxes assessed on the value of the smelted copper.

Nothing was ever simple. Three years before, sex work had been legalized. The reasoning was that the unmarried Drekavac soldiers were going to be serviced by sex workers anyway, and it was better to have it legally regulated rather than allowing women to be forced into it. And there were women who had been raped and would not be able to find husbands, and this was a way for them to be self-sufficient. What we didn't foresee was that once we passed a law legalizing sex work, then we had to pass laws to protect sex workers and their clients from disease. Then we had to pass more laws to protect the women and boys from violence. Then these laws needed to be enforced, so money had to be allocated to pay soldiers to protect the workers. As legislators, we were becoming aware that if we passed a law then other laws needed to be passed to enforce the law, and then more laws to deal with the unintended effects of the laws.

As a member of council, I represented the interests of mages and witches, but I usually remained silent during the debates, as did Tessia unless they involved foreign relations, the military, or law enforcement—her domains.

Generally, the system worked reasonably well, for which we could thank Tyrmiss the dragon, who, as a final gift to the kingdom, dictated the laws, then allowed us to discuss, debate and amend them as we saw fit.

As I walked into the council chamber, I realized that the topic under discussion was, not surprisingly, the assumed arrival of Tyrmiss after her twelve-year absence. Farmers were worried she might prey upon their sheep and cattle, so they had to be assured that their livestock were safe because Tyrmiss ate only fish and venison. The Drekavac militia who guarded the countryside expressed concern their warriors would be attacked—not unreasonable considering how many Drekavacs Tyrmiss had killed in the days of Ludek's rule.

Much less reasonable was the argument by one councilman, a married man known as a frequent patron of sex workers. "Shouldn't we be concerned," he asked in a voice that dripped insincerity. "That the dragon, being able to read people's dreams, will use the information to blackmail upstanding citizens and destroy marriages?"

At this display of overt hypocrisy, Tessia caught my eye and suppressed a smile. Why is it that the politicians who speak loudest in favor of marriage and family values are always the worst spouses? Fortunately, the other council members ignored his hypocritical attempt to uphold family values.

I was pleased to see Princess Kana sitting on her throne beside the Queen. Kana, as she insisted I call her when we were alone, had brought a welcome influence to the kingdom. Whereas her predecessor Princess Taja had been a beautiful aloof figure whose golden hair and regal height struck awe in anyone who saw her, Princess Kana was a warm and slightly plump woman whom everyone liked. If needed, Kana could dress up for formal occasions. Right now, for example, she was resplendent in a light-yellow gown that set off her olive skin and black hair. But on most days, Kana wore a simple belted dress typical of the farmgirl she once was, and you were more likely to find her in the kitchen overseeing the evening meal than in the stateroom entertaining dignitaries.

Idella and I were pleased to have introduced Tessia and Kana. The daughter of a prosperous farmer, Kana had been working in Idella's bakery when the queen stopped by for an inspection—a formal duty the queen performed at regular intervals to show support for local businesses. As the Queen walked by, I saw Kana catch her eye before looking down in respectful submission. Tessia had responded with a small secret smile. The signal, no doubt missed by everyone except Idella and me, was subtle but clear. Later, Kana was invited for dinner at the High Tower of Windkeep Castle.

After the marriage, Princess Kana had taken over the huge responsibility of managing the royal household with an enthusiasm the dozen members of the staff had never seen before. The kitchen became a matter of special attention by the princess, and as a result, the High Tower had become Idella's best customer, and the two women had become close friends.

As for Tessia, I was glad to see that a bad first marriage had not embittered her. She was never one to hold onto the past, which was fortunate for me since I had made many mistakes in our long friendship. For example, once I accidentally turned her into a dragon with the head of a lion. But Tessia generously let bygones be bygones, realizing that sometimes magic spells have a will of their own.

Kana was listening carefully and approvingly as her wife, Queen Tessia, addressed the council.

"Dear friends and neighbors," Tessia began. "It is not for nothing you call me the Dragonqueen. Tyrmiss was my best friend in the time of wars. She carried me into battle in the revolution that overthrew the evil wizard Ludek. She flew me to the land of Sheonad to take captive the weather witches." At this, she nodded to the witches Evanora and Zamarrra, who were now important allies of the kingdom although neither Tessia nor I completely trusted them. "And I rode the dragon against King Kazko of Osterbo when he kidnapped Tyrmiss's baby dragonlings. I was present, as most of you were, when the dragon Tyrmiss first dictated the new constitution that established this Council as the ruling body of the kingdom.

"It is not an exaggeration to say that without Tyrmiss's wisdom and courage, this kingdom would not exist as a free and independent nation. So, it is with great concern that I hear members of this council talk about the dragon Tyrmiss as if she were an enemy to be feared, rather than a friend to be welcomed. If the rumors are to be believed that Tyrmiss is nearby, then we should welcome her as the guardian of this kingdom. We should treat her with the respect and gratitude she has earned. I do not know why she would return to this kingdom, but if she has, it may be to ask us for help. And if this is the case, then we owe it to her to listen and give her what aid we can."

As Tessia sat down on her throne, she shot me a glance which I knew was my cue to speak.

I rose to my feet. "Esteemed members of the council," I said, speaking loud enough to hear my words echo from the rafters of the great hall. "Our queen has spoken the truth. The dragon saved us more than once against our enemies and taught us how to live together in peace. I, too, know the Dragon Tyrmiss. The queen and I have at times bonded our thoughts with hers. We know her to be brave and honest. If the dragon comes here and asks for a favor from the kingdom, we are honor-bound to grant her request if we are able."

The hall was quiet. Then Queen Tessia proposed a resolution to welcome the dragon Tyrmiss as an honored guest if she arrived in our kingdom, and the resolution passed unanimously.

Chapter Two

After the council meeting, I went to the Dungeon—a cavern beneath the stone tower—where my second-year students waited. These students had begun learning potions and spells, and if their inexperience with magic caused a disaster, then the thick cave walls would, in theory, prevent innocent citizens from being hurt.

The students had completed their first year under my tutelage, so they were familiar with the philosophical and ethical issues which constituted the foundation of magical studies, at least in the way I taught it. Most students, of course, never completed the first year because they found these issues boring; they just wanted to learn a few tricks that would impress their friends or make them money. I sent these students off with no hard feelings; after all, philosophy is not for everyone, but teaching students how to influence the world through magic without their understanding the purpose of magic is a recipe for disaster. I had seen in my brother Ludek what could happen to a gifted magician who never learned to respect the Goddess, and I wasn't going to be responsible for creating another wizard who lusted for power.

In the second year, the students started with healing potions, a practical skill that they, most of whom had grown up on farms or small villages, could learn easily. From a young age, they'd been helping their mothers and grandmothers gather edible greens, seeds, and berries from the fields and had learned to spot the small clues that made the difference between enjoying a salad and vomiting on the dinner table. They were well aware, for example, that the red berry of a yew tree is poisonous, but the red currant which it resembles is nutritious. This kind of knowledge had been passed down through the generations, and I tried to build on the young people's existing skills. I taught them to how to find yarrow and prepare the leaves as a poultice to help wounds heal, and how to prepare a tea from the yarrow root to lessen the despair that comes over new mothers.

Today's lesson focused on the potion made by mixing an infusion of the leafy river creeper with a small amount of ground semoseed, a rare spice imported from the East. This mixture was combined with the spore of an appeath mushroom.

"Isn't that mushroom poisonous?" one of the students asked. "It grows in the woods near our house, and my grandmother told me never to touch it."

"Your grandmother is right, of course," I said, nodding to him encouragingly. "Grandmothers usually are. But the semoseed neutralizes the poison."

Once the mixture was complete, I decanted it into small clay cups which I distributed to the six students. They looked at the dark liquid in the cups suspiciously.

"What is this going to do to us?" asked one of the young women whose name was Cleamine or Cleatis… or something. It was a constant source of embarrassment to me that after years of teaching hundreds of students, I had given up learning most of their names, a failure which puzzled me because I knew the names of thousands of plants and could recite hundreds of spells in ancient languages. Yet, somehow, the many Helmuts and Heathers had blurred together in an endless parade of youthful faces and adolescent dramas. Nevertheless, I tried to be kind to them, and every now and then, a student came along who showed real talent and passion.

"Are we supposed to drink this?" one of the Heathers asked.

"Is this going to turn me into a frog?" one of the Helmuts asked.

"That would be an improvement," his buddy, also named Helmut, cracked.

I raised my eyebrows and looked at both of them in a slightly disapproving way, and they, having been properly raised by their hard-working no-nonsense mothers and their stern strong fathers, straightened their backs, and wiped the grins off their faces.

"You do not have to drink the potion," I said. "In fact, you should never drink a potion or give a potion to someone else which you are suspicious of. However, I have consumed this potion many times and I've prescribed it to other people, and I have never seen an adverse effect. Instead, the effect is mild and fleeting." I paused to create suspense and looked around at the students to make sure they were paying attention. "The effect of this potion is that it makes you smarter."

I let excitement ripple through the room, lifted my cup in the air and downed the shot of elixir. Then I looked at one of the Helmuts, whose name I suddenly remembered was actually Tamás Bertalan, and I recited his family's history in the valley. "Your great-great-grandfather, Egyed Bertalan, emigrated to the Bekla Valley from a southern fishing village after his brother drowned at sea," I intoned. "Not wanting to suffer his brother's fate, Egyed started working as a farm hand. His son Jónás, your great-grandfather, fought in the Great War against the Drekavacs and brought home enough plundered silver to buy a farm in the Bekla Valley. His son, your grandfather, expanded the farm downriver and become wealthy. But your father, Varga, who had been a younger son, and therefore did not inherit, learned the trade of leatherworking and is now a respected craftsman who on Saturdays sells his trade goods in the market square."

The boy was flabbergasted that I could spiel off his family history so easily, but I felt the effects of the elixir wearing off, so I had to change tacks.

"Now, if you wish to, you may drink the elixir and then pair off. I want you to impress each other with how much you know."

Every student lifted a cup and drank, then turned to another student and started talking. The room filled with excited babble, a bedlam of astronomical tables, family histories, folk poems, and songs in foreign languages. One boy was actually speaking in Minnimaic, a language even Drekavacs no longer spoke. Then, after a few moments, the room grew quiet and the students, stunned, looked at each other. A few had tears in their eyes.

"Wha… what happened, Professor?" one of the Heathers asked.

"You just found out how much your minds hold that you are usually unaware of. This discovery may make you feel sorrow," I answered, nodding at a girl in the front row whose bottom lip was trembling.

"C-can we take this elixir every d-day?" she asked.

"No, no," I responded quickly. "As Tamás pointed out, the elixir is slightly poisonous. Let your body cleanse itself. You don't want to take the elixir again for at least a month."

"Will you give us another dose in a month?" she persisted.

"We'll see," I said, seeing that her fascination with the elixir could become a problem. As the Goddess teaches us, *never encourage excess.*

My afternoon class was followed by a meeting with my two post-graduate students, my daughter Ena and her friend Adamu, each of whom had shown exceptional ability after formally studying magic for five years.

We started with a prayer to the Goddess asking for wisdom in using her gifts. I prayed only with the advanced students. Praying with the apprentices would have been a waste of effort because they had not yet experienced the Ecstasy. Given time, some of them may eventually have a true connection with the Goddess, and then they would be ready for the real work of being a mage. Until then, they were being trained to go back to their farms and villages to bless the fields and tend the ill and injured—important work, of course, and I'd traveled the Bekla Valley for years doing those very tasks, but now I was exploring new ways to use magic, and I was grateful to have young companions to help me.

Most afternoons I met with Ena and Adamu in the top floor of the High Tower because I wanted to make clear to these two talented young people that they were no longer students, but mages in their own right. Clearly, they were proud of their growing skills. However, this morning Ena seemed uncomfortable when I looked at her. *Good*, I thought, in the mild indifference to discomfort so many fathers specialize in. She and I had not yet had a chance to talk about her desire to work for Heikum as a serving wench at the Silver Pony. I thought that perhaps a little anticipatory discomfort was a good thing for her to experience, and then I caught myself. *Oh no, I'm acting like my father. Stop it, you fool. Be kind, Norbert, be kind.*

I smiled at my daughter, which seemed to relax her slightly. *She is so beautiful*, I thought. She reminded me so much of my mother, who died when I was a child. Ena's red hair spilled over her shoulders in a lush cascade, and her freckles, which she hated, covered her face when she spent time in the summer sun. I suspected that she and Adamu were more than just classmates, judging by the way he looked at her, but she had not deigned to tell me about their relationship. I wanted to know, of course, but was afraid of the answer, so I didn't ask. *Ah*, as the poet says, *an only daughter is the needle of the heart.*

She and Adamu were the same age. *When did eighteen become so young?* I wondered. He was a tall dark boy (*Was he a man yet?* I wasn't sure) from a small village downriver from

Dragonja City. His father was a weaver, a quiet deliberate man who was very proud that his son was training to be a wizard. *A mage,* I kept reminding him, we don't allow wizards in the kingdom. After being ruled by my evil brother Ludek for years, the kingdom had had enough of wizards.

One thing I liked about working with the two of them was that they approached magic from very different perspectives. Ena was the practical one. She could mix potions and cast spells almost as well as I could. Invisibility spells, healing potions and truth charms gave her no problems at all. She even discovered spells on her own. I remember years ago, I walked behind our house to the rocky hill to gather minerals and came across her, no more than a wisp of a girl, holding a hickory wand which she must have cut and enchanted herself. With the wand, she was throwing small fireballs, not much larger than sparks, at a boulder. She had heard somewhere that I had protected the queen in the last war by throwing much larger fireballs at Drekavacs attacking her. My enterprising daughter had sequestered herself in the royal archives in the castle and found the spell in an old manuscript. I watched her for a while, but she was concentrating on mastering the spell and didn't notice me. I never mentioned the incident to her because it was obvious she wanted to master magic on her own, as every mage ultimately has to.

Adamu, on the other hand, was merely competent at practical magic. He could mix an elixir or make a sack of coins look like laundry well enough, but his real strength was in philosophy. When Ena and Adamu went to the archives together, she looked for spells she could master while he collected ancient prayers and songs. Evidently, he'd experienced the Ecstasy at a young age, and it had changed him, as it normally does. He'd never told me how the epiphany happened, but when I first met him, he had seen no more than eleven summers, and yet I saw a light in his eyes. It was as if the Goddess looked out from this boy. There are ancient stories about gods and goddesses who want to experience the world as a human, and he, I surmised, was one the Goddess had chosen as her vessel. But being chosen by a god makes a person ill-suited for human society. Sometimes, when Adamu spoke, it was as if his voice was coming from far away, and often he sat in the corner of our tower room, looking out the window at the river stretching down the green valley, talking to himself in a faraway voice.

When I first met Adamu's father, the old weaver pulled me aside and asked if I knew why his son was so odd. "An excellent worker," his man said. Then he tapped his head, "But he may be slightly touched."

I assured the man that his son was not possessed, but gifted, and he would become a respected mage. His father beamed at me, and from then on, always treated his son with gentle respect and encouragement. A good father wants his son to exceed him.

"Let's take another look at the plans for the new aqueduct," I said to my two young colleagues.

Ena unrolled the long vellum where the detailed schematics of the watercourse were laid out. One of the instructions Tyrmiss the Dragon had given the council before she left was to build a wooden aqueduct to bring fresh water from the mountains. At the time, people were getting sick from drinking river water. The aqueduct had served the city well for twelve years, but now it had become rotten and leaky in places. Because the city often had no fresh water, people were getting sick from drinking river water again, so the council had asked the court mages, that is Ena, Adamu, and me, to design a stone aqueduct which would replace the wooden one.

Adamu was squinting at a specific place in the design. He seemed troubled.

"What is it?" I asked.

"The angle of the water flow here," he said, putting his finger on the schematic, "where we've planned to build a bridge for the aqueduct to cross the gorge, is too acute. The water is going to slow down here and spill out of the channel. In the spring when the mountain snow is melting, we are going to lose a third of the water in spillage."

Ena looked at Adamu, looked back at the drawing, then looked back at him, smiling. She loved his intelligence. She and I had learned to trust his intuitive calculations.

"What's the solution?" I asked, looking from Adamu to Ena.

"We could make the walls of the channel higher, so the water doesn't spill," Ena suggested.

Adamu squinted his deep-set eyes, did a quick calculation and responded, "That would make the aqueduct very heavy in that spot over the gorge, increasing the danger to the construction workers by creating an unstable structure. The aqueduct will be made of stone, so we need to use as little material as possible."

"What's another solution?" I asked.

"We could flatten the slope slightly uphill from the gorge and deepen the slope slightly downhill, so the water flows more quickly," Ena said, giving the problem another try.

"Yes," Adamu said. "A slight change in the angle would solve the problem."

Ena beamed. It was important to her that Adamu respected her ideas, but she knew that he was too honest to patronize her. If he thought she was wrong, he would say so.

"Good, make the adjustments on the vellum," I said, amazed at the brilliance of my two assistants. "I'd like to take the plans to the queen tomorrow. If she approves them, we'll present them to the Citizens Council at their next meeting."

Ena, Adamu and I had been working on the aqueduct design for months, so we were excited to be close to finishing it.

"We need to start planning for the actual construction. Have the Blue Witches taught you how to cut and move stone?"

They nodded.

"Any problems you foresee?" I asked.

Adamu looked at Ena before saying, "It's actually not very complicated. Just three spells: cutting, cracking, and lifting."

"The weight of the stone is not a problem?" I asked.

"If all three of us are casting the lifting spell at the same time, we should be able to handle the blocks of stone easily," Ena said.

"All right, then," I said, smiling. "Barring any silly politics from the Council members, we should be able to start the new aqueduct in a few weeks."

As Ena was rolling up the vellum, I asked Adamu whether he would like to join us for dinner.

"I'm sorry, sir," he said, glancing at Ena. "I've made other plans. Perhaps another time."

Ena looked at me. I knew that look. She was struggling with wanting but not wanting to have a serious talk with me.

"That's fine, Adamu," I said. "Ena and I have a few things to discuss anyway."

After the young man left, Ena asked, "Has mom told you I'm planning to move out?"

"Yes," I said, trying to sound neutral in my tone. "She said you plan to move into the Silver Pony. Heikum has offered you a job."

She nodded, then delved into the middle of the issue. "Queen Tessia was only seventeen when the two of you came to Dragonja City. And you both worked at the Silver Pony for months. I'm eighteen, so I'm sure I can handle it."

Of course, my daughter and I both knew we were doing a dance for which there was only one possible outcome. She would be leaving her childhood home to start her own life. Nevertheless, I felt I had to follow the steps one at a time. I was also afraid that if I gave into my fear of her vulnerability, then I would risk poisoning the love and trust between us.

"That was a different time, sweetie," I said. "Tessia's father had been kidnapped by Ludek, and she never knew her mother. Heikum and Femke were the only people we knew in the city. Tessia took the only job available."

"You worked in the Silver Pony as well," Ena pointed out.

"Yes, I did. I entertained the patrons in the tavern by playing my lyre and singing."

I looked at this young woman and saw the little girl I'd carried in my arms years before and felt a strong urge to protect her.

"There are other jobs you could take," I said.

"Like what?"

"You could work as an assistant to your mother. She always needs more hands in the bakery."

"Dad, I've been helping Mom with her business since I was four. It's time for me to find other work."

"Perhaps there's work that I could get for you in the castle. Perhaps, Queen Tessia could take you on as one of her advisors."

"Dad, if you ask Tessia to hire me, she will, because she owes you her life, but it wouldn't be because she needs me. She already has plenty of advisors, including you."

"Working as a serving wench is very rough," I said, shaking my head in disgust. "The men in the tavern will treat you badly. You know what happened to Tessia when she worked as a serving wench at the tavern, don't you?"

"I know, I know," she said, rolling her eyes. She recited the story in a singsong voice, indicating she had heard it a thousand times. "Every evening, men pinched her butt and made jokes about her sexual habits until she finally had enough abuse and hit a drunken patron with a tankard of ale. His friends tried to attack her, and she stood on a table, fighting them off single-handedly until Femke came out of the kitchen with a broom and the two women cleared the bar."

We laughed at the story which had become a legend in the tavern, if not the whole city. Then Ena grew serious. She looked at me with level eyes and said, “Dad, that’s not going to happen to me.”

“Oh, why not? Have drunken men learned to behave themselves in the last twenty years? We have a whole new generation of enlightened men now?”

She laughed. “I doubt that. It’s just that I’m different than Tessia. She is a warrior, and I...”

Obviously, she didn’t want to brag.

“You are a mage,” I said, finishing her sentence.

“Yes,” she said, almost inaudibly. “I am a mage like you.”

“Well, I think you know the ethics of using magic for violence. It is only to be used in defense of yourself or of innocent beings. You should never use a spell against someone for merely being rude to you.”

“You mean I can’t turn a drunken patron into a donkey?”

“From what I’ve seen, most of the patrons in the Silver Inn are already donkeys. It would be nice, though, if you turned them into men.”

My daughter laughed and came into my arms. We both knew that the necessary *pas de deux* was over, and she would soon be leaving home and starting her own life.

Chapter Three

After dinner, Idella and Ena went off to talk about what she would need at the Silver Pony. She would be staying in the same room where Idella and I had sheltered during the wars, a small but pleasant space with a lovely view of Windkeep Castle. I knew she would have to make decisions about which, if any, of her girlish things to take with her. Through the years, she had accumulated a plethora of dolls, figurines, pillows, paintings, and mementos, and leaving behind most of these things would be difficult. I remembered twenty years ago, Tessia showing up at the Silver Pony with nothing more than a change of clothes, extra weapons, and a fierce determination to free her father from prison. But, as my daughter rightly pointed out, she and Tessia were very different people.

I was enjoying my second ale of the evening—which I felt I was entitled to since I'd had to skip my midday meal to attend the Citizens Council meeting—when there was a loud knock at the front door. Since we lived a good walk upriver from the city gates, it was unusual to have unexpected visitors after dark. Idella and Ena stuck their heads out the doorway of the bedroom. Idella's eyes were wide in fear, but Ena's eyes were narrow. I noticed she'd grabbed her wand and was holding it in front of her. I remembered her joke that afternoon about turning a drunken patron into a donkey, and I wondered whether she'd actually discovered a spell to do that very thing in her research.

I unsheathed my wand and held it behind my back as I

opened the door. A Drekavac whom I recognized as a sergeant of the Queen's Guard stood in the moonlight framed by the door.

"Sir Mage," the veteran guard said, "Her Majesty wishes for you and your daughter to come to Windkeep."

"My daughter?" I asked, turning around to look at Ena who shrugged, obviously as puzzled as I was. "Are you sure the Queen wants both me and my daughter?"

"Yes, Mage," he replied firmly. "She was very clear she wanted both of you to come to Windkeep immediately. I am to accompany you."

I invited the Drekavac into our home, but he declined and stationed himself a few steps away from the door.

"I am in the middle of moving, Dad," Ena said. "I'm starting my new job tomorrow."

"I know, but you can't ignore a request from the queen."

Idella and I exchanged a look that spoke more than a library of old scrolls. Whatever this royal request was, it was sure to change our lives forever.

Ena and I followed the Drekavac sergeant down the river road to the East Gate of the city. He spoke briefly to the sentry, and we were let through the narrow door. We walked quickly through the market square, past the Silver Pony and through the gate in the curtain wall leading into the courtyard of Windkeep Castle, and finally to the High Tower. But instead of stopping in the council chambers as I had earlier in the day, or in the royal chambers where Idella and I were sometimes invited to dinner, we climbed the stairs to the dragon lair, unused for twelve years. And there, lying on the stone floor with the large entrance behind her open to the night air, was the dragon Tyrmiss. Tessia sat beside her, and in the far corner, Adamu sat on a bench looking as baffled and frightened as a puppy in a lion's den.

"Hello, Norbert," Tyrmiss rumbled. "Oh, by the Holy Talon, is this little Ena?"

My daughter had grown up hearing tales of her father's friend the legendary Tyrmiss, but it was assumed that the dragon was gone from our lives forever. Now, faced with a legendary being she never expected to see again, Ena stood just inside the dragon lair as still as a stump, that is, if a stump could have its eyes and mouth wide open in shock.

"Don't be frightened, dear," Tyrmiss said. "Come a little closer so I can see you." And the dragon bared her teeth in a grimace which I knew she intended as a disarming smile, but actually, the sight of a double row of dagger-like teeth terrified Ena and Adamu.

"Don't worry. I don't bite," she said. And I thought *That's true. I've never known her to bite a human. She lights them on fire, yes, but she never bites.*

To reassure Ena and Adamu, I walked over to Tyrmiss, put my hands around her large scaly head and gave her a hug. Ena moved a little closer to the dragon, but still kept her distance. Adamu wasn't about to get up from the bench against the far wall.

"Where are Rozae and Banos?" I asked.

"Rozae is staying with friends," she said.

"What about Banos?" I asked.

"Banos died a few years ago, I'm afraid. But I'll tell you about him later. I'm actually not here on a social call, Norbert, and I need Rozae to stay out of the coming storm." Her large right eye close to my head turned to me, and I caught a glimpse of a weyr of dragons flying toward a faraway castle… Was this image something from her memory as a youngster? I remembered she was the sole dragon survivor of the war between men and dragons thousands of years before.

"Stop reading my mind, Norbert," the dragon said. "It's very rude to read a dragon's mind without permission."

"Well, you're the one who taught us how to do it, Tyrmiss," Tessia chided her friend.

"Yes, yes," Tyrmiss replied. "It's rarely a good idea for dragons to teach humans anything. It usually comes back to bite us in the tail."

To emphasize her point, she gave a twitch of her tail which stretched across the wide floor.

An hour later, after Tyrmiss had eaten the large roasted salmon that the kitchen sent up, and we had had a chance to summarize what had happened in the kingdom since she'd left twelve years before, Tyrmiss gave a rank smoky belch, and settled into a comfortable position.

"As you guessed, Norbert," the dragon began. "I need your help."

Having seen that Ena and Adamu became nervous when she spoke directly to them, she addressed herself to Tessia and me, ignoring the young people for the time being.

"When Rozae, Banos and I left the two of you on the mountainside twelve years ago, we flew to Sheonad, the ruined castle of the Blue Witches, in the Nordtoppen. They weren't using it anymore, and the mountains and glaciers there offered us privacy with plenty of space in the tunnels the witches had dug into the mountain. We were quite comfortable there. For food, we flew down to the valley where the Renetu lived.

"As you remember, the Renetu are quite a sophisticated people—they have been there for thousands of years. They are so sophisticated, in fact, that they've given up all technology and live a simple life. They know that a warm hut, good food, and wise stories and songs passed down through the generations are all that humans need to live a good life. The Renetu, being close to nature, have great respect for dragons. The villagers would see us skimming the river for fish or hunting elk in the mountains, and they'd wave to us, letting us come and go as we pleased. But over time, traders from Osterbo City started making more frequent trips to the Renetu, exchanging metal tools and implements for the furs of animals which have been completely hunted out in the lowlands. I was afraid we would be spotted by the traders, so the dragonlings and I moved further west into the mountains, then seeing traders there as well, we moved deep into the mountains where men rarely go.

"One morning, the twins showed up at the cave excited. They told me that they'd found a dragon lying beside the river that ran beside our mountain. They said he was very old—even older than me." Tyrmiss gave a deep chuckle. "Of course, children always think their parents are ancient, but in my case it's true." She tilted her head toward the frightened young people and winked. "I am, after all, ten thousand years old."

Resuming her tale, she said, "The dragonlings led me to the place where the dragon lay, and I was surprised to see that they were right. He *was* old. I've never seen so many wrinkles on a neck. And he was strange looking. His head didn't look like mine, but like a turtle's, and his legs and wings were small.

"He couldn't move, and he could barely talk. I sent the little ones down the river to catch fish, and I sat with the old dragon. As the morning passed, his ragged breath came more slowly. I carried water in my mouth from the river and let it fall a drop at a time into his toothless mouth. He had no teeth, just a small sharp beak. In a hoarse rasp, he thanked me and said his name was Tudhoiphug which means *Lord of Snow*. He'd left his tribe to be by himself, so he could die. Between coughing spells, he told me he was one of the first dragons created by the Goddess. 'Before she got the hang of it,' he joked. I looked at his terrapin-like head, his small wings and short legs and thought that he did indeed look like a primordial ancestor of dragons.

"'I thought all the dragons had been exterminated except for my children and me,' I told him.

"'No,' he said. 'Only the Eastern Dragons were wiped out in the war with men these seven thousand years past.' He spluttered and coughed but finally said the thing that surprised me almost as much as finding my children's eggs, 'The Western Dragons still live in the mountains. They have tried to stay far away from men, but now…' His voice trailed off, and he mumbled something incoherent about a dragon army.

"I felt my heart jump when I heard this. I asked whether the Western Dragons look like me, and he answered, yes, very much so. 'It is only I,' he said, 'who looks like a turtle.' He gave a small chuckle, but it was too much and he started coughing.

"When he breathed evenly again, I asked him where his homeland was. He gestured to the west and said it was two days' flight from where we stood. 'You'll know you've arrived when you see the mountain that looks like a she-wolf with her nursing pups,' he whispered and closed his eyes.

"I sat with him most of the day, shielding him from the sun with my wing. Rozae and Banos returned with a fish Rozae had caught in a mountain lake. When he woke, I tore off a small piece of fish and fed it to the old dragon.

"'Last meal,' he said. 'I always loved the taste of raw bass.' He closed his eyes a last time, and by evening, he was dead.

"Rozae, Banos and I gathered driftwood from beside the river and piled it on him. I let the twins blow flames at the pyre and we stood back and watched Tudhoiphug return to the earth and air from whence he came. I said a short prayer to the Goddess, thanking her for our lives. I wished Tudhoiphug Lord of Snow a safe journey home, and we flew back to our cave.

"I thought for weeks about what Tudhoiphug had said about his tribe and his homeland. Could it be true? Was there actually a tribe of dragons who lived just two days flight from here? I wondered how they would feel about three dragons joining them. Would they welcome us? Or would they think of us as interlopers? Would my children be safe among them?"

"It was a summer afternoon, and the twins and I were flying back to our lair when Banos suddenly faltered in midair. He lost momentum and started falling. I folded my wings close to my body and went straight down after him. I was an arrow aimed at the earth while he was a twisting thing tumbling through the air, so I caught him soon enough in my talons, carried him down to earth and gently put him down on a wide boulder. Rozae landed beside us.

"'What happened?' I asked him softly, stroking his head.

"'I don't know,' he sobbed, frightened out of his wits. 'I was just flying along and suddenly my shoulder froze up, and I couldn't move it.'

"I inspected his shoulder and the long stretch of his right wing. 'I don't see anything wrong, Banos,' I said gently. 'Has this happened before?'

"He nodded. 'Sometimes my right wing just stops moving.'

"I tried not to show how worried I was. Instead, I reassured him that these things happen, and he shouldn't be frightened. 'Maybe it would be better if you don't fly for a while and let your shoulder rest,' I said.

"When he was calm, I encouraged him to climb on my back, and I flew my little ones home to our cave. That was when I decided we were going to find the Western Dragons. I hoped there would be a wise old grandmother in the tribe who would know how to heal my son."

"It was a long flight, longer than the two days that Tudhoiphug had indicated. We flew due west for three days, with Banos on my back and Rozae struggling to keep up behind. When I realized we had somehow missed the mountain that looked like a she-wolf with her nursing pups, we turned around and flew back the way we came for two days. Then I chose a path to the southwest and flew two days. We saw lots of mountains, but none looked like wolves. Then after days of staring at mountains, I thought they all resembled wolves.

"We turned around again and started flying northeast and finally when Rozae was completely exhausted, we stopped to rest. During the entire five days we had been flying with only brief stops to rest, she'd never complained. I was proud of my daughter, scared for my son, and starting to get very angry at an old dead dragon who'd given me bad directions. Then I saw a dragon, or what might be a dragon, or maybe it was just a glint on the horizon.

"We hoped to get closer to get a better look, but the figure on the horizon disappeared. I noted the landmarks where we last saw the dragon, and we flew toward them. I wasn't sure whether we were going in the right direction until I started to hear voices in my mind getting louder and louder the closer we got. It had been seven thousand years since I'd heard an entire tribe of dragons chatting, arguing, explaining and complaining. I slowed down, so Rozae could catch up to me.

"'What is that, Momma?' she asked. 'Are those dragons I'm hearing in my mind?'

"'Yes, dear,' I said. 'We're almost there.'

"'I can hear them too,' Banos said, still holding firm to my back.

"We came over a high ridge, and below us, we saw hundreds of dragons, some in the air, others sitting on ledges, and at the bottom of the valley next to a stream, there were dozens of dragons of all ages, from old ones like me to adolescents like my twins to babies being nuzzled by their mothers. I gave a gasp. I had not realized how much I missed being part of a tribe."

Tyrmiss paused in her story, her eyelids drooping. "I'm too sleepy to continue this evening," she said. "Let's continue tomorrow."

When Ena and I got home, Idella wanted to know what happened, so Ena repeated Tyrmiss' story to her.

"What does she want from you?" My wife asked, her eyes narrowing.

"We don't know yet," Ena said. "I don't understand why Tyrmiss would come all this way to tell us these things."

"We'll go back again tomorrow," I said. "We better get some sleep. I have a feeling we're going to be taking a long journey soon."

I waited until Ena had gone to bed, then I kissed my wife on the cheek and turned toward the door.

"Are you going to pray?" she asked.

I nodded, left our house, walked toward the orchard, and sat on the stone bench beneath the ancient oak tree where I prayed most evenings. With all that had happened during the day, it took me a while to find the quiet place inside me. At last, Nilene appeared in front of me, beautiful as ever in her shimmering gown and the garland of ivy holding back her hair.

"Thank you, My Lady, for guiding me through this life. I owe you everything."

"So, you and Tessia are going on another quest," Nilene, Mother of All Life, said.

"It would appear so, my Lady."

"Aren't you getting a little old to be running off to war with Tessia? You have responsibilities here, Norbert."

"Tyrmiss needs us, my Lady. She has done so much for us; how can I refuse her?"

"I suppose you feel you must go, but you need to be aware that this quest is different than the others. It is far more dangerous. And you have much more to lose if things go badly."

"What do you mean, My Lady? Will I be killed on this quest?"

"No, Norbert. You will not die on this quest, but others will, and their deaths will change you. You will suffer more than you have ever suffered before."

"Will Ena be hurt? Will she be killed?"

"That has not been determined yet. You and Tessia must protect her."

"Can you protect her, My Lady?"

"No, I cannot," Nilene sighed. "War is not my domain. I have no more say over what happens in war than you do."

"Is there another god I can…" I stopped when I saw the anger on her face.

"Norbert, I am the only deity you may pray to. If you pray to another then I will take back the gifts I've given you."

"I am sorry, my Lady," I said quickly, sliding off the bench and falling to my knees in front of her. "You have given me so much. I don't want to seem ungrateful."

Nilene reached her hand out to touch my head. "All is forgiven, Norbert. I feel a little jealous of your affection. My brother and I have had arguments about you."

"Your brother?" I asked, puzzled.

"Yes, you will be meeting him soon, I think," she said. "And when you do, keep in mind to whom your fealty lies."

"Yes, my Lady, I will," I said, but she was gone.

The next morning, Ena and I had a light breakfast of bread and pears and headed to the dragon lair where Tyrmiss was waiting for us and immediately picked up her story where she'd left off the evening before.

"The tribe of Western Dragons accepted the three of us right away," Tyrmiss continued. "They were aware my tribe had been exterminated thousands of years before, and they were glad to discover there had been at least a few survivors. I told them about meeting Tudhoiphug on his last day in this world. They seemed grateful we had eased his passing and built a pyre for him.

"The females accepted me quickly and I was grateful because I felt I had much to learn from them. One day, shortly after we arrived, I asked one of the old wise ones, whose name is Qerlun, which means Lady of the Skies, whether she'd ever seen a young dragon suffer a paralyzed wing as Banos had, and she nodded sadly. Every now and then, she said, every hundred years or so, this ailment affects one of their young males. No one knows what causes it, or how to cure it. She said that when one wing is paralyzed, the other wing is soon paralyzed as well. Then the neck and the talons, and eventually, the dragonling cannot move at all. When the paralysis spreads to the abdomen, then the youngster can't breathe anymore, and he dies.

"Qerlun said this to me softly, gently communicating through her thoughts, as well as her eyes, a great deal of sympathy. I turned and saw my son Banos, only ten summers old, happily playing a game of demon stone with his new friends. I felt a great weight come over my heart. 'How long?' I asked, barely able to form the words in my mind. 'How long will he live?'

"'By the end of summer,'" Qerlun said. "'He'll be gone.'"

"Rather than letting Banos become frightened by reading my thoughts, I felt it kinder to explain to him what he could expect. Brave little dragon that he was, he listened carefully, asked a few questions, then comforted me as I wept. He never shed a tear for himself. His only concern was for the welfare of his mother and sister."

Tyrmiss lay her head on her fore talon and wept, large tears falling on the stone floor, blessing Windkeep with their magic.

"Should we stop for today and continue the tale tomorrow?" Tessia asked, wrapping her arms around her friend's scaly neck.

"No, no," Tyrmiss said, lifting her large head and gathering her composure. "It is urgent that you know what is happening to the Western Tribe. We must save them." After a few moments, she continued in a level voice: "Two years after Banos passed away, a terrifying thing happened to the tribe of Western Dragons. We were discovered by humans.

"For thousands of years, the Western Dragons had lived

deep in the mountains, far beyond the reach of humans who lived on the coast. But over time, as humans settled in the river valleys further and further inland, the dragons became aware of the threat the presence of the humans posed to them. The dragons saw columns of smoke on the horizon as cities burned in human wars, and they came across slaughtered humans who had been hunted down by their enemies. Dragons smelled the rivers polluted by the farm animals and heard the dreams of humans as they plotted and schemed against each other. The Western Dragons all knew what had happened to the Eastern Dragons, so they had done their best to keep their existence a secret. But now the secret was in danger of coming out.

"Then the inevitable happened: A young dragon with an interest in birds had followed a flock of starlings into a fragrant valley, and there he was, perched on a ledge looking down at the swirling flock following the river when he felt someone watching him. Although he'd never heard the thoughts of a human before, he knew immediately what he was experiencing. And as sure as day, across the narrow valley, a hunter was looking up at him.

"The young dragon flew home immediately and told his neighbors what had happened.

"'Why didn't you kill the hunter?' Another young dragon, known for his impetuosity, asked.

"'Because that is not our way,' one of the elders explained patiently. 'We do not kill a being to protect a secret.'

"And the other elders nodded their heads sagely. But truth to tell, I was not the only dragon who later wished the young dragon had killed that first human because much trouble came from that chance encounter."

"As the months dragged on, bands of hunters were seen following the river valleys into the mountains, and it was only a matter of time before more dragons were spotted. We are large beasts who are most comfortable flying through the air. Even at night, it is difficult for us to hide.

"There was much discussion about moving deeper into the mountains, but many were reluctant to give up our beautiful region where there were quick-running rivers and deep lakes. Salmon, pike, and bass were plentiful, as were elk and deer. The Western Dragons had lived in this region since the Age of Ice, and our species is attached to our traditions. We do not adapt to change easily. The beauty of the mountains and forests had brought us much happiness, and in this place, we felt close to the Goddess.

"However, as we discussed and debated what we should do, the men were getting closer, encroaching on our ancient hunting grounds. A young female dragon never came back from gathering dinner for her children. An old bull dragon fought five hunters, killing one and chasing off the others. Men were learning that bows had little effect on us, barely penetrating our thick scaly hides, but a well-placed spear-thrust could kill us, tear our throats open, or pierce one of our two hearts.

"Now we knew we must either leave our valley or go to war against men.

"In our council, we put the question to a vote. All of the dragons but one voted for war. I was the sole dissenting voice. I argued with my brothers and sisters, my whole adopted tribe. I told them I had seen war. I repeated the stories of my own tribe, the Eastern Dragons being wiped out in a great battle with men, and how I had been the sole survivor. I told them how I had also gone to war to fight the enemies of my friend, Tessia the Wise, whom they call Dragonqueen, because I allowed her to ride on my back against her enemies who were also my enemies. I killed many men in these wars, and I was standing in the council of elders to tell my adopted brothers and sisters that war is a terrible thing that must be avoided at all costs.

"I also told them that men and their allies, the Drekavacs, are used to war, and many of them live for war. They teach their children that war is glorious and good, and fighting for land and riches is a noble endeavor. Their children are given toy weapons to play at war, and their songs and stories celebrate massacres and laying waste.

"'Dragons,' I said to my adopted brothers and sisters. 'We have no culture of war. We teach our children to play with each other peacefully. We teach them to honor the Goddess and all living things. We kill nothing for sport. We thank the salmon and the elk who give their lives for us to live. We take no pleasure in killing as men do.'

"But the dragons did not listen to me, for I was new in the tribe and not yet fully accepted as kin. And so, the dragons began their war against men, hunting the hunters, killing them with fire and talon. And then one day, a scout who had been sent to the coast returned to our valley, and she asked to meet with the council of elders. She told us she'd flown out of the mountains and all the way to the sea, further than any of our kind had ever been in a thousand years, and what she saw had terrified her. She said there were great walled cities on the coast where thousands of humans and Drekavacs lived. And there were sailing ships coming and going from the cities. And roads that led from the cities and followed the rivers into the mountains, *our* mountains. And there were soldiers and machines of war.

"Now the council of elders realized it had been a terrible mistake to attack men. Our thousand dragons would have no chance of defeating their army. So, the elders sent an emissary to the king of the nearest city, a place called Hoclav, but the emissary never returned.

"Then the elders decided that since war was upon us, we would need allies. An emissary was sent to the trolls that live deep in the mountains. Another was sent to the whales and dolphins who live far out to sea. And I was sent as emissary to Queen Tessia the Wise, who is known as the Dragonqueen because of her friendship with me."

At this point, Tyrmiss bowed her head until it almost touched the stone floor in front of Tessia's feet, a position of supplication I had never seen her make before. She said, "I beseech you, mighty Queen, if our friendship means anything to you, please come to fight for my cause, as I have fought for yours in the past."

Chapter Four

Tessia, Ena, Adamu and I were stunned. We stood gaping at Tyrmiss, whom no one in the kingdom had seen in twelve years, and who had returned with this tale of her quest to find a home for her and her children. And now she was asking us to go to war to save her adopted tribe.

Shaking off her surprise, Tessia reached out her hand and touched Tyrmiss's broad scaly head, "Arise, my friend, you should bow to no human. Of course, I will join you on this quest as you have joined me in the past. We shall fly to victory together."

As Tessia turned to look at me, I realized she was expecting something like this request from Tyrmiss. Why else would she have invited me? But why are Ena and Adamu here? I saw a moment of silent communication between Tyrmiss and Tessia, and Tessia turned pale.

"We will not win against this army of men with sheer force of arms," Tessia said, catching my eye. "The Eastern Dragons of old were slaughtered by men in a face-to-face confrontation. Instead, we will need to use guile and magic to win. Norbert, will you join your queen and her dragon in this quest to save dragon-kind?"

In that moment, my mind went back to the first time Tessia asked me to join her in a quest. She was only seventeen and I was only ten years older. We set out to free her father from Ludek's prison, but little did we know that before we could free her father, we would first have to free the kingdom. Once a quest is begun, no one can foresee where it will lead.

"I would be honored, Your Majesty," I said, bowing my head.

Tessia turned to Ena. "Mage, we will need you to come with us. We will be facing a huge army with only a thousand dragons. Your ability to learn new spells quickly will be invaluable. Will you heed the call of your queen?"

Ena hesitated, looking from Tessia to Tyrmiss. "I don't know..." she began.

Then looking into Tyrmiss's eyes, Ena blanched. I caught merely a glimpse of the terrible images that Tyrmiss had projected into Ena's mind. Soldiers were shooting great bolts from ballistas at dragons flying overhead, and the dragons were crashing to the ground to be swarmed by soldiers who slaughtered them where they lay. I knew these were Tyrmiss's memories of the great battle between men and dragons seven thousand years before.

Ena bowed her head and said, "I will, Your Majesty."

"Wait," I said. "Her mother will never agree to Ena leaving on a quest."

Ena looked at me in anger, and Tessia said, "Your daughter has seen eighteen summers, Mage Norbert. Under Dragonja law, she is an adult and can make her own decisions."

Turning to Adamu, the queen said, "Mage, I understand your magic includes mathematics and philosophy. You have an understanding of the underlying structures of things and their past and future. What do you call this magic?"

"I call it Silver Magic, Your Majesty, because it brings light to the matters at hand."

"And you are eighteen as well?"

"I am, Your Majesty."

"Very well, then, we have need of logistical and engineering support."

Adamu bowed his head in acquiescence. He needed no convincing. Wherever Ena went, he would go as well, but I feared what Idella would say about Ena flying to the other side of the world to fight an army.

"What about your responsibilities as Queen of Dragonja?" I asked. "Remember what happened last time you left on a quest. The kingdom descended into chaos."

"I'm appointing Princess Kana as regent during my absence," Tessia said turning to me. "Your son Alaric will remain here as General to protect the kingdom. The Citizens Council is doing a fine job in running the city. They don't need me here.

"I've already discussed this change of leadership with the princess and Alaric," Tessia added with a glint in her eye. "They've accepted the responsibility of leading the kingdom in my absence. I have also sent a formal letter to Councilwoman Femke who will read it to the council tomorrow."

I realized that Tessia and Tyrmiss must have shared their thoughts on the quest during the night, and Tessia had put the wheels of governing the kingdom in motion this morning. So, Tyrmiss's story and Tessia's kneeling before her in fealty were a bit of theater to convince Ena, Adamu and me to join the quest. Not for the first time, I'd been outmaneuvered by Tessia and Tyrmiss.

"How many soldiers will accompany us in our quest?" I asked, trying to adjust to the new situation.

"None," the queen responded curtly. "We have no way to transport them to the other side of the world.

"And besides," she said, looking at her three mages and her friend Tyrmiss. "Each of us is worth a regiment."

Idella was understandably upset at the idea of her husband and daughter going across the world to fight an army with only their wands to protect them. "This family has given so much to the queen's causes," she pointed out. "You fought in the revolution against Ludek, the war against the Blue Witches, the war against Kazko, and I…" She trembled as she remembered what Ludek had done to her when she was his captive, and I trembled as well. It had been only a few years since we told Ena that she was my brother Ludek's child. It had been the most difficult conversation of my life.

"Mother..." Ena began, then stopped. What could she say that was both reassuring and true? The truth was that she would likely die in this quest, as would her father. She understood that her mother, who had seen war close up, was horrified at what might happen to her family if we joined Tessia. But Idella also knew that her family and everyone else in the kingdom owed Tyrmiss everything. We could not refuse to help her when she needed us.

"The Queen already has you, Norbert," Idella said. "You were at her side in every battle she has fought. Why does she need Ena as well?"

"She didn't tell me, but knowing Tessia, she probably is already forming a strategy and whatever that strategy is, it requires three mages."

"THREE?" Idella gasped in panic. Obviously, she was worried that our son Alaric was being recruited for the quest as well. Even though he'd never studied magic, he had certain gifts that made him invincible.

"Tessia has asked Adamu to accompany us," I hurriedly added. "And the Queen has asked Alaric to remain in the Kingdom as its defender."

"Oh," Idella said, relaxing slightly in relief. "I thought... Alaric..."

"I know, love. Alaric will remain here—with you."

Idella turned to Ena, gulping to swallow her tears. "Are you sure you want to go on this quest? It will be full of hardship. You may be killed."

Ena nodded her head. "Yes, Mother. I am being called to serve the Queen and the dragon Tyrmiss. We owe them everything, so I have no right to refuse." Her shoulders slumped slightly, and she added, "Besides, I've finished my studies and the only job I could find was work as a serving wench..."

For the first time, it became clear to me that Ena hated the idea of working at the Silver Pony, but it had been the only option in front of her. Now, she had the opportunity to pursue glory and adventure, and she was excited. And I felt dread rise in me. My darling little girl was going to see war close up, as her mother and father had. It was going to be an adventure certainly—a horrible, bloody, terrifying adventure.

The next day, Ena, Adamu and I met Tessia and Tyrmiss in the dragon lair. We would be flying a very long way, and we needed to discuss logistics.

"Tyrmiss has told me we can't fly directly across the Nordtoppen mountains to the west coast because the mountains are too high and the winds too strong and cold for humans to tolerate," Tessia explained.

"So what is the best route?" Adamu asked.

"We'll have to go the long way around, flying to the southern coast and following the strand west and eventually north to get to our destination. The journey will take weeks," Tessia paused and a slight smile played at the corners of her mouth as she added, "And it happens that this route will take us past the Blessed Isle where my uncle Zygmunt lives."

Tessia looked up at me and the smile grew. Her uncle had been the leader of the revolution against the Wizard Ludek a generation before. He was certainly the most admirable man I had ever known: a brilliant strategist, an inspired leader, a skilled fighter, a man of vision and integrity.

Besides being a legendary figure, Zygmunt was also someone I was proud to call my friend, and I was looking forward to seeing him again after twenty years.

"General Zygmunt?" Adamu said, exchanging glances with Ena. The two of them had never met Zygmunt and knew him only from the stories every Dragonja child was told at bedtime. He was the greatest hero of our time, perhaps of any time.

"He is often called the founding father of Dragonja," Adamu murmured in awe.

"And for good reason," I said. "After we'd taken the capital and established order, General Zygmunt had the integrity to turn all power over to Queen Varvara, the rightful ruler of the kingdom. The Wise Queen, as she came to be known, adopted Tessia as her heir, and when Queen Varvara died, Tessia inherited the throne. The ascent of the two wise queens and all they've done to make Dragonja a free and prosperous kingdom has been possible only because General Zygmunt declined to rule."

"Enough history," Tessia said, unrolling a large map on the stone floor. "Let's talk about our route. First, we will fly to the pass between the mountains, and there we will visit our old friend Hamlin the Bear. His position allows him to keep an eye on the travelers and traders between our valley of Dragonja and the valley of the Iskar River on the other side of the ridge, as well as enabling him to see a long way up the Iskar. He can tell us what to expect as we travel toward the Round Keep where the magical beasts live. Our friend Narrra, the mimic sheep, can tell us who has passed through the valley. Then we will follow the Iskar River to its source in the Nordtoppen mountains. There is a high pass near there where we can cross out of the mountains to the shore of the Southern Sea. We'll follow the coast until we come to the Blessed Isle, the place where my uncle Zygmunt lives with his companion Wessel. My uncle led a small army of partisans with the aid of only one dragon, Tyrmiss, against the wizard Ludek's much larger army behind the high walls of Dragonja. I'd like to discuss strategy with Zygmunt and get his advice on how best to capture Hoclav City."

"Excuse me, Your Majesty," Adamu asked. "What is Hoclav City?"

"Hoclav is the largest city on the western coast," Tessia responded. "It is ruled by a king named Beyazit."

Tessia looked up at us, obviously uncomfortable. "You need to know that the people of the west are very different than we are. We easterners are farmers and tradesmen, people of the valleys. We are practical and skeptical of anything we cannot see. We worship Nilene the Mother Goddess, who ensures that our crops grow and our businesses prosper. The people of the west, on the other hand, have a close connection to the sea. They are traditionally sailors and fishermen. Their stories and songs are those of coming from far away where sea-monsters rule. They worship demi-gods, such as Wolios, God of Wind, and Rutia, God of Battle. Their patron is Thortia, Mistress of The Sea."

Eva, Adamu and I looked at each other, puzzled. "Why are you telling us this, Your Majesty," I asked.

"Because there are stories that Tyrmiss has told me, things she's heard in dreams…"

We waited for Tessia to explain, but she looked at the floor.

"What Tessia doesn't want to say," Tyrmiss said in her deep rumbling voice, "is that King Beyazit claims he is descended from sea monsters."

"What?" Ena asked, shocked. "Is it true? Is this king a sea-monster? Is he some kind of shark or squid?"

"Maybe he's a giant clam," Tyrmiss said, wryly.

All of us chuckled, but I, for one, take rumors and legends, even self-serving ones created by megalomaniacs, seriously. They are usually not factual, but they often hint at the truth.

In any case, this was going to be a very interesting journey.

We took a break to eat a midday meal, and while we were finishing up the last of the salmon and greens, a

Drekavac soldier, one of the queen's guard, came into the dragon's lair with two wooden boxes which he laid in front of Tessia. She acknowledged him with a nod, cleaned her hands on a linen napkin and opened the larger of the two boxes.

Inside were three exquisitely crafted brooms. Tessia proudly distributed them to Ena, Adamu and me and read the dedication written in a florid hand on an enclosed vellum sheet:

> *"These brooms were made with loving care by the Blue Witches Evanora and Zamarrra who now gift them to the queen's mages in friendship and gratitude. May you use them well."*

I held the broom in my hands, feeling its balance and admiring the way the oak handle had been carved with runes. The brush was a carefully chosen assemblage of various stems and herbs. I couldn't wait to give it a try. Ena and Adamu were also admiring their respective brooms. Both of them were accomplished broomists. Ena had been flying since she was a child, and Adamu had mastered the art of flying last year in his final training as a mage.

"What's in the other one?" Ena asked, nodding toward the long narrow box at Tessia's feet.

Tessia leaned down, lifted the lid and pulled out the most exquisite Voprian sword I had ever seen. Her father Kerttu was the legendary smith who discovered the Voprian alloy and hammered out many fine swords. In fact, every man and Drekavac who served in Tessia's military was issued a Voprian blade. The alloy was so hard and strong the swords could be as thin as two fingers and flexible as a bough in the wind. They kept their edge permanently, almost never needing to be sharpened.

Tessia lifted the blade from the box and balanced it in her hand. The hilt was engraved with a small figure of a woman, lithe and beautiful as Tessia herself. The handle was encrusted with purple jewels. Tessia whipped the blade through the air a few times, the surface of the blade shimmering with blue light and the sword singing as it moved. Of all the swords her father had crafted, this one was clearly Tessia's favorite.

Tessia looked up at me, her green eyes shining. "I shall call her Agatha the Righteous," she said.

Part Two: The Blessed Isle

Chapter Five

The first leg of our journey was a short one. Tessia rode on Tyrmiss's back while Ena, Adamu and I rode our brooms. We flew to the pass between the mountains known as the Two Thumbs of the Giant to visit our friend, Hamlin the Bear. Having lived as a man and then as a bear, it was clear to Hamlin that being a bear suited him better. Ten years before, he had taken a mate who bore him several pairs of cubs. But now, his mate was dead, his offspring had spread through the mountains, and Hamlin once again lived alone. It was a beautiful spot with a clear stream nearby and lots of nuts and berries in the forest and fields. Years before, I'd disguised the entrance to the cave with the illusion of brush and boulders, so Hamlin was safe here. He couldn't speak, but he understood human speech perfectly well.

We told Hamlin about our plan to fly south down the Iskar River Valley and over the southern ridge to the sea where we'd meet Zygmunt to ask his advice about developing a strategy for conquering King Beyazit of Hoclav. At the mention of Zygmunt's name, Hamlin grew sullen. He had never forgiven Tessia's uncle for having his lover Anja executed for spying on the rebels.

It was midday, and we were getting hungry. Hamlin signaled we should follow him into a nearby field where moon berries were ripening. We didn't bother to put the berries in a basket, but rather ate them the way bears do, putting our lips over the small white orbs, using our teeth to pull them loose from the stems, chewing them and letting the juice run down our chins. After we'd had our fill, we went back to the meadow and sat in the grass.

Tessia asked Hamlin whether he had seen anyone crossing the pass recently. With a single talon, he drew stick figures of two men leading mules. These figures represented traders who carried goods between Dragonja City and the Iskar Valley, not unusual this time of year.

"Anyone else?" Tessia asked.

Hamlin drew a stick figure of a dragon and glanced at Tyrmiss.

"Yes, I passed through here a few days ago," Tyrmiss confirmed.

Hamlin thought for a minute, then he sketched a broom and looked at the ones Ena and Adamu were carrying.

"I haven't ridden a broom over this pass in years," Ena said, puzzled.

"And I've never ridden a broom in these mountains," Adamu said.

Hamlin then drew two more brooms in the dirt.

"Witches?" Tessia asked. "Witches flew over this pass? How many?"

Hamlin slapped his paw on the ground at least a dozen times.

"A coven of witches flew over the pass?" Tessia asked, starting to sound worried. "Did you recognize any of them?"

Hamlin hit his paw on the ground once. *Yes.*

"Was Evanora one of them?"

Yes.

"Was Zamarrra one of them?"

Yes.

"Anyone else you recognize?"

No.

We sat quietly while we sorted through the new information. The Blue Witches were very powerful. They could influence the weather, quarry stone, manufacture brooms…

"It's possible they are going back to Sheonad," Tyrmiss offered.

"Possibly," Tessia said. "But why? They abandoned that city because they couldn't stop the glacier from burying it."

The Blue Witches had conducted a war against Dragonja City a dozen years earlier and caused terrible damage to our kingdom through drought and flood. We finally were able to conquer them, but as part of the peace treaty, Queen Tessia had granted them caretaker rights to their ancestral homeland in the Dry Hills. In the decades since, the Blue Witches had turned a wasteland into a cedar forest, and it was now a beautiful place. My son Alaric had worked with them, leading a group of young men who did the hard work of planting the forest, while the witches encouraged the weather to favor the forest. The magical skills of the witches had become a great asset for the kingdom.

But having fought them in the war, Queen Tessia had never completely trusted the witches. They were, in her view, vicious and unreliable. She was always worried the witches would eventually try to take over the kingdom as they had in ancient times. So, why were they now leaving the kingdom and flying in the direction of Sheonad, their abandoned city?

We slept in the cave that night and woke the next morning to the smell of fresh fish cooking on the stone in the middle of the front room.

"Breakfast anyone?" Tyrmiss offered, slicing the large salmon into pieces with her talon. She lifted a large piece and swallowed it whole. The rest of us gingerly picked up pieces with our fingers, blew on them until they were cool, and ate them. After we had finished and the cooking stone was cool, Hamlin bent his head down and ate the rest of the fish. There was nothing left but an oily spot on the stone.

Tessia went into the back room and emerged holding a sack of gold coins. This cave was one of the places where she stored her personal wealth; whereas the treasury of the kingdom was held in a vault below the High Tower and protected by spells I had cast.

"I think we may need gold at some point on this quest," she said, handing the sack to me.

I cast an invisibility charm on it and put it in my kit next to my smaller sack of gold.

Outside, we mounted up, and Tyrmiss flew off into the Iskar Valley with Tessia on her back. Ena, Adamu and I followed on our brooms. We could see to our right the northern flow of the river past farms and villages. As we came closer to the river, we turned left into the southern reaches where no humans or Drekavacs lived. It had been the domain of the witch Tatatungia for many years, and she'd enchanted the animals living there. Although Tatatungia was long dead, the valley was still full of residual magic left over from her experiments.

Tessia looked back at me, and I knew she was feeling the same trepidation I felt, but this was the fastest route to the southern coast.

Since the mimic sheep were terrified of dragons, we landed downriver, and Tyrmiss said she would use the time to scout the route ahead. Tessia, Ena, Adamu and I walked toward the Round Keep through a forest of tiny oak trees. I took the lead and instructed the others to stay in single file and step in each other's footprints in order to minimize the damage to the forest.

As we drew close to the keep, I heard a voice, "Norbert? Norbert Oldfoot? Is that you after all these years?"

"Hello, Narrra!" I shouted and led our party out of the forest of tiny oaks and into the green meadow where the mimic sheep lived.

"You remember Norbert. Don't you, dear?" Narrra said to

her companion. "He's the nice mage who visited us looking for Zamarrra so many years ago."

Narrra turned to me and asked, "How is Zamarrra?" Narrra had been Zamarrra's foster mother until Evanora took the child away to live in Sheonad.

"She's well. I saw her at the Council meeting yesterday." I told Narrra about Zamarrra and Evanora settling in their ancestral home, and how they'd turned the Dry Hills into a beautiful cedar forest. I didn't tell her about the wars her foster daughter had caused or how she'd almost destroyed our kingdom through drought and flood.

"You haven't seen Zamarrra?" I asked, innocently. I was thinking that if the witch flew this way, she might have stopped to greet Narrra.

"No, no…" Narrra said. "I haven't seen her in many years. I think the last time was when you and she came here together, and she said there was a great war going on and she had to do her part."

I thought *Zamarrra did her part alright and almost got Tessia and me killed.*

Changing the subject, I said, "You haven't changed a bit in the last twenty years, Narrra."

"Oh, you flatterer," she demurred. "You know I'm over a hundred years old. The old witch bred us to live a very long time." She looked at me coquettishly. "And as you know, we give the sweetest milk and the softest wool."

I reached up and touched the wool behind her ears. She closed her eyes in ecstasy.

"May we stay here tonight?" I asked.

"Of course, you may," she purred.

The next morning, we breakfasted on sheep milk and oats, then walked single file through the grove of tiny oaks to the tall woods where Tyrmiss was waiting. Along the way, Tessia decided we would stay with our original plan and ignore the Blue Witches for the time being.

We mounted up and flew south, following the Iskar River. This was unknown territory to all of us except Tyrmiss who said she hadn't been this way in a very long time. For a being that is ten thousand years old, "a very long time" can be a long time indeed.

Below us the forest gave way to more open territory and the mountains on either side of the river grew steeper until we were flying over a gorge that cut through a desert. The river filled with rapids as we went into the high country. At midday, we landed in a wide level spot where a stream came down from the mountains to form a waterfall that fell over the lip of the gorge and joined the river below.

I distributed dried fruit and nuts from my pack and each of us took a long drink from the stream. The water was clear and sweet. Tyrmiss was looking at the high peaks to the west with a nostalgic look in her eyes.

"I was born not far from here," she said.

I remembered what she'd told me about the dragon tribe in which she was raised.

"The ice towers of Qodosh were in those mountains?" I asked.

Tyrmiss nodded, "In ancient times before men arrived, Qodosh was carved by dragon breath from a tall glacier. In its glory days, it had ten thousand dragons occupying its towers. Dragons lived quite differently than men, you know. We were a peaceful society, loving music and art. Every evening bards would sing a paeon to the Goddess, and dancers would fly in elaborate choreography above the city. We loved our young and our old alike, each dragon treasured for being unique. Fighting was unknown to us until men arrived."

Not for the first time, I felt a flush of shame for the irreparable damage men and women had done to the earth. Why did the Goddess still favor us after so many assaults on her creation? This was a mystery I would never understand.

Tyrmiss shifted her gaze to Tessia who stood close by listening to us talk. "How are we going to defeat the armies of men this time, my friend?" Tyrmiss asked. "In the last war between men and dragons, they slaughtered us."

"I'm not sure yet," Tessia admitted. "This is the reason why we need to talk with my uncle Zygmunt. He'll help us develop a strategy." She turned and leveled her green eyes at Ena, Adamu and me. "The only thing I am absolutely sure of is that you three mages are needed."

Somewhat rested, Ena, Adamu and I straddled our brooms; Tessia climbed on Tyrmiss's back and we lifted off, Tyrmiss in the lead and setting a fast pace. We reached the base of the southern ridge as the sun was casting long shadows across the valley. Tyrmiss landed in a mountain meadow that overlooked the river valley we had been following all day. The Iskar River had become a stream, then a dry gulley and finally nothing at all, just a wide spot in the desert. Up here on the mountain though, the melting snows kept the meadow green all year.

I used my wand to start a fire, and Ena and Adamu gathered fresh greens. There were moon berries at the edge of the aspen forest. Tessia used her bow to shoot a few grouse. She gave two to Tyrmiss and the other one she gave to me for the cookpot. I gathered a few herbs and roots, washed them in wet snow and added them to the mix. By the time the light faded, we had a nice soup, and for dessert we had berries. It reminded me of my younger days, walking up and down the Bekla Valley with my donkey Ottolo loaded with pots and pans and other trade goods. In those days I ate whatever I could find in the fields and forests unless a kind family invited me to their table in exchange for news from afar and a couple of old songs for entertainment.

As if she read my mind, Tessia called out, "How about a song, Mage?"

I never had to be asked twice to sing. I brought out my lyre and strummed a few notes, waiting for what words might come. I've always believed that song and story are gifts of the Goddess, no less than rivers and forests.

I remembered an old folk song about Milon Redshield, the shining king who led the army that defeated the dragons. A key passage in the story involved Milon chaining the dragon Morf to a heavy cairn for forty days until the dragon consented to allow the warrior to fly on his back. In the great battle between men and dragons, Morf turned on Milon and the hero killed the dragon with a spear through his right heart.

The song had been a crowd pleaser at the Silver Pony, and I had sung it many times in the days before I met Tyrmiss. Once I became friends with her and she told me that Morf was actually one of her littermates, that is, her brother, I never sang the song again. But I had often thought the song would be even better if it were told from the point of view of Morf. Now that my sympathies lay with dragons, why not make him the hero? In the years since I was the bard of the Silver Pony, playing for copper coins and a bowl of soup, I had played with the lyrics a little. A tweak here and a reversal there, and I had a pretty good song about Morf, the dragon hero of the Bekla Valley. If there was ever a time to try out the new version, this was it.

I strummed the lyre a few times and gave a standard invocation to the Goddess and then launched into the song. It had two themes, a rollicking rhythm, and violent images to describe the battles, with a gentle rhythm and lots of nature images to mourn the captivity and death of Morf. I never claimed to be a great musician or poet, but I could carry the crowd for a while. As the old saying goes, "When the poem fails, stomp the rhythm and sing louder."

As I hit the last mournful notes, I looked around. Tessia, Ena and Adamu were silent, still feeling the tragic death of the great Morf. Tyrmiss was sobbing, large tears falling on the dust at her feet.

After a few moments, Tessia said, "And this, my friends, is why we are flying to the aid of the dragons."

Chapter Six

The next morning, we flew over the high pass of the Southern Ridge and saw the sea in front of us like a blue dream that stretched endlessly to the horizon. For land people like us, the sea is a wondrous and terrifying thing. At first, we couldn't take our eyes off it.

On our brooms, we followed Tyrmiss as she banked to our right, starboard as the sailors call it, and followed the coast as it led us west. By midmorning, we saw a wooded island. Drawing closer, we could see that the Blessed Isle, as befitting its name, was beautiful, a green gem in a sea of light. Orchards of blossoming fruit and nut trees swayed in a gentle breeze. And beyond, a forest of ancient trees lay at the foot of snowcapped peaks towering over the warm southern waters. It was not only a beautiful island, but also, the legends say, a magical place. The elemental spirit Liatris resided here. I closed my eyes and felt her presence like a whirlpool beneath the surface of the sea.

We circled the island once and landed beside a small castle, just a single keep like a stone box with the ruins of a curtain wall around it.

Tessia climbed down from Tyrmiss's back, stretched her legs and looked around. "Is this the Blessed Isle?" she asked. "Is this where my uncle lives?"

Before Tyrmiss could answer, a narrow door in the keep opened, and two men came out, a tall muscular man with a Voprian sword at his belt and an older man with white hair. I recognized the tall man as Wessel, General Zygmunt's companion, lover, and bodyguard who happened to be deaf and mute. Zygmunt had found Wessel when he was a homeless boy living in the alleys of Dragonja. Zygmunt had taken him in, given him food and shelter, and later as Zygmunt built the rebel army that eventually took back the kingdom from Ludek, Wessel became his adjutant. Wessel was completely devoted to the older man and had saved Zygmunt's life more than once.

The older man, though, did not look familiar to me. Could this old slightly stooped man be Zygmunt? When I served under the General, he was tall and vitally alive. His thick black mane, which Tessia had inherited, was like a dark crown that caught the light. He was dearly loved and admired by the men and women under his command, and he moved among them and fought beside them with skill and grace. Even the Drekavac soldiers looked up to him.

I did a quick calculation of the years. Tessia had now seen thirty-seven summers, and I was ten summers older than she. I had always assumed that Zygmunt was about twenty summers older than me which would make him sixty-seven. My goodness, I thought, the years have not been kind to him. I remembered my last conversation with him when I dressed his wounds after the battle for Dragonja. His wounds were not only of his body, but also of his spirit, feeling responsible for the deaths of so many.

He and Tessia embraced affectionately. He had been her mentor when she was young, teaching her how to fight, first with her hands and feet, and later with a sword, and he had been a strict commanding officer to her when she joined the rebel army. He had never shown any favoritism, making her earn every promotion. His attitude toward me had been far more lenient, recognizing I was valuable as a healer, but not cut out for military discipline.

"Welcome," the old man said and came over to me. "Norbert, it has been so long since we last saw each other. How are you?"

I recalled the last time I saw him at the end of the war, and I immediately recognized the warm brown eyes meeting mine, and the gracious manner of Zygmunt, my dear friend. "I'm well, General," I said.

"I am simply Zygmunt now," he said, waving his hand and giving a small smile at being addressed by his old rank.

"We've been expecting you," Zygmunt said graciously. "Tessia was kind enough to send a message by pigeon to say you would be paying us a visit."

He went to Tyrmiss, bowed his head slightly and greeted her warmly although the two of them had never been friends. He had tried aggressively to recruit her services for the rebellion years before, but she refused. It wasn't until Tessia befriended her that Tyrmiss had joined the fight and played a key role.

Zygmunt moved to Ena and Adamu, introducing himself and extending his hand. They were both instantly smitten. *He hasn't lost his charm*, I thought.

"You must be exhausted," he said to all of us. "Wessel will show you your quarters where you can refresh yourselves, and then we will catch up on what has happened these many years over dinner. Tyrmiss, please let me show you the stables which we use as a storage space. It's the only place we have large enough for you, and there have not been any horses on the island in decades. I hope it will be adequate for you."

In my room, I unpacked my kit, putting Queen Tessia's sack of gold coins behind a table against the wall. The invisibility spell was holding, so I thought the gold would be safe there. I left my own small sack of coins in my kit.

As I was leaving the room, Ena came walking down the hall.

"Why exactly are we here?" she asked. She wasn't uncivil in her tone, merely puzzled. We'd discussed this part of the quest before, but I supposed she was having trouble imagining that Zygmunt, the great hero of the revolution, was the charming old man she'd just met.

"We are here to ask Zygmunt's counsel," I explained. "He has the greatest military mind Tessia and I have ever encountered, and we are about to fight a large army with a small army. We need his help."

We met the others in the garden where a table was laid out resplendently with a variety of foods grown on the island. In this southern clime, tiger grapes and candy lemons, black melons and pepper pomegranates thrived. And mussels, tuna and sunfish were laid out in the center of the table. Nearby, a separate table for Tyrmiss had a large, seared tuna and a giant tureen of spring water.

Tessia told Zygmunt what had happened in the kingdom since he left twenty years before. The reign of Wise Queen Varvara, whom he had installed on the throne after the revolution, had been a great success, and she passed the crown to her adopted daughter Tessia. Clearly though, it wasn't working to have all power residing in the throne. So, with Tyrmiss's help, we instituted a new constitution which established rule by the Citizens Council.

"And has that worked for you?" Zygmunt asked.

"Oh yes, I hated having to govern, and truth to tell, I wasn't very effective as a peace-time ruler," Tessia said. "I'm an excellent general, but administrative duties bore me."

Next Zygmunt turned to me, "Norbert, how is Idella? As I remember, she is a baker."

He was the most gracious host I've ever known. Remembering my wife's name, as well as her profession, after twenty years was extraordinary. He drew me out to talk about my son Alaric, whom he'd known as a boy, and once he heard that I'd founded a school for mages and had two dozen students, he wanted to know all about it. I found it very easy to talk with him and I burbled on about the challenges of teaching magic. When

I paused to take a breath, he gracefully turned his attention to Ena, asking about the aqueduct project I had mentioned, and then bringing Adamu into the conversation to explain the mathematics of the project. We were delighted by the conversation, the food, the ocean breeze, and the sweet wine imported from the mainland. Well into the evening, I stifled a yawn.

"Oh my, I apologize for keeping you up so late," Zygmunt said, graciously. "But you are all so interesting, and rarely do we have guests these days. Perhaps tomorrow we can talk about the strategy for helping the dragons in their war? But tonight, you must rest."

Walking back to our rooms in the keep, Ena said, "What a fascinating man! A charming host and a war hero. Hmmm… I know a number of attractive older women who would love to meet him."

I laughed. "Zygmunt and Wessel have been lovers and companions for many years, my dear. So, the general is not…"

"On the market," she finished my thought.

"Exactly," I said, pecked my daughter on the cheek, and went to my room. After checking to make sure Tessia's sack of gold was still invisibly sitting under the table, I went to bed and slept, snoring like a Tyrian troll.

The next morning, I woke shortly after dawn and looked out the window. In the garden, the large table was set with piles of zeolon oranges, durian sorrow fruit, and slices of heart pumpkin. On Tyrmiss's smaller table, a bucket of mango eels squirmed. I washed my face in the basin, dressed and went into the hall where I saw Tessia.

"Morning, Norbert," she said, yawning. "I think I ate too much last night."

I laughed. "The food was delicious. I wonder…" I stopped myself, not wanting to be a prying guest.

"You wonder how my uncle came to occupy this island?" she said, finishing my thought. "I actually asked him that very question at dinner last night when you were talking with Adamu. Zygmunt said Queen Varvara gave him the island as a reward for his service to the kingdom. A number of years ago, he sent a message to me that he and Wessel were safe and living here. He invited me to come visit him, and I always meant to come, but..."

"You've been rather busy with your job."

"Yes," she grew thoughtful. "That's exactly what it's been. A job. Being queen is not what it's cracked up to be."

We laughed, but I knew she was telling the truth. Many times, I had the impression that the happiest times of her life were when she was a wild young girl running through the hills with Hamlin and Anja. She was carefree then. Now, she was a woman of substance, a woman with responsibilities, a queen, a general, a legend. I had often noticed that Idella and I, as well as her wife Kana, were the only friends Tessia had. Everyone else, sometimes even Heikum and Femke, treated her as if she were an institution rather than a person.

At breakfast, Zygmunt kept the conversation light, asking about the cedar forest in the Dry Hills which he remembered as a desert. He wanted to know how the Blue Witches had been able to bring rain to the desert, but I confessed that this kind of magic was beyond my skill. He also asked about Tyrmiss's daughter. Somehow, he surmised that her son had died, but he was far too tactful to bring up the subject. It was wonderful to see Tyrmiss speak with pride about Rozae while slurping down eels. It seemed that Zygmunt had enchanted the dragon as effectively as he had the rest of us. I was glad to see this warmth between them because in the old days, Tyrmiss had not trusted him.

After breakfast we moved to a different place in the garden where stone benches were placed in a semicircle. Zygmunt nodded to me, and as we had previously arranged, I lifted my wand and drew a square in the air. I tapped it twice, said the words *Tablă de cretă*, and a chalk board appeared. I handed him my wand and he began to draw a map, rudimentary at first, but once the board understood the task at hand, it voluntarily began filling in details and illustrations and when it reached the edge of the board, it extended until Zygmunt had a detailed map of the Dragonja and Bekla river valleys.

"Tyrmiss," Zygmunt began. "I've studied the songs and tales of the great battle between dragons and men that occurred seven thousand years ago. You were there, participating in that battle. How would you describe it?"

Tyrmiss looked at the ground and muttered, "It was a nightmare."

"Excuse me?" Zygmunt said.

"It was a nightmare," Tyrmiss repeated more loudly. "A slaughter. A bloodbath."

"How many dragons were killed in that battle?"

"There were ten thousand dragons, more or less, and I was the only one who survived."

"How many men were killed?"

"Perhaps a few hundred," Tyrmiss said. "Let me say that dragons have never taken relish in war as men and Drekavacs do. We kill only to eat…" Her voice trailed off and I knew she was thinking about the Drekavac soldiers she'd killed twenty years before in revenge for her beloved Rilla's death. She hung her head, realizing she was no better than the Drekavacs she'd killed. Tessia went to Tyrmiss and put her arms around the long scaly neck and whispered words of comfort in the upright ear. A tear rolled down Tyrmiss's cheek. Tessia caught the dragon tear and massaged the liquid into the scales above the eyes. Dragon tears were known to heal, and Tyrmiss was experiencing grief for her mate Rilla, her son Banos, and her tribe all over again.

"Tyrmiss," Zygmunt said soothingly. "We need for you to remember the battle, so we can learn from it. We don't want a repetition of that slaughter. Tell us what happened seven thousand years ago."

Tyrmiss shook off her grief and looked at the map that floated in front of us. "There were ten thousand of us spread across the mountains above the Dragonja River. Down below, there were many more men spread in long lines in the river valley. We could see their shields flashing in the sunlight."

The map filled in the details as Tyrmiss described them.

"What time of day was it?" Zygmunt prompted.

"It was morning. The sun was in our eyes, but we could see that the men had hundreds of the… what are they called? The giant crossbows?"

"Ballistas," Tessia suggested.

"Yes, ballistas," Tyrmiss closed her eyes, remembering. "We flew toward the army of men, and they let loose arrows, huge clouds flying at us like bees. The arrows stung as they hit our hides, but the arrows could not kill us unless they hit us in the eye or tore a wing. Some of the dragons crashed to the ground and the men with spears finished them off. But it was the ballistas that killed most of us. The bolts from the giant crossbows flew at us, hitting us in the throat or in the belly."

"How close together were you flying?"

"Very close. We flew wingtip to wingtip. Yrilla, our leader, our general as you would say, divided us into squadrons and told us to stay together so we could protect each other."

"And you flew straight at the army of men? There was no flanking of the enemy? No attempt to roll up their line?"

"I don't know what that means, Zygmunt."

"Was there any attempt to get behind them? Attack them from their rear?"

"Not that I know of… Dragons know nothing of these things. We have always lived at peace with each other and with other living beings until men arrived."

Tessia again put her arms around her friend's neck and whispered in her ear. It was obviously painful for Tyrmiss to have to relive that terrible day so long ago.

"What about intelligence assets? Did you have any way to know what the enemy's plans were or where their weaknesses were?"

"No, none of that," the dragon said, sounding puzzled. It was obvious that the art of war was a complete mystery to the dragon.

"Did you have a fifth column in the ranks of the enemy? Turncoats who would fight against their own side once the battle started."

"No. Not that I know of."

I remembered that in the revolution against Ludek, Zygmunt had recruited a platoon of Drekavacs who gave important intelligence to the rebels, and once the battle started, the turncoats opened the city gates and let our troops in.

Seeing that Tyrmiss's head was sinking lower and lower as it became clear to her that the dragon leaders she'd trusted in her youth had known nothing about war, Tessia requested a break and Zygmunt agreed.

I left Tessia comforting her friend, and I walked away from the garden and out into the orchard of orange trees. The fruit was everywhere, and I wondered what they did with all this excess. As far as I could tell, the only residents of the island were Zygmunt and Wessel. I wondered whether they traded the surplus of fruit for the wine and seafood which they seemed to have in abundance. Who was preparing our food? It seemed unlikely that Zygmunt and Wessel were putting much time into preparing meals and setting tables. Just then, I heard a humming sound and saw a quick flash of light on my right. When I turned, there was nothing there.

At that moment, I realized that this island, this Blessed Isle, was not only inhabited by the elemental spirit Liatris, as the legends say, but it was also enchanted.

When I returned to the garden, Tyrmiss had calmed down, and Tessia was sitting with Ena and Adamu quietly talking. Zygmunt and Wessel arrived shortly after I did.

"First, I want to apologize to Tyrmiss for interrogating her about the horrible day of that battle. I didn't mean to delve into such painful memories, but I thought it was important to understand why the battle went so badly for the dragons. We need to make sure that such a thing doesn't happen again. Now, based on what we know about that battle, we can devise a new strategy that may go much better in the coming weeks.

"The first thing we need to understand is that the most important principle of war is deceit. Deceiving your enemy encourages him to make mistakes, so you can exploit his weaknesses and keep him off-balance. Be aware of how your enemy perceives you and use that knowledge to do the unexpected. When your enemy expects you to strike on the left, strike on the right. When he expects you to strike him in the front, strike him in the back. When you are weak, make him think you are strong. When you are strong, make him think you are weak. In this way, a small army can conquer a large one.

"What happened in the ancient battle between dragons and men is well known. The lore has been passed down through the generations. The generals of the army of men will try to repeat that battle which ended so disastrously for the race of dragons. Your strategy will be to let them think that the current battle will go the same way. You should give them every chance to become overconfident."

Zygmunt looked at Tyrmiss and said, "There were a number of mistakes the dragons made in the war against men seven thousand years ago. We must make sure these mistakes are not repeated. One of the most obvious mistakes was that the dragons did not understand the power of the ballistas, nor did they understand their limitations. Ballistas are powerful weapons, but they are not accurate at a distance. When the dragons charged at the army of men, they clumped together thinking that when they came close to the ground to spread fire among the men, they would be able to help each other. But the fact is, being clumped together in the air made it easy for the men to shoot bolts at the squadrons and hit the dragons. Their lack of accuracy was not a problem because all they had to do was shoot a ballista at a squadron of dragons, and they were likely to hit, or at least graze, one of them. But this time if you charge the army of men, spread the dragons out with lots of space between them, so the bolts will likely miss you."

Tyrmiss nodded, beginning to understand a few of the principles of war. It was obvious that she had never thought about such things. Nor had any dragon.

"Another thing," Zygmunt continued, "The line of dragons should be longer than the line of men, if you can do so without weakening the middle of the line where the attack by the men is likely to be focused."

Zygmunt turned to the chalk board and with a wave of the wand he'd borrowed from me, erased the map and drew instead a series of dragon stick figures in a long line, and facing them a series of men stick figures in a slightly shorter line. The magic square interpreted his intention and turned the stick figures into beautiful illustrations of dragons and soldiers.

"You see," he said, pointing the wand at the end of the line of dragons. "If the ends of your line extend beyond the enemy line, you can flank your enemy, bending your line so that it attacks the end of their line on three sides. Then you continue this process down their line, always outnumbering the enemy at their weakest point. This is called *rolling up the line*. It is basic military strategy."

Zygmunt looked at Tyrmiss, making sure she was following his explanation. "If the enemy understands your strategy, then he will move his forces toward the end of the line, trying to stop your attempt to flank him. When he does, he will leave a weak spot further down his line. This weak spot is the place you attack with your main force."

Tyrmiss was beginning to understand. "So," she said, "the enemy is faced with two alternatives, neither of them advantageous to him. Either let us flank him and roll up the line. Or weaken his line to defend his flank."

"Exactly," Zygmunt said, glancing at Tessia. He knew she was already familiar with these basic strategies, but he was wondering whether she agreed that this strategy would work in the coming battle between the dragons and the army of men. When Tessia nodded, he continued. "Of course, in the smoke and confusion of battle, it's difficult to know exactly what is going on, so you have to look for small clues that tell you what's happening."

"What kind of clues?" Tyrmiss asked.

"It's hard to say," Zygmunt said. "You may see a flashing of shields in a place where they weren't before. Or perhaps there's a bugle call or a quickening in drumbeat signaling a pre-arranged order to change positions… But you, my friend, have a special advantage which you should exploit as thoroughly as possible in the coming war because it will make the difference between winning and losing."

"And what is my special advantage, General?" Tyrmiss asked.

"Dragons can hear the dreams of men."

Zygmunt went on to suggest a number of strategies to employ our special advantages. We had, after all, three skilled mages, as well as Tessia who had the reputation of being the greatest warrior of our time. Since the enemy would not be expecting humans to be allied with the dragons, the general recommended that we infiltrate the enemy forces. Two of the mages, Ena and Adamu, could be a mobile force behind the enemy line throwing fireballs, digging ditches, and carrying out assassinations against enemy officers, in other words, creating as much destruction and confusion in the enemy army as possible. Meanwhile, Tessia and I could infiltrate the castle in order to attack the king, his guard, and his ministers while his generals were in the field. We would also look for targets of opportunity: for example, stealing gold and silver coins from their treasury and tossing them into the streets to create a riot, or releasing prisoners from the dungeon, or pulling down the stone blocks from turrets onto soldiers below. He encouraged us to use our imaginations to create as much panic and havoc as possible.

When Zygmunt finished explaining overall strategy, he encouraged us to break into groups and develop specific tactics. Ena and Adamu sat on a stone bench and excitedly exchanged ideas about the ways they could be saboteurs behind enemy lines. Meanwhile, Tyrmiss grilled Zygmunt about battlefield tactics, and Tessia and I talked about the best way to get into the castle.

"By the way, Uncle," Tessia said. "We suspect that two Blue Witches have flown to the Western Coast."

"Blue Witches?" Zygmunt asked. "The Weather Witches? Do you suspect they are helping King Beyazit in his war against the dragons?"

"We don't know," she answered.

"I've heard of the weather witches, but I've never met one." Zygmunt said. "How effective are they at carrying out war?"

"Very effective. Very dangerous," Tessia replied. "Twelve years ago, a witch named Zamarrra nearly destroyed our kingdom through drought and flood. After we won the war, the witches became our allies and have restored the cedar forest in the Dry Hills, but I've never trusted them."

Zygmunt thought about strategy for a moment, then looked at me. "One of the first things you need to do when you get to the west coast, Norbert, is to determine whether the witches are there, and if so, where their allegiances lie. If they are allied with the king, then you will have to deal with them first."

Late in the day, none of us having eaten since breakfast, Zygmunt called for a break. He said that dinner was being served. Immediately, I wondered who had prepared the meal since Wessel had been silently standing guard nearby all day, and I hadn't noticed any servants or workers on the island. Could they have a cook who moved so unobtrusively that he or she was invisible? I was becoming convinced there was magic happening on this island, but of a subtle kind, invisible even to me. My professional curiosity was aroused, and I wondered how I could ask Zygmunt about this magic without seeming rude or ungrateful.

When I went back to my room to freshen up for dinner, a strange feeling came over me. Something was different about the room. I reached under the table to feel the sack of gold coins. It was gone. Someone or something had taken it. I thought about who could have done it. Tyrmiss cared nothing for gold, and besides she could not have squeezed her bulk through the window. Zygmunt or Wessel? It was unthinkable that these honorable men were thieves. Ena? Adamu? Equally unthinkable. It was Tessia's gold, so it was possible she had taken it, but surely, she would have mentioned it. As I walked down the hall, I saw my three companions and told them the sack of gold coins was missing from my room.

"Do you know anything about the gold?" I asked.

Ena and Adamu shook their heads, puzzled. Tessia narrowed her eyes in suspicion. Due to her first wife Taja's betrayal, this was a sensitive issue for Tessia.

"Don't worry," I told her, not wanting to upset her. "I'll solve the mystery and report back to you."

In the garden, I approached Zygmunt and asked whether we could talk privately. He nodded and we walked a short distance out of hearing of the others.

"Tessia's gold is missing from my room where I'd hidden it. I'm wondering whether there might be servants or helpers who moved it for safekeeping?" I never mentioned the words "stolen" or "thieves," but the implication was clear to him immediately.

He leaned toward me and said softly, even though we were a good distance from the others, "I know who might have taken the gold. After dinner, we'll talk to her sister."

Whoever was preparing the meals was an extraordinary cook. On the table, there was an assortment of seameats—tuna steaks, oysters on the half shell, large red crab claws. There was a mountain of fresh greens, and a sea vegetable dish that was tangy and delicious. There were fruits from the orchard—zeolon oranges, durian sorrow fruit, and slices of heart pumpkin. There were breads and puddings even Idella would've been proud to have baked—loaves with fruit and nuts, cheese rolls and finally when we thought we could eat no more, a huge pastry with a creamy filling that tasted of honey and lemon.

After feasting for longer than I should have, I noticed Zygmunt signaling me with a tilt of his head. It was time to unravel some of the mysteries of this island.

Chapter Seven

"I'm very sorry this happened, Norbert," Zygmunt said as he led me through the orchard. "It's been a number of years since Wessel and I have had guests here, and I had hoped this time it would be different.

"When Queen Varvara gave me this island twenty years ago, she warned me that it was reputed to be haunted, but she dismissed the rumors as being nonsense. As you remember, she was a very practical woman who looked for sensible explanations for supernatural phenomena. The island had been in the possession of her husband's family for generations. She knew it was uninhabited because people were afraid of the elemental spirts who supposedly live here. Since I was recovering from the wounds that I incurred during the revolution..."

He looked at me meaningfully, and I remembered how at the end of the war he'd had his lover Anja executed as a spy. The wounds that Zygmunt still carried were to his spirit, not his body, not uncommon for men and women who had gone to war. I suffered these kinds of wounds myself, as did Tessia.

"The Wise Queen thought the solitude here would help me heal." Zygmunt looked around at the beautiful orchard, the perfect gardens, the misty blue mountains in the distance, the waves crashing on the sea-cliffs. This jewel of an island was perfect in every way. And now, I thought, he was going to show me the fly in the ointment.

"Are you familiar with elementals?" Zygmunt asked.

"No. In fact, I've never known whether they exist at all except in stories."

"I'm not sure what the stories say about elementals, but the ones who live here are very protective of the island. They don't let just anyone live here. Twenty years ago, when Wessel and I first arrived, the ship captain made us swim to shore because none of his men would row to the island. We found the place to be spectacularly beautiful with orange groves and well-tended gardens and an empty keep that was fully furnished. But the first night, strange things started happening. First our money was stolen. Then Wessel was attacked outside the keep. I knew there was something here that didn't want us to stay. So, the second night, I walked out into the garden, and prayed to the spirits who live here. I thanked them for their hospitality and asked permission to live here. The next day, nothing happened to us, and in the evening, instead of Wessel and me having to prepare dinner, a wonderful banquet appeared. And now, every night I go into the orchard and thank the spirits for allowing us to live here, and twice a day an abundance of food appears for us.

"Several times as I prayed, a beautiful woman has walked up to me out of the dark forest. She has dark skin and wears a shimmering dress. Her name is Liatris. When you and the others first showed up on the island, I came here to the edge of the orchard, and asked her permission for your visit. She graciously allowed it. My guess is that her sister who takes care of our needs saw your gold and took it, perhaps not even realizing its value to you."

We were standing in front of a stone cairn taller than a man and covered in acanthus vines. Acanthus is known to have its roots in the spirit world, and I've often used its leaves in potions. Zygmunt and I kneeled before the cairn, and he gave a short prayer of gratitude. As he had described, a woman walked out of the forest and stood in front of us. I was shocked that she had the exact appearance of Idella, my wife, but I knew that the elemental spirit had read my mind and taken on the appearance of a woman I love. I wondered how the elemental queen appeared to Zygmunt. Had she taken the form of his mother or another woman he loved?

"Thank you, Liatris, for coming to us in answer to my prayer."

"I know why you're here, Zygmunt. And I know why you've brought this mage," she said inclining her beautiful head toward me. "You've come about the gold, haven't you?"

"Yes, I have, my Lady."

"I'm afraid there's not much we can do about the gold," Liatris said. "My sister Purpura, who is what you might call a *woodland sprite*, found it, and she plans to keep it."

"What was Purpura doing in my room?" I asked, but I regretted my tone immediately. After all, I was a guest on the island and had no right to claim a piece of it.

Liatris looked me up and down for a few moments, thinking no doubt about how to respond to my impertinence. When she finally spoke, it was with a gentle tone. "Mage, the room is not yours, but rather it is part of this island, known as the Blessed Isle, on which we elementals have lived since long before the age of ice. It is your own fault that Purpura claimed your property. After all, by casting a spell of invisibility, you made the gold part of the invisible world where we live."

She gave a small indulgent laugh. "You mages want to have it both ways. You want to live in the world of things with your friends, but you want to dip into the invisible world to perform your magic when it suits you. You are like apes who use straws to fish out termites from the earth without any regard for the many lives underground you are disturbing." I looked into her eyes which were exactly like the eyes of my beloved Idella but infinitely older. Liatris was as old as the earth itself; in fact, she was not so much a being as a vision, a dream of the Blessed Isle and all it had seen through the eons.

"My sister is not going to return your gold. She wants to

keep it because she thinks it is pretty. But I know you feel you have been betrayed. Your friend Tessia, the one they call the Dragonqueen, entrusted you with the gold, and you feel it is your duty to protect it. So, I am going to give you something much more valuable than the gold Purpura took. I am going to give you a boon."

I waited and when she didn't explain, I asked, "What kind of boon?"

She shrugged. "Whatever you wish. There will come a time in the near future when you suffer a great loss, and you wish the harm to be undone. When you suffer in this way, come to me on the Blessed Isle, and I will try to help you."

Zygmunt and I looked at each other in surprise. She was indeed giving me something of great value.

I bowed my head to her and said, "The harm was actually done to my queen. It was her gold that was stolen."

Liatris shrugged. "Your queen will not miss her gold. She can easily get more from the dragon with whom she has allied herself. The harm was done to you because you felt you had failed your queen whom you love. She will be happy you traded the gold for something much more valuable."

Liatris turned and walked back into the dark woods. At that moment, I decided to save the gift she'd given me for a time when it was most needed.

Part Three: The Valley of the Dragons

Chapter Eight

In early evening, we said goodbye to Zygmunt and Wessel. Tessia swung onto Tyrmiss's back. Ena, Adamu and I straddled our brooms, and we lifted off, heading west then north over the sea, flying parallel to the coast. We flew high, using cloud cover as much as we could, not wanting to alert any of King Beyazit's sailors or soldiers below. We flew all night without stopping, landing shortly before dawn on the rocky shore. We made a fireless camp, ate bread and fruit Wessel had given us, laid out our blankets and rested through the day. After dark, we ate the last of the fresh food, mounted up again and flew through the night. Around dawn, we landed on a sandy beach below a high cliff.

"You must be very quiet here," Tyrmiss whispered. "There's a busy road that runs next to the cliff above us. The road follows the coast north to Hoclav City where the king holds court."

After making sure we were safely hidden, Tyrmiss, taking advantage of the last of the darkness, slid into the surf and disappeared. She planned to swim out to sea, then take to the air and fly toward the city to reconnoiter while we rested. Tessia, Ena, Adamu and I settled into the shade of the cliff, ate dried fruit and hard tack that Ena had brought, and waited for Tyrmiss to return.

It was well after dark when we heard the beating of her wings approaching. She landed in front of us, and after she'd caught her breath, hoarsely whispered to us, "Thank the Goddess we've arrived in time. The king is still marshalling his forces. There's a sizable army of perhaps twenty thousand soldiers who are camped upriver from the city, and a camp nearby where war machines are being constructed. I counted over one hundred ballistas."

So Zygmunt was correct, I thought. *The king plans to use the same strategy that our ancestors used to defeat the dragons. Draw them out to the open plains and shoot them down as they attack. It was essential that Tyrmiss get the word out to the dragons that they should not fly in tight formation, but rather spread out so they will be more elusive targets.*

Tyrmiss nodded at me, having heard my thoughts. She knew she had to fly to the mountains to warn the dragon-leaders. Also, we needed to coordinate our behind-the-lines infiltration with the dragon's frontal assault.

"Also, you need to know I saw the two Blue Witches," Tyrmiss said.

"Where were they?" Tessia asked.

"They were standing on the castle battlements looking out at the bay. The water was strangely calm. My guess is that the witches are protecting the harbor from storms, so Beyazit's ships can bring in supplies."

"For a sea-faring people, the weather witches would be valuable allies," I said. "Did you see the king?"

"Yes, he was on the battlements talking to the witches. He's a monstrous fellow, half man, half squid."

As we mounted up again, I was struck by the incredible endurance of Tyrmiss. In the last two nights, she'd flown hundreds of leagues from Zygmunt's island, then reconnoitered the city and surrounding plains while her human companions slept, and now she was prepared to fly with Tessia on her back into the mountains to rejoin her adopted dragon-tribe. But Tessia had told me that the sleep cycle of dragons is different than that of humans. Tyrmiss would stay active for weeks, then curl up in her lair and sleep for a week. I wondered how long it would be before she needed to rest.

It was a moonless night, perfect for flying over a large plain full of enemy soldiers. We flew high, straight inland, and by morning we were in the mountains. There was no need to be surreptitious now, so we flew through the day stopping only to drink water and arrived at the dragon's home valley early the next morning.

After being impressed by Tyrmiss's tales of the great ice palaces created by the dragons of old, I was disappointed to find the Western Dragons living in caves which looked as if they were nothing more than large holes in the cliffs scratched out of the rock by generations of dragon talons. *This way of life*, I thought, *does not represent civilization, but merely subsistence.*

As we dismounted, we four humans—Tessia, Ena, Adamu and I—looked around at the squalor. "What is the name of this place?" I asked.

"We call it *home*," Tyrmiss answered simply. "Mage, I know that this... way of life is not impressive. You were expecting to see a magnificent city, and I've brought you to an encampment. But keep in mind dragons have been hiding from men for thousands of years, and we couldn't afford to make great cities which would have been easily spotted. We survived by being almost invisible. We've become masters of the unobtrusive. But now, men have discovered us, and just as men do with everything they discover, they want to destroy us."

"Now," she said. "I need to see my daughter." And she hurried off toward one of the caves.

I suddenly felt a rush of pity for Tyrmiss and her adopted tribe who wanted nothing but to be left alone but now were on the verge of extinction, and I reaffirmed my vow to do everything I could to help them.

A young dragon named Oroz, perhaps ten years old, showed Tessia, Ena, Adamu and me to a small cave where we would be sleeping. Soon, he brought a fresh fish, laid it on a flat stone and cooked it with his dragon breath until it was brown and crispy.

"Would you like for me put some moon bark on the hot stone?" he asked. I noticed his eyes were purple and shone with an inner light, like a cat looking at the moon.

"What's moon bark?" Tessia asked.

The young dragon looked surprised. Evidently, in his world, everyone knew about moon bark.

"It's the bark from a tree that grows on the edge of the timberline," he explained. "We heat it on a hot stone, and it gives off a delicious aroma. It makes us feel good."

We declined his offer, but I wanted to know more about this herb. We invited the young dragon to eat with us, during which he explained that almost everyone breathed the vapors of moon bark, except baby dragons.

"I'm not a baby anymore," he said, proudly. He looked at Ena. "Could you teach me magic?"

"I could probably teach you a few basic charms," she said politely. She glanced at me, and I nodded.

After we ate, I walked to the river, which flowed clean and clear here, high up in the mountains, and followed the shore a distance, stretching the cramps from my legs. I stopped and took a long drink and looked around. Away from the dragon camp, which was muddy and littered with fish bones, the valley was quite beautiful with aspens climbing the slopes and everything bathed in a clear light from the bright sky.

I saw Ena and Oroz below me in a meadow. Ena was pointing her wand at a boulder while explaining something to the young dragon. I noticed they were the same height, but Ena was a grown woman while Oroz was clearly immature, rocking back and forth on his back feet, full of the swagger of a little boy and lacking the restrained wisdom of the ancient dragons raising him. The boy-dragon watched my daughter with wide blue eyes. If he'd been human, I would have said he was developing a crush on this pretty redhead who was showing him friendly affection. Ena shot a small fireball at the boulder, flames licking the stone before dissipating harmlessly in the air. Oroz started jabbering excitedly, his eyes wide. He had just recently developed the hard flat teeth at the back of his mouth that would function as a striking surface to ignite the gases coming up from his belly. I didn't see any harm in Ena teaching him basic fire safety. I assumed we would be living here only a few weeks, and then the war would be over, and we could go home.

Returning to the cave, I saw that Adamu had laid a pile of dry wood next to the entrance. He pointed his wand, igniting the wood, and soon, we had a warm place to rest until Tyrmiss could call a meeting of the elders.

"I don't see why we have to fight these humans," Komroisder, known as The Scowler, an old male with a bald wrinkly neck, was saying. I had seen only a few dragons in my lifetime, and I hadn't realized that as they get old, they lose their scales. "Why don't we just move further inland as the witches and the trolls have?" he asked.

"Because now that the humans know we exist, they will hunt us down wherever we go," a young female argued. "We must wipe them out, the same way they want to wipe us out. I have two dragonlings. I cannot abide their growing up never knowing whether they'll be attacked and killed."

"There are far too many of the humans to kill all of them," said an old female named Yvnede the Dark One who seemed to be leading the meeting. "Even if we were to wipe out all of the humans on the coast, there would be other humans in other lands, who would hear about the massacre and come here to avenge their kind. We must fight this King Beyazit until he can fight no more, then negotiate peace. We will kill no more humans than we have to. In this way, we can free ourselves of the constant threat without creating a situation that stirs humans in other lands to attack us."

A number of the council members nodded at the wisdom of Yvnede. Having attended many raucous Citizen Council meetings in Dragonja City, I was impressed by the courteous way the dragons addressed each other, quietly listening and waiting their turn to speak. After a long silence while the dragons considered what had been said so far and what still needed to be said, Tyrmiss was recognized to speak.

"My friends," she said, lifting her head above the other dragons, so she could be heard, "I am so grateful to you all. When my dragonlings Rozae and Banos and I arrived in this valley three years ago, you took us in. The mother-dragons in particular treated us with kindness and generosity. When my dear son Banos was suffering with illness, the mother-dragons cared for him as though he were their own son. And when he finally died, the mother-dragons brought food and sympathy to my daughter and me. We had no one else, and we may have died of grief and exhaustion without your love. My own Eastern Tribe, as you know, was exterminated seven thousand years ago in the Great War with Humans, and I had lived with my wife Rilla until twenty years ago when she was killed by a Drekavac soldier. Having spent eight years in the company of humans, my dear friend Queen Tessia and her court, I had forgotten what it is to live in a community of dragons. As grateful as I am to Tessia for giving me a place in her castle Windkeep, and as grateful as I am to the Mage Norbert," Tyrmiss nodded to Tessia and me. "Still, I am not human. I found many of their ways puzzling, and I yearned to be with my own kind.

"Humans—and I include Drekavacs here because as we all know they are merely different races within the same species—have a need to dominate and control. They act this way with each other. For example, humans have relegated Drekavacs to a second tier in their society. Drekavacs are allowed certain jobs, such as being soldiers and guards, but they are not allowed to own land or to found businesses, and even when the laws of humans give them that right, the customs deny it. And humans have the same need to dominate other beings. To them, the natural beasts of the fields and forests, birds, bears, rabbits and deer, are there for the taking, and humans don't even bother to thank the departing spirit of the animal they've killed, as we do when we take fish from the river.

"Yes, humans are strange, not like dragons or dolphins or whales or other sentient animals, nor are they like the beasts of the field. In Queen Tessia's kingdom where I come from, humans burned the great cedar forests a thousand years ago simply because their enemies, the Blue Witches, worshipped trees. But now, the queen has wisely allowed the witches to return to their ancient homeland to replant trees and turn the desert once again into a forest. But Tessia will be the first to tell you that she did this not out of love for the witches, for they had betrayed us, stealing my dragonlings and bringing drought and flood to the kingdom. Instead, the wise queen made peace with the witches and allowed them to return to their ancient homeland because her kingdom needs the forests to be restored. So, when I point out the failings of the humans, keep in mind I am not talking about Queen Tessia, nor the Mage Norbert who advises her, nor the mages Ena and Adamu whom he has taught.

"Most humans are not wise like these four beside me, nor are humans wise like dragons. We serve the Goddess, and we respect all life, even human life. However, humans have disturbed the balance and broken the circle of life. They tear up the soil with their plows, leaving the wounded skin of the earth unprotected. They cast nets into the rivers, taking not just what they need to survive, but all creatures, and the ones they do not want, they kill. They drag heavy nets across the ocean floor destroying the coral that gives life to all. They lay out poisoned meat for wolves to eat, killing them and their pups. They train dogs to hunt large cats. Men kill even the sentient creatures—whales, dolphins, elephants, and dragons. Humans have no respect for Creation, and this is why we are here today discussing war against them.

"The problem, though, is that dragons know little of war. In our long history, there have been no wars between dragons. We have no songs passed down through generations telling of heroic battles and conquered cities burning through the night. We have no armor, nor weapons, nor shields, nor helmets. We have no battlements and turrets, nor machines of war. When we lift our voices, we do so to sing praises to the Goddess. We list every blessing she has given us, and our songs rise into the heavens to please her.

"Men, on the other hand, study war. There are entire colleges devoted to learning how to kill and conquer, just as there are colleges devoted to learning how to destroy forests and mountains. For men, war is a game, a contest of will, ferocity and intelligence. Recently, I spent a few days with the great human general Zygmunt, renowned among his people as a great conqueror. He is Queen Tessia's uncle and a friend of Mage Norbert, so the general shared with us a few strategies he thought we could use in our war. We need to consider his suggestions carefully. We cannot make the same mistakes that dragons made in the Great War with the Humans. I was there. I watched my brothers and sisters, my neighbors and our leaders killed, one after the other, until I was the only one left.

"My hide bristled with arrows. My wings were torn. I flew from the battlefield and lay down in a meadow beside a stream to die. Fortunately, Rilla, who was just a dragonling at the time, found me and nursed me back to health. Rilla eventually became my wife, my lover, my partner, and we were happy together for thousands of years until a soldier stumbled upon her sleeping in the very spot beside the stream where she had found me long before. And the soldier killed her with a spear through one of her hearts for no reason other than he could.

"I will not, I cannot, watch another slaughter of dragons at the hands of men. We must flee, or we must study war as men do. If we decide to stay in this valley, then we must have a strategy that hurts them so badly they sue for peace."

Tyrmiss lowered her head. Her face was covered in tears. Tessia reached up and put her arm around Tyrmiss's neck and drew her face close to hers. I looked at Ena and Adamu. Their faces were covered in tears, and lifting my hand to my face, I was surprised to discover I was silently weeping as well.

There was a long silence after Tyrmiss finished speaking. Yvnede finally raised her head above the others and said, "Our sister Tyrmiss has given us much to consider. It is clear we cannot stay in this valley where men can find us easily. We must either move inland and find a new home, or we must go to war against men to defend ourselves. Do other elders wish to speak of this decision?"

An old male raised his head. "I want to thank sister Tyrmiss for speaking so eloquently about her life. She has much more experience in dealing with men than the rest of us. She spoke of developing strategies of war we would need to bring against men. May we hear more about these strategies?"

Tyrmiss glanced at Tessia who gave a small nod. This was what we'd hoped for, a chance for Tessia to address the council. "Respected Elders," Tyrmiss began. "We are fortunate to have with us my friend Queen Tessia, who is known as the greatest warrior of our time. She studied with her uncle General Zygmunt, and she has led men into battle many times. I am proud to have served with her. And I might add, she has never fought against dragons, only men.

"I know it is not the custom to have humans address this

council, but we are living in perilous times when we must get used to accepting actions and attitudes we find odd. We must become comfortable with being uncomfortable. Therefore, I request that the council allow Queen Tessia to answer the excellent question about what strategies we should use in the war against men."

Again, there was silence, then Yvnede said, "If there is no objection from council members, then the Queen may address this council." She looked around, but no dragon objected. Instead, they looked interested in what this human Queen might tell them about the strategies of war.

Tessia stood up, so she could be heard and seen by the council members. "Dragon-mother Yvnede and esteemed council members, I would like to start by explaining why the strategy of the Eastern dragons turned into a slaughter. Then I would like to explain a better way of carrying on battle, one which may lead to the victory we need. And finally, I would like to explain how I and the three mages," she said, moving her hand in the direction of Ena, Adamu and me, "will attack the army of men from behind, causing them to become confused and disorganized."

Tessia went on to recount what Zygmunt had explained to us about spreading out the line of dragons to make them a more difficult target for the ballistas, as well as flanking the enemy in order to roll up their line. And then, Tessia added a tactic of her own.

"I'm going to explain a tactic that your general," she nodded at Yvnede, "may want to consider. The first part is a double charge, and the second part is a feigned retreat and forced rout. Here are the steps: first the dragons fly once over the men using fire and talon to cause fear and destruction, then after passing the main part of the enemy's army, the dragons should bank in an orderly way and turn back to fly over the enemy again raking them with fire and talon, doubling the amount of damage."

"It's like Tsolonyi!" one of the dragons said, and a number of the council members nodded in agreement.

"What's Tsolonyi?" Tessia asked.

"It's a game dragonlings play on the river," Yvnede said. "They fly from one bank to the other and then fly back. In both directions, they drag their talons in the water. It's a race, but you lose if you lift your talons out of the river. All the dragonlings have to turn in one direction so they don't run into one another."

"That's right," Tessia said, smiling. "I want you to play Tsolonyi with the enemy, but instead of dragging your talons in the water, you rake the enemy with your talons and breathe fire on them."

The dragons were getting excited. They now knew exactly how to attack the enemy.

"And the next step," Tessia added, "is the feigned retreat. The dragons return to their starting point in the hills and wait for the men to charge, then the dragons retreat, and retreat again, letting the men tire themselves out as they climb the hills. Then, the dragons attack again. By this time, the men have hopefully forgotten about their ballistas which they left on the plain, and they'll have nothing but bows and arrows to defend themselves. Most of them will try to hide, or they will turn and run. You should be able to finish off the enemy at this point."

Years later, this strategy of raking the enemy with a charge of calvary, turning for a second charge, and then feigning a retreat became a standard tactic taught in colleges of war around the world, but my impression at the time was that Tessia had thought of it at that moment in council. She was truly a brilliant general. She went on to explain what she and the mages would be doing behind enemy lines. The dragons listened, rapt with curiosity. Like Tyrmiss, they had never realized before that there is an art to war. I wondered, though, whether in teaching the race of dragons how war is conducted, we'd woken a sleeping giant.

Walking back to our cave, Tessia said, "That went well."

"Yes," I said. "We were lucky the council vote was unanimous. Tyrmiss told me that if there is even one dissenting vote, then the council will continue discussing the issue until everyone agrees."

"Oh," Tessia looked puzzled. "I didn't know that."

"Tyrmiss thought it was better you didn't know until after the vote. She didn't want you to feel too much pressure."

The corners of Tessia's mouth tightened. She didn't like being kept in the dark.

"Tessia, my friend," I added quickly, thinking she shouldn't dwell on the idea that Tyrmiss had kept something from her. "Your discussion of strategy was brilliant. You explained all the relevant principles simply and thoroughly. You showed the dragons how to win the war. Even your uncle could not have done a better job. Thank you."

She looked pleased, then laughed. "I did do a good job, didn't I?"

I laughed and we entered the cave. We needed a good night's sleep. Tomorrow we were going to war.

Chapter Nine

Following Zygmunt's advice, I woke before dawn, dug the small bag of coins from my kit, the last of the gold I'd brought, flew on my broom to the harbor and waited for the two witches to arrive. Before long, they came down from the castle and as they drew near, I pulled back my hood so they could see my face. Zamarrra and Evanora were startled to see me. It was barely dawn and no one else was on the docks, so they walked up to me with their eyebrows raised in a silent question.

"Hello, Witches," I said. "Nice day for casting spells on the water, wouldn't you say?"

They silently waited for me to explain. "I'm here because I'm wondering why you are here," I said.

"We were hired by King Beyazit to calm the waters in the harbor," Zamarrra replied carefully. "Why is this your concern?"

"Did you know the King is going to war against the dragons?" I asked.

"Yes," Evanora said. "But we have no part in the war." She looked at me with narrow eyes, sizing me up. "Are you allied with the dragons?"

"Yes, I am," I said. "If you value your lives, then you should leave this kingdom immediately."

"We can't leave yet. We haven't been paid," Evanora retorted.

"How much did the king promise you?"

Evanora hesitated for just a moment, tipping me off that she was about to inflate the sum. "Twenty gold coins," she answered.

"Queen Tessia will pay you ten gold coins to leave the

kingdom," I said, my hand on my wand. Ten coins was all I had. If they wouldn't accept it, then there would be trouble.

Evanora laughed. "Why should we accept less than what the king promised us?"

"Because you'll live to spend it," I answered, watching their eyes carefully. I knew that in a wand-to-wand fight, I could beat them easily, but a battle between us would be loud and call attention to my presence. Also, they were doing important work restoring the forests in the Dry Hills of Dragonja. It would be best for everyone if the two witches left quietly.

"Can you pay us now?" Zamarrra asked. When I nodded, she said, "Come, Mother, let us take the gold he offers, and go home. This is not our fight."

I escorted the two witches away from the city, flying high on our brooms across the broad plain, and looking down, I saw thousands of soldiers and tents spread in every direction. And worse, I counted more than fifty ballistas.

When Zamarrra, Evanora and I were over the Valley of the Dragons, the two witches veered off to the mountains on their way to visit their old home of Sheonad while I landed outside the cave which served as the meeting place of the Council of the Elder Dragons. The Elders were already in session and were startled by my bursting in. Evidently, they were used to a certain slow decorum in their meetings, and I was being rude by speaking quickly without being recognized. "We must act quickly," I said, almost shouting. "Thousands of soldiers are already encamped next to the river, and more are arriving today. We must either attack them or retreat. If we stay here, we'll be trapped in this valley."

Tessia nodded to me, then turned to Yvnede, her head bowed, and the two of them spoke quietly. Yvnede quickly called the meeting to order. It was clear by the serious expressions on the faces of the elders they'd already made a decision, and my announcement merely confirmed the urgency of the situation.

"I move that we declare war on the humans," Yvnede said. "Are there any further comments on the issue?" She looked around the room. "All those in favor?" Every council member raised his or her head. It was unanimous. The dragons were declaring war against the humans, and their attack would start immediately.

"Now I turn the floor over to Queen Tessia who has already explained the tactics we will use," Yvnede said, nodding to Tessia who stood and faced the council of elders.

"It is essential," Tessia explained, "that we spread out the dragons in the frontal assault. There should be at least five wingspans between each dragon."

"Perhaps you can explain the flanking strategy again?" a young female in the front row said.

"I'll be glad to," Tessia said. "We will have a long line of dragons flying toward the much denser line of humans. At each end of our line will be a squad of dragon warriors who will veer off and fly around the line of men. The purpose of these squads is to outflank the soldiers; that is, to get behind their line and attack from there. Since dragons can fly much faster than a man can run, outflanking them should be easy," Tessia explained.

"Please tell us again about the feigned retreat," Yvnede requested.

"When the signal is given, all dragons should disengage from the enemy and fly back to the mountain ridge. We will reorganize there on high ground. With luck, the humans will think they've routed us and will charge up the slope to finish us off. Since they cannot move their ballistas quickly, the men will be charging uphill without ballista support. At the signal, we will swoop down on them."

"You said earlier that we may not use a feigned retreat," Yvnede pointed out.

"A feigned retreat depends on our maintaining discipline. Otherwise, it will turn into chaos. The commander will have to decide whether we have sufficient discipline to pull off the ploy."

Looking around the council room, I noticed Ena and Adamu in one corner of the cave and almost laughed. At my instruction, the two mages were wearing long green robes and high conical hats strapped under the chin. The fabric, which I had designed years before, was covered with moons and stars. The purpose was to make it clear to anyone who saw them that they were masters of magic. The effect was intended to scare our enemies, and it usually worked. I didn't have time to change, so I would go into battle in my daily attire: a linen shirt and breeches, short leather boots, a simple peaked cap, and a brown hooded cape. It would have to do.

"Your Majesty, we are counting on you and your mages to attack Beyazit and his commanders directly," Yvnede said. "We want their army in the field to be leaderless and confused."

"We understand," Tessia said, graciously. She had actually invented the strategy but seemed willing to let Yvnede take credit. The old dragon seemed unsteady on her feet as if she were inebriated, and I hoped she would be able to follow through with the strategy.

"Your Majesty," Yvnede said, her purple-rimmed eyes filling with tears. "It is likely that neither you nor I will survive this battle, so I want to say that we dragons are very grateful for your help."

Tessia nodded and shifted her feet. She wasn't comfortable with emotional goodbyes, so she thrust her fist toward the grandmother dragon and said. "It's a good day to die."

The old dragon bumped her talon against Tessia's fist. "It's a good day to die," Yvnede echoed, taking a deep breath and standing taller.

Part Four: The Burning Plain

Chapter Ten

As the dragon-army rose from the valley and headed west over the mountains toward the Hoclav Plain, our small contingent separated from the main force and flew north, Tessia and Tyrmiss in the lead and Ena, Adamu, and me following on our brooms. Clumping together would make an easy target for the ballistas, and we didn't want to be spotted by soldiers, so we spread out and flew through the mountains until we were far from Hoclav City, then veered west toward the sea. Once we were out of sight of land, Tyrmiss led us back in the direction of the city. By then it was midday. We skimmed the surface of the water, almost invisible to the guards on the battlements until we were on them. We lit the poor devils on fire and landed on the balcony of the highest tower where Yvnede had told us the king held court. Tyrmiss perched on the rail of the balcony in case we needed a quick retreat while Tessia charged through the doorway with her sword, Agatha the Righteous, at the ready and her three mages close behind.

The last thing that Beyazit expected was to have a warrior and three mages enter his throne room from a balcony high in the air. The first guard gaped at us and had his head neatly separated from his shoulders by Tessia's blade. The next one lowered his halberd only to have Tessia lop off the hand that held it. I rushed past Tessia into the large room in time to see the courtiers running toward the far exit, and the king glaring at us, outraged at this intrusion. It probably hadn't crossed his mind that the dragons might have human allies.

Then King Beyazit stood up and I saw he didn't have legs but tentacles, eight of them, and he could move quickly on them. He ran, pushing past his courtiers who were crowding the exit, knocking them down as he got into the hall. I ran after him, my wand at the ready, with Ena and Adamu close behind. The courtiers, seeing three mages rushing toward them, scattered, leaving an opening through which I ran in hot pursuit of the king.

Not knowing in which direction he'd turned, I said, "Ena, Adamu, go that way. Find him! We can end this war quickly if we can catch him."

I ran toward the wide marble stairway and looking down, saw the top of his head. A group of Drekavac soldiers saw me and charged up the stairs. I pointed my wand at them and shot a ball of fire into their midst, lighting several of them on fire. The whole squadron turned and ran back down the stairs with me not far behind. From above, I heard the singing of Tessia's Voprian blade and realized that some of the courtiers must have regained their nerve and turned to face Tessia's attack. Big mistake. Tessia would dispatch them quickly, covering our retreat.

More soldiers were coming up the stairs. I shot a couple of fireballs at them, but they hid behind their shields and kept coming. At this point, I realized I wasn't going to catch up to the king. I turned and ran back down the hall and entered the throne room in time to see Tessia wiping blood off her blade. There were dead and injured soldiers and courtiers lying around the room, and the floor was slippery with blood.

"Where are Ena and Adamu?" Tessia asked.

"I sent them down the back stairs in pursuit of the king," I answered.

The exasperated look in her eyes confirmed my growing feeling I should have kept Ena and Adamu with me. They had no fighting experience, and there was no way to know how they would react in their first battle.

"We need to find them," Tessia said, heading into the hall, and when I pointed at the service stairway where I last saw my young charges, she ran toward the door and opened it. A huge cloud of black smoke came out of the stairway.

Tessia ripped the scarf from around her waist and covering her mouth and nose with the cloth, entered the cloud of smoke. I used my cloak to cover my face and followed her.

The smoke blinded us, and we both started coughing violently. At the next floor down, to get away from the smoke, which was coming from further down in the castle, Tessia opened the door.

We found ourselves in a large kitchen with rows of ovens on the right wall. A line of tables ran down the middle of the room, and on each table sat a pile of raw dough in various stages of kneading. On the left wall there were storage bins. And the far wall there were three doors. I guessed the middle door led to the marble stairway where I'd been before, and the right and left doors were for storage. I wondered whether we should check to see whether Ena and Adamu had taken shelter in one of the storage rooms.

Tessia must have been thinking the same thing. Holding Agatha at the ready, she quickly opened the right door. There was nothing but barrels of flour and sugar and baskets of apples. Moving left, she again held Agatha at the ready and quickly opened the middle door. Inside were three fat women dressed as cooks, each holding a large knife. As soon as the door was open, one of them lunged at Tessia, ready to slice her face off. Tessia slammed the door and leaned against it, keeping it closed while the cooks inside pushed against it. Tessia struggled, but she was clearly not going to win this shoving contest. I pointed my wand at the door and said a locking charm which would hold the door closed for a short time, and Tessia opened the left door which brought us to the marble stairway where I had been shooting fireballs at Drekavac guards earlier.

"We can't spend any more time looking for Ena and Adamu," Tessia said. "The king seems to have escaped. Let's go back and find Tyrmiss. We need to get out of this tower and join the fight."

I knew she was right, but I worried my daughter was in danger. I could only hope she and Adamu had found a safe place to wait for the end of the battle.

We ran back up the service stairs and down the hall to the throne room. We had to be careful stepping over bodies and walking across the floor slippery with blood. Out on the balcony, Tyrmiss was lying behind the stone balustrade, trying to make herself as small as possible.

"The soldiers on the rampart spotted me up here and started shooting at me with a ballista. I had to hide," she said.

I looked around for my broom which in the excitement of our first attack, I had left here on the balcony, but it was nowhere to be seen. I wondered whether Ena had her broom. Could she have flown from this tower? I was beginning to panic, thinking about my daughter being hurt and I was powerless to protect her.

"By the Goddess, there goes Beyazit," Tessia said, pointing over the rampart to the harbor below. I looked over the edge and saw the king scampering on his many legs across the dock. When he reached the edge of the water, he dove in and disappeared. The water roiled and a large sea monster, perhaps it was Thortia, the city's patron demigod, emerged from the dark surface. She had the seaweed-covered head of a woman but the claws of a crab. I wondered whether she was capable of climbing out of the water.

"What do you want to do?" Tyrmiss asked Tessia.

"Let's do our job," she answered. "Let's fly down to the rear of the army and cause confusion and havoc. Just make sure we don't collide in midair with another dragon." Tessia climbed on Tyrmiss's back in her usual place holding onto one of the spines on the dragon's neck. Then, she turned to me and extended her hand. "Norbert, get behind me."

Grabbing her hand, I climbed up and sat behind her, settling between the wings with my arms around Tessia's waist. Twenty years before, Tessia and I had flown into battle on Tyrmiss's back a number of times. I settled into the familiar spot and gripped the belt around Tessia's waist. It felt like coming home.

Tyrmiss leaped off the balcony and went into a dive, gaining speed as she went straight for the soldiers on the rampart with the ballista. There was no time for them to aim, so the bolt they fired missed us, flying wildly over our heads. Tyrmiss bore down on them, breathing fire, setting the ballista alight. The soldiers hit the floor, and we flew on, leaving the city walls behind and heading for the battle on the burning plain before us.

The battle had become a melee: wounded dragons on the ground were being swarmed by Drekavac soldiers; other dragons wheeled overhead, swooping down to breathe fire; archers fired at the dragons whose hides bristled with arrows. The tactic of Tsolonyi, in which the dragons would have flown in wide formation raking the soldiers, had been abandoned, as had the feigned retreat to the hills. Instead, it was chaos on the battlefield, and the dragons, who were hugely outnumbered by the soldiers, were losing by attrition.

Tyrmiss flew low over the soldiers raking them with her talons and breathing fire. Tessia shot her bow with deadly accuracy to the left, and less accurately, I shot fireballs from my wand to our right. We were clearing a swath as Tyrmiss headed toward the nearest ballista. Seeing the dragon coming straight at them, the soldiers on the platform lost their nerve and dove for safety, just as Tyrmiss set the war machine on fire. Swooping to our right, she set out for another ballista, but this time, the soldiers kept their nerve, aimed at us and let loose a bolt straight at us. If Tyrmiss hadn't swerved just in time, the bolt would have gone right into her neck. I had given up holding onto Tessia's belt. She was moving around so much that I would have been whipped off Tyrmiss and fallen into the swirling mass of soldiers and dying dragons below. I grabbed Tyrmiss's bony shoulder, pressed my knees into the base of her neck, and held on for dear life, shooting fireballs at the soldiers below as best I could.

And suddenly, we were hit. A ballista bolt grazed Tyrmiss's neck and went through Tessia's calf. Tessia's artery was squirting blood, and I shouted at Tyrmiss, "Tessia is hit! We need to land!"

Tyrmiss ducked a ballista bolt which flew past her head, and we went down quickly, crashing into the battlefield. I was banged up, but not seriously hurt. Tyrmiss sat on her haunches breathing fire at the soldiers who tried to approach us. Tessia's calf was spraying blood from the artery—even if the soldiers didn't kill Tessia, she would bleed out quickly if I didn't save her. I dragged her a few feet to the safest place I could think of, directly beneath the neck of the dragon. I knew Tyrmiss would defend her friend to the death. With my right hand, I pushed the slippery ends of the severed artery together and used my wand to cauterize them. The bleeding stopped. I looked up in time to see two soldiers approaching us from behind in Tyrmiss's blind spot. I pointed my wand at them and shot a fireball quickly. It was a wild shot that went over their heads but gave them notice to back off.

I pulled Agatha from her sheath and placed the pommel in Tessia's right hand. She'd lost a lot of blood but was still conscious enough to smile wanly at me. "If the soldiers get past Tyrmiss and me, you'll have to use your sword. Understand?" She nodded, the old look of fierce determination coming over her face. I looked behind Tyrmiss and again soldiers were cautiously approaching. I pointed my wand and fired twice, the first shot went over their heads, but the second one caught a soldier squarely in the face, making him scream and fall on his knees. His friends knocked him down and put out the fire, then dragged him to safety. I grabbed a shield lying on the ground and stationed myself behind Tyrmiss, hiding from the arrows shot at me. I shot a fireball every now and then, but the number of soldiers was overwhelming, and I knew it wouldn't be long before they overwhelmed us.

Then I remembered the dragons could speak to each other through their thoughts. "Tell Yvnede to call a retreat!" I shouted to Tyrmiss. "Tell them to go back to the low hills as we planned!"

Tyrmiss's eyes, blood red from anger and fear, squinted, and I could feel her sending out the thought to Yvnede. She knew as well as I that when the dragons retreated, some of the soldiers might follow them as we hoped, but many would stay on the battlefield to finish off the wounded dragons, including Tyrmiss. With Tyrmiss dead, Tessia and I would not stand a chance of survival behind enemy lines.

And then with no warning at all, Ena and Adamu dropped out of the sky on their brooms. Adamu stationed himself to Tyrmiss's left and waved his wand at the dust on the ground, stirring it up into whirlwinds. As the whirlwinds grew in size and power, they picked up dirt and rocks, spears and swords, helmets and severed hands, a tornado of battle-debris. Then he sent the dynamos out into the battlefield, forcing soldiers to cover their eyes and fall back. In their need to protect themselves from the tornados, they forgot all about Tyrmiss and her companions. Meanwhile, on the other side of Tyrmiss, Ena was busy as well. Pointing her wand at a dark cloud overhead, she twirled it saying an incantation I didn't recognize. Then she brought down her wand eye-level. I could see the fear in the soldiers' eyes as they saw what was about to happen.

Down came a lightning bolt, hitting in the mass of soldiers, exploding with a loud clap that shook the ground. Soldiers, weapons, dirt and debris went flying into the air. As Ena lifted her wand again to the sky, the soldiers turned and ran, a lightning bolt exploding behind them.

And then it was quiet all around us. We could hear the distant shouts of soldiers charging toward the hills where the dragons had retreated and were waiting for them.

Tessia, meanwhile, had passed out from lack of blood, but her leg was no longer bleeding. I checked the rest of her to make sure there were no other wounds, and then I turned my attention to Tyrmiss. The dragon had a long gash across her throat, but it hadn't hit an artery. Fortunately, dragon hide is very thick and covered in scales, so a laceration has to be very deep to do serious damage. She let me treat the wound with a salve from my kit and sew up the hide with shark-gut. She also had a small tear in her right wing which I stitched up. She would be completely healed in a matter of weeks. Tessia, on the other hand, was in danger from loss of blood. I needed to get her to a place where she could rest and consume fluids, and I could check on her every few hours.

I looked around at the carnage of the battlefield. Thousands of men and hundreds of dragons lay on the ground. Many were dead, some were barely moving. In the distance, there were squads of soldiers giving the *coup de grâce* to wounded dragons, cutting off their heads or running a spear through one of their hearts. I felt utterly exhausted. What a pity. What a waste. This is the thing that poets sing of and boys dream of? War is not a thing of glory, but an ugly disgrace. The world writhes in agony in order to satisfy the pride of kings.

I looked off into the hills. The dust the charging soldiers were raising was well into the distance, and there were no sounds of battle yet. It appeared that the dragons' feigned retreat was working. The soldiers were being drawn away from their war machines, and soon the dragons would turn and attack the disordered ranks of men who would have little defense against fire and talon coming down on them from the air.

Chapter Eleven

Ena and Adamu arranged a sling between their brooms, and we laid Tessia carefully down. They would carry her back to the Valley of Dragons where she could rest. I gave them careful instructions how to make the yarrow root poultice to help her wound heal.

"It's best to let the body heal itself," I said. "Don't use your wands unless you have to."

The advice was, of course, unnecessary. They were both accomplished mages I had trained myself, but they understood my instructions came from love for the queen and not from a lack of confidence in their abilities. So, they indulged me and nodded solemnly at my instructions.

After Ena and Adamu flew off with Tessia suspended between them, Tyrmiss and I waited on the battlefield. The King's cleanup squads finishing off the dragons stayed well away from us. The word was out this dragon was under the protection of powerful magic. I found a wineskin nearby and tasted the contents. Sweet brandy wine. I took a large burning gulp and used the rest to wash Tyrmiss's wound. I knew she was thirsty, but dragons can't drink the stuff because their stomachs are full of flammable gas, and alcohol combines with it in disastrous ways. Tyrmiss would have to bear her thirst until we could get back to the hills where there were streams to drink from.

Shortly before evening, Adamu returned on his broom, carrying Ena's broom strapped to his back. Soon, Adamu and I were using a lifting spell to carry Tyrmiss in a sling between us, flying slowly back to the Valley of the Dragons. As we passed the hills, I could hear the screams of men rising into the air and realized the dragons must have doubled back to attack their enemy. The slaughter of men had begun.

A few days after the battle, Yvnede called a Council of Elders meeting. She began by welcoming everyone back to the valley and graciously recognizing Tessia, Ena, Adamu and me for our valor in battle. The dragons seemed surprised that humans would fight so fiercely against their fellow humans, but they were eloquent in their gratitude, nevertheless. I noticed that many of the dragons, including Yvnede, had the purple shining eyes I had come to recognize as a symptom of moon bark intoxication.

It took most of the evening for Yvnede to call out the names of the dragon dead. Hundreds had been killed in the plains, and a few more in the hills. As each name was called, Yvnede paused and let the sobs and wails die down. These were the names of fathers and mothers, brothers and sisters, children, friends and neighbors. As tears rolled down the scaly cheeks, talons caught the tears and carried them to the wounds left from the battle. I knew that dragon tears help to heal body and spirit, so I caught a few of Tyrmiss's tears and gently rubbed them on her wounded throat and Tessia's torn calf.

With equal parts shame and gratitude, I realized once again that I had been to battle and returned without a scratch while others were killed or wounded. Was I under a spell that protected me? Or had fate or bad luck just overlooked me for the time being? In any case, I gave silent thanks to the Goddess for protecting me, whatever she had in mind for my future.

After the roll call of the honored dead was complete, Yvnede asked Jyrross the Gifted One to compose a song to commemorate the dead. The song was to be performed in two weeks, and it would be accompanied by a dance on the waters of the river performed by his sister Nyme the Graceful One. The two artists bowed their heads in silent acceptance of the commission.

Next came the announcement of the news that Beyazit had sent a courier with a short letter asking for a parlay. He wanted to discuss the terms of peace. Most of us had not heard of this development, and a ripple of excitement went through the cave.

"This is what we hoped for!" A young matron new on the council exclaimed.

"I don't trust them," the old dragon Komroisder said, shaking his head so vigorously loose scales fell off his neck. "What if it's a trap?"

"We will proceed cautiously," Yvnede said, and many dragons nodded in agreement.

"Does he want to meet with you?" I asked.

"Yes," Yvnede said. "He wants to hold a parlay in three days at the clearing in the woods where the river emerges from the cliff."

"Do you feel safe there?" Tessia asked.

Yvnede thought about it a moment. "I think we can station sentries on the cliff that overlooks the clearing. They should be able to keep an eye on us. If we are attacked, they can easily fly down and protect us."

"May Tyrmiss, Norbert, and I come with you?" Tessia asked. "We have the most experience in fighting, so we can help to protect you."

Yvnede nodded. "Thank you, Queen Tessia. We welcome your help and your experience. The courier is waiting at the head of the valley for our response. Should I tell him that we agree to the parlay?"

All the elders agreed that talking with the humans was a good idea. The dragons could get what they wanted, which was to live in peace, and the humans could have the same thing. This is what every species wants, isn't it? To be free to thrive? Humans were essentially no different than dragons, the dragons asserted, nodding. But I noticed that Komroisder, the old male dragon who didn't trust humans, said nothing, but just watched his friends and neighbors who seemed happy to end the war.

Walking back to our cave, I asked Tessia, "Do you think that King Beyazit actually wants peace?"

"It's possible," Tessia said carefully. "His army was thoroughly defeated in battle. Thousands of his soldiers were killed. Most of his war machines were damaged or destroyed. Crops and pastures were ground into mud pits by the marching men. He must be feeling the damage. Suing for peace with the dragons is the practical thing to do at this point. His soldiers did fight bravely and killed many dragons, so if we offer him a peace that is not humiliating, then he can claim at least a partial victory."

"I'd like to hear what Tyrmiss thinks of this agreement to meet with King Beyazit," I responded. "She voted for it, as did all the dragons—even Komroisder."

"As we know, dragons like to reach consensus," Tessia observed. "Even when they disagree with a proposal, they will vote for it if the other dragons want it passed. They seem to have an aversion to discord."

"It would be nice if the council in our kingdom felt the same way," I said, and we both laughed, thinking of the raucous debates in the Citizen's Council. There were times when members almost came to blows over a vote.

"Hello, Tessia. Hello, Norbert," Tyrmiss said. She was reclining on a large shelf of rock at the back of her cave watching her daughter Rozae scorch a salmon.

"Are you hungry?" Rozae asked, looking up at us.

"I could eat a little," Tessia said and I nodded in agreement. The fish smelled good.

"Rozae is really getting the hang of searing fish," Tyrmiss said, looking with pride at her daughter.

"There's really nothing to it, Momma," Rozae said.

Tyrmiss glowed with pride. She loved being called *momma* and why not? She had waited ten thousand years for the privilege.

Over dinner, Tessia asked, "What do you think of meeting with the king for a parlay?"

"I'm for it," Tyrmiss answered, watching us eat. Her own portion of the fish had gone down in one gulp. Dragons weren't much for chewing. "Why? Do you suspect a trap?"

"Always," Tessia said, ruefully. "But I think we can protect the negotiating party, and I don't see what Beyazit would gain from an attack."

"You know there are elders who still believe we should move further into the mountains, don't you?" Tyrmiss asked.

I nodded, remembering Komroisder's skepticism. "It may still be a good idea," I said. "The further from men the better. We've won one battle, but we may not win the next."

Tyrmiss sighed. "In the end, dragons will disappear altogether. We are not suited to live in a world dominated by men. They will always want to kill us. I don't know why. It seems to me we should be able to live side by side in peace, but men have never wanted peace with dragons. Men want only to destroy what they cannot control."

I knew exactly what she meant, and not for the first time I felt ashamed to be a member of a species that destroyed the earth for no reason other than we can.

"Tyrmiss," I asked. "Do a lot of the dragons use moon bark?"

My dragon-friend nodded her head sadly. "Moon bark has been used since ancient times as a way to understand dreams, and on special occasions to heighten the sense we are part of the spirit-world. But more and more young people use it just for fun, or perhaps as a way to ease their despair."

"They are grieving because the Old Way is disappearing?"

"For young dragons, it is very painful to think of the future. Have you noticed how dirty the village is? Fishbones and dragon waste everywhere? Old dragons tell me that it didn't used to be this way. Dragons took pride in themselves and their race. Now dragons have lost hope. We have no sense of a future for our kind."

"What about the elders? Do they use moon bark as well?"

Tyrmiss looked uncomfortable talking about this. "It's well-known that Yvnede has been using moon bark. She is still effective as a leader, but I fear she may make mistakes in judgment."

We sat for a long time in silence, feeling the sadness of Tyrmiss. She had at last found a tribe of dragons, but they were on the verge of disappearing just as her own tribe had.

"Do you know this place that Beyazit has chosen for the parlay?" Tessia asked, always the tactician looking for the advantage of terrain.

"Yes, I've been there many times. It is a favorite fishing spot for young dragons. There's a deep pond at the base of a waterfall and a cliff that looks down on the clearing. Yvnede is right. The terrain favors dragons. We can watch the proceedings from the top of the cliff, and if trouble breaks out, we can easily swoop down to protect our delegation."

"Will you be able to listen to their thoughts and determine if they plan to betray us?"

Tyrmiss slowly shook her head. "Perhaps, but I wouldn't depend on it. It's not difficult for a dragon to read another dragon's thoughts, but we have trouble listening to the thoughts of humans. Your thinking is so muddled with thoughts appearing and disappearing quickly, and often you believe things which are obviously not true, but you hold onto them anyway because they make you feel good," she said, sounding exasperated. "Something that dragons can never understand is that humans often lie to themselves. Lie to THEMSELVES! Can you imagine it? Why on earth would an intelligent species want to convince themselves of things they know aren't true just to make themselves feel better?"

Tyrmiss lifted her talons into the air as if beseeching the Goddess to explain the inexplicable nature of humans.

"Dragons can listen to the dreams of humans if they are close by, but dreams are undependable in revealing the truth. Although with humans, they are more likely to tell the truth when they are sleeping than when they are awake."

"So, I take it the answer is no," Tessia said, suppressing a smile.

Tyrmiss looked at her friend out of the corner of her eyes in an imitation of irritation, then they both laughed.

After dinner, Tyrmiss asked me to sing a song. Dragons prefer lyrics about the beauty of nature and the gifts of the goddess, so I sang an old one, an elegy about the passing of a girl who fell from a cliff trying to save a lamb. The girl then wanders the beautiful woods looking for the entrance to the underworld. She finally finds it, says goodbye to her mother and leaves this world forever.

It's a lovely song and my voice in those days was still strong, so it brought tears to everyone's eyes. Tessia and I bade goodnight and left Tyrmiss' cave.

I needed to talk to Ena and Adamu before going back, so Tessia nodded and walked on while I ducked into their cave. The two young people were snuggling together in their blankets at the back of the cave. I realized I should have asked permission before entering. As a father, it's sometimes easy to forget or ignore your daughter's right to privacy, but this time, no harm seems to have been done, and so I forgave myself, perhaps too easily, and greeted them.

"When Tessia, Tyrmiss and I go to the parlay in a few days, I need for the two of you to stay here, alright?"

They both nodded, then waited for my explanation.

"There are a lot of wounded dragons in the valley who need attention. Bandages need to be changed, infections treated, splints maintained, stitches removed."

"What about the nursery?" Ena asked. "Do the eggs and the new dragonlings need care?"

"As long as the eggs remain buried in the boxes of sand, they should be fine, and the dragon-mothers instinctively know how to care for their newborns. Make sure, though, that the newborns' air passages are clear before the mothers take charge of them. Their fire-glands sometimes move up into the throat and block the air. If that happens, just place your finger against the gland and push it back down the throat." I laughed. "And then pull your finger back quickly. Baby dragon teeth are sharp!"

"What about preventing infections? Does a yarrow root poultice work with dragons the way it works with humans?" Adamu asked.

"You can use yarrow root in a pinch, but I find a mix of equal amounts of oholi leaves and ivory sage flowers works better. Just mash them up in a stone bowl with a little wine and spread the paste on the wound. Cover it with a bandage."

"What about spells?" Adamu asked. "What works for dragons?"

I shook my head. "With humans, spells are essential as a placebo. Humans don't heal well unless they think magic is happening. But dragons are more sensible. They can spot mumbo-jumbo in the blink of an eye. So, with dragons, just stay with basic medicine, and let the Goddess handle the magic."

They both smiled. They knew that wounds usually heal by themselves. All we can do is to help nature along a bit by preventing infection. For people in our line of work, humility is always called for.

The next few days were quiet, so we settled into the regular routine of the village. Each morning around dawn, the dragons started stirring. A few went flying downriver to catch breakfast. Others went into the mountains to hunt deer and elk for dinner. I had been told that dragons didn't hunt bears because they were sentient beings. Thinking of my friend Hamlin, I was relieved to hear of this stricture.

Days were languid. We lay on the riverbank watching the dragonlings play in the river. They skimmed the surface with their talons making a steady spray which tickled their bellies, or they played tag, racing up and down the river valley laughing excitedly. They also loved to swim tucking their wings against their sides and wriggling through the water like snakes. A little way upriver, a family of otters lived, and the dragons considered them neighbors. The dragonlings and baby otters often played together, sliding down the mudbanks to land in the river.

The adults spent their time lying on the riverbank in the cool of the morning or napping in their caves in the afternoon. I was beginning to realize that many of them were intoxicated on moon bark, but it didn't seem to do them any harm, so I didn't say anything about my concerns. After dinner, as the long shadows of the mountains crept across the valley, I could hear songs rising in the air, beautiful dirges for the dragons lost in the battle and elegant celebrations of the beauty of creation. All dragons sang, it was their natural language. Legend has it that the Goddess gave dragons the gift of song, but they learned to speak from men. Jyrross, known as the Gifted One, was acknowledged as their best poet, and his songs were something to marvel at. I've been praised for my songs, but they were nothing compared to his. Listening to his voice floating through the valley in the evening took my breath away, and when his voice was rising in the mountain air, all the dragons stopped what they were doing to listen.

One evening I wandered upriver looking for catkin roots

and watercress leaves and other edible plants we humans need to thrive. We were tired of eating only fish and meat as the dragons do. We needed fresh vegetables. On the water ahead I saw a movement, and as I drew closer, I could see it was Jyrross's sister Nyme, known as the Graceful One. She was slowly moving across the water, barely touching the surface with her talons. Her wings were moving very quickly and yet she was staying in the same place, hovering over the water. She looked for all the world like a dragonfly, and I wondered how long she had practiced that movement to show such beauty and grace. I realized she must be practicing for her performance on the river that Yvnede had requested.

Chapter Twelve

On the day we were scheduled to parlay with King Beyazit, Tessia and I rose before dawn, ate a simple breakfast, and left the cave. I was glad to see her leg was healing, and her limp was barely visible. I had patched her up a number of times and was always surprised at how quickly she healed—one of the many gifts that made her the perfect warrior.

Next to the river a large group of dragons was gathering. I noticed it included all the best fighters in the tribe. Yvnede called to us, and we went over to stand in front of her. Her eyes were purple. I looked around and saw that many of the dragons had the same moon bark eyes.

"Are all of them coming with us to parlay with the king?" Tessia asked, gesturing toward the dozens of dragons standing nearby. There were more joining the group every few moments.

"Yes," Yvnede said. "We have to be prepared in case the king is planning to ambush us."

Tessia looked up and down the valley, her tactical eye sizing up the situation. "Shouldn't you leave some of our best fighters behind in case the king attacks the village?" She asked.

"We are leaving quite a few behind to defend the village," Yvnede answered. She sounded slightly defensive. She obviously didn't like this foreign queen, a human no less, questioning her tactical decisions. She looked at me and said, "Two out of three of the mages are remaining here. Besides, if the humans were planning to attack the village, then we would know it. We would have heard their thoughts."

She turned to the dragons nearby, "Have any of you heard any soldiers nearby?"

One of the dragons, a tall male with scales that came down from his chin like whiskers said, "We saw a small party of hunters in the pass a few days ago. We watched as they went into the woods at the end of the valley. They seemed harmless, so we left them alone."

"That's all? Just one small party of hunters?" Yvnede asked, looking around at the other dragons.

She waited for a moment, then looked at Tessia and said, "See? The village will be safe. It's the negotiating party that's vulnerable. We need to concentrate our strength where it is most needed. Now, if *Her Majesty* has no objection, let us get started."

Tessia looked at the ground and nodded. She had no standing to make decisions here, and she had to trust Yvnede to make the right ones. Tyrmiss was sympathetically looking at Tessia, embarrassed for her friend, but I was looking up and down the valley, thinking that Tessia's tactical instincts were rarely wrong. I excused myself and hurried over to Ena and Adamu's cave to warn them to stay on guard. They weren't in their cave, and I didn't see them near the river. They must have gone to check on injured dragons. I thought about searching for them, but Tyrmiss signaled that I should come back. Tessia was climbing on her back. The dragons were ready to fly. I walked over to Tyrmiss.

"Should I stay here in case the soldiers attack the village?" I asked Tessia.

Before she could answer, Tyrmiss growled, "Stop dithering, Norbert. Either get on my back or stand clear. We need to go."

Rationalizing that Yvnede sounded absolutely positive that the village would be safe for the day, I climbed behind Tessia and tapped Tyrmiss on her shoulder next to me, signaling I was ready to go.

Yvnede divided our force into three contingents. A brigade

of dragons was stationed in the mountain pass between the plains and the Valley of the Dragons. The brigade would cover our retreat if needed. A second group, the best flyers, were positioned on the cliff above the meeting place. They had a clear view of the proceedings and could easily attack from the air if fighting broke out. The third group, the smallest, was made up of Yvnede, two of her closest advisors, Tessia and me. We were the negotiating party. Yvnede had said she wanted Queen Tessia and me, wearing my full wizard regalia, to be present in order to show the king that dragons had powerful allies.

There was no one at the meeting place, so we sat down and waited.

Half to herself, Yvnede muttered, "I'm going to gain an assurance that dragons will be left in peace in perpetuity. No man or Drekavac will be allowed in our valley. This ban will be for all time."

"You know, Yvnede, humans have short lives and cannot as a practical matter bind their descendants to any treaty." Tessia said, trying to be helpful. "And therefore, the kind of agreement you want would be impossible to enforce…" Tessia's voice trailed off as Yvnede glared at her.

Yvnede straightened up in order to give Tessia a sharp retort, but suddenly the dragon's ears perked up. She looked up at the sentry on the clifftop. He was evidently giving her a thought-message. "Pay attention," she said to Tessia and me, not having to say anything to her two dragon-advisors who would have heard the thought-message. "The other party is approaching."

When the king's negotiators arrived, I was surprised there was only one negotiator in the party accompanied by ten heavily armed guards.

"My name is Kugel," said the negotiator, a short man in a large tricorn hat with a feather almost as big as he was. He didn't bother to introduce the ten soldiers standing at attention behind him.

"I am Yvnede known as the Dark One, and I represent the interests of the dragons. My advisors are Qayrgoin, Eater of Sheep, and Zeommarrelth, the Strong Minded."

Kugel smirked at the names of dragons. *This bigot hates dragons,* I thought. *He is here only to insult and cheat us.*

"And Tyrmiss of the Eastern Dragons," Yvnede said.

Kugel looked surprised, "I thought the Eastern Dragons were wiped out in the Great War."

"Oh no," Tyrmiss lied. "We are legion."

This was the first time I had ever known a dragon to lie outright. *Tyrmiss has learned a lot while living with humans,* I thought bitterly.

"And Norbert the Green Mage," Yvnede said, nodding to me in my conical hat and long green robe with moons and stars. "You may have heard of him."

Again, Kugel looked startled. It was clear that Beyazit and his advisors had no idea whom they were fighting.

"And finally, our honored ally Her Majesty Queen Tessia of the Dragonja and Bekla Valleys, known as the Dragonqueen. You may have heard of her as well."

Kugel looked at Tessia. It was clear he was tempted to bow to her, but was holding himself back, not wanting to show the fear bordering on awe he was feeling.

Yvnede nodded to me, and I pointed my wand into the woods, picked up a log and carried it to the clearing. I carved out a comfortable seat on the log and used the shavings to construct a back rest, creating a crude but serviceable throne. This was pure theater, done for Kugel's benefit. I could have done this simple chore earlier, of course, but Yvnede wanted me to perform it in front of the envoi to show him what he was up against.

I bowed to Tessia in a manner befitting a queen. She walked over to the makeshift throne and gracefully sat down. I stood behind her. I indicated to Kugel he should sit on the ground opposite us, but he remained standing. Yvnede and Tyrmiss sprawled in the grass behind us with their heads sticking up above ours. I could see that Kugel with his increasingly nervous guards behind him, felt intimidated. So far, so good.

"I am disappointed King Beyazit could not be here," Yvnede said. "I suppose his envoy will have to do."

"The king had other business to attend to," Kugel said, nervously. "If I may, he has entrusted me to proffer the terms of a treaty to your tribe."

"Go ahead," Yvnede said.

"The King offers you two valleys east of here," Kugel began, hesitantly.

"What?" Yvnede said. "What two valleys? You mean he expects us to move our village further inland?"

"Yes," Kugel was barely audible. He looked nervously from Yvnede to Tessia, his superior attitude had faded; obviously he'd just realized that the king's offer was insulting to the dragons, and quite possibly Kugel's own life was in danger from these three dragons.

"I don't understand," Yvnede said. "The valleys east of our valley are not King Beyazit's to offer. Those valleys are now occupied by the trolls and witches who fled there years ago, trying to get away from the depredations of humans. And now, the king offers those lands to us? This offer makes no sense."

"Nevertheless," Kugel said, shrugging his shoulders in feigned indifference. "That is the king's offer. It is not negotia..."

Without warning, Yvnede breathed a large red flame at the little man. Later, all I remembered was his plumed tricorn hat going up in flame. The soldiers behind Kugel lowered their spears and charged us. One of them lunged at Tessia who drew Agatha and lopped off the blade of the spear. Before she could slice off his head, he jumped back, knocking over one of his fellows. I drew my wand, but before I could think of a spell, Yvnede, Qayrgoin and Zeommarrelth had breathed fire at the soldiers who fell down, rolling in the grass, trying to put out the flames. Taking pity on them, I pointed my wand at the nearby stream and brought a heavy spray of water down on them, dousing the fire. I looked up and saw the dragons from the cliff dropping into the meadow, but by then, the men were all either dead or so badly burned they were no longer a danger to us.

Tessia, Tyrmiss and I looked aghast at Yvnede who seemed preternaturally calm in the aftermath of the fiery slaughter. "Do you have any idea what you've done?" Tessia asked.

"Yes," Yvnede said, almost indifferently. "His offer was insulting."

"And so, you killed him?"

"Of course," Yvnede said. "What would you have done, *Your Majesty*?"

I looked at the old she-dragon closely. Her purple eyes were shining. "You are intoxicated," I said.

"I am not," Yvnede said.

"It doesn't matter now," Tyrmiss said to me. "We've killed the King's envoy and his guards. Let's think carefully about what we should do next."

As Qayrgoin and Zeommarrelth used their talons to put the burned soldiers out of their misery, Tessia looked at me, puzzled.

"Their offer made no sense," she said. "Surely they knew the dragons would not accept it. So, why did Beyazit bring us here?"

No sooner had she asked the question, then the answer was obvious. "It was a diversion!" we both said simultaneously.

"Yvnede" Tessia said. "We need to return to the valley of the dragons. They are under attack!"

"But wait," Yvnede said, "if the king planned for us to be here while he was attacking the village, then isn't he expecting us to return at some point?"

"Good point," Tessia said. "The humans are probably planning to ambush us when we get back to the village. If I were planning to ambush dragons in a valley, then I would place ballistas on the mountainsides, and soldiers hiding in the forest next to the river."

"Why didn't the dragons hear the thoughts of the soldiers as they were moving into the valley?" I asked, looking at Tyrmiss.

"The king's soldiers must have found a way to quiet their thoughts. The dragons weren't expecting the soldiers to be nearby, so they weren't listening carefully. Also, there's a lot of noise with the dragons communicating with each other."

We all looked at Yvnede who was looking off in the distance, her eyes filling with tears. "I should have seen this coming," she said sadly.

"Never mind that now," Tessia said. "If we're right, then we need to go quietly back to the valley of the dragons, find the ballistas positioned on the mountainside, and take out the soldiers in the valley."

"And what do you think has happened to the dragons we left in the village?" Yvnede asked.

Tessia didn't answer. Instead, she looked at me with alarm. We were thinking the same thing: *What has happened to Ena and Adamu?*

Chapter Thirteen

Yvnede and the dragons gathered at the pass that led into the valley of the dragons and sent Tyrmiss, carrying Tessia and me, to reconnoiter. It didn't take long for us to confirm that Tessia's tactical analysis had been correct, as it usually was. Staying out of sight by flying behind a screen of trees, Tyrmiss said she could hear the faint thoughts of the soldiers manning the ballistas on the mountainside below us. We could also see the village below. We were too far away to make out details, but it was clear there had already been a battle. We could see dead dragons lying beside the river and there were scorch marks on the rocks and trees around the village.

Flying back to meet Yvnede and the other dragons in the pass, Tessia, Tyrmiss and I were silent, each of us feeling worried and afraid.

"How did they carry the ballistas up the mountainside?" Yvnede wondered.

"They must have dismantled them and divided the pieces between soldiers," Tessia answered.

"How many ballistas are on the mountainside?" Yvnede asked.

"We counted five ballistas, two on one side of the valley, three on the other."

"And what do you suggest we do, Queen Tessia?" Yvnede asked in a mild tone. She evidently had accepted that Tessia understood the tactics of warfare better than she did, and she was now open to advice. Her eyes were no longer purple with the effects of moon bark, but had turned blood-red. I knew from long experience with Tyrmiss that when a dragon's eyes turn red, her mood is dangerous.

"I suggest that the mage and I take out the two ballistas on the east slope and you, Qayrgoin and Zeommarrelth take out the ballistas on the west slope. There will be three soldiers assigned to each machine. If we approach them from above, we can catch them by surprise. Use your dragon breath to light the ballistas on fire. Not only will this destroy them, but it will cause a distraction to the soldiers in the valley. They will be expecting the attack to come from the west and to be carried out by dragons. While their attention is on the west slope, Norbert and I will come down the east slope and attack the soldiers from their rear. Once you see and hear that we've engaged them, then fly down the slope, cross the river and attack their front."

Tessia turned to the other dragons and said in a loud voice that could be heard even in the back of the brigade. "Stay here in the pass until you see and hear that we have engaged the enemy. Then, fly as quickly as you can into the valley and kill as many of the soldiers as you can."

Tessia turned to Yvnede and bowed her head, "Of course, these are merely suggestions, Dragon-mother. It is not my place to issue orders to dragons."

Yvnede gave a small smile of gratitude for the generous humility of Tessia and said, "My friends! You heard the Dragonqueen! Nerdyn, Lord of the Skies, wait here at the pass with your regiment and prepare to fly into the valley once the enemy is engaged. Qayrgoin and Zeommarrelth, come with me to the western slope and we will each take out one ballista by killing the soldiers and setting the machine on fire. Then, once the enemy is engaged in the forest next to the river, we will fly down to attack. The Dragonqueen and the Mage will fly on Tyrmiss to the eastern slope, stealthily take out the ballistas, then make their way down to the forest where they will be the first to engage. Everyone understand? We are fighting for our home. We are fighting for our brothers and sisters. We are fighting for the survival of dragonkind!"

As Yvnede turned away, I heard her say under her breath, "By the Holy Talon, I hope we are not too late."

From the pass, Tyrmiss followed the same route we'd flown when we reconnoitered, using the tree line as a screen to cover our approach. She dropped me off above the first ballista. I found a rough trail down the mountain, and tried to move as quietly as I could, but the slope was steep and full of loose gravel, and I kept losing my footing. By the time I could see the ballista through the trees, the soldiers had heard me coming and had swiveled the machine around to point in my direction. They were obviously expecting a dragon to come at them from above the trees, not a man bracing himself as he moved from one tree to the next down the slippery slope.

About fifty paces from the soldiers, I stopped. With my left arm, I hugged a pine tree. With my right, I pulled out my wand. I wasn't worried about the ballista aimed at me. They were never designed to pick off individuals hiding behind trees. When I saw a soldier pulling the lever, I stepped behind the pine tree and the bolt went flying by, completely missing me.

I stepped from behind the tree and used an atlatl spell to lift a fist-sized rock and fling it at the soldier who had pulled the lever. The rock hit him in the shoulder, knocking him backward. In quick succession, I lifted two more rocks and flung them at the other soldiers. Each hit a soldier in the chest and the soldiers were knocked backward. I scrambled down the slope trying to keep my footing and clung to another tree where my aim would be better. As the soldiers stood up, slightly stunned, I flung rocks at them, hitting each one in the forehead, just below their helmets.

I approached the ballista cautiously. Close up, these soldiers could be deadly with their swords, but each one was lying motionless on the ground, his head bleeding. The ballista rested on a large flat boulder that created a ledge. From here, the soldiers could see the entire valley, and even more important, the misty air above the valley.

After employing a disassembling spell to take apart the ballista, I used the atlatl spell to fling the pieces in different directions into the woods. Then I started the descent down into the valley. About halfway down, I began to pick up signs of the army below, a glint of light from the blade of a spear, the shifting around of dark shapes, a few whispered voices. Not for the first time, I thanked the Goddess for Tessia's insight into battle tactics. It often seemed she could almost read the mind of the enemy leader. She once told me, quoting her uncle Zygmunt, that three warriors could defeat an army if they had a good strategy and worked together.

I sat down in the shadow of a dead tree and waited for the signal to attack. I carefully studied the valley below, looking for Ena and Adamu. Although there were a number of dead dragons in the valley, I didn't see any sign of my daughter. Perhaps she and Adamu had been able to get away safely? Perhaps they were hiding up in the mountains right now, watching? Perhaps they were in one of the caves, huddled down with dragonlings, ready to protect the young ones? Perhaps... But I feared the worst. Looking at the many bodies of dead dragons below, I realized it was unlikely my daughter had survived the bloodbath.

Before long, three columns of smoke rose from high up the western slope of the valley. This was the signal. Our friends Yvnede and her cohorts had taken out the three ballistas on the western slope and set them on fire. I moved a little lower on the mountain and took a position behind a pile of boulders directly above the soldiers. Looking at the pile of rock, I realized it wasn't very stable, and I could, using a lever spell, push the boulders downhill, starting an avalanche. I was close enough now to see individual soldiers, their sergeants telling them to stand in line and get ready to march. I had to make my move now, or the moment would be lost. I tested a few spots on the pile of rocks and found a place where the rocks seemed ready to move. All they needed was a lift and a push and the whole pile of rock would start rolling and sliding downhill, taking rocks, gravel and trees below with it. I planted my feet firmly on a ledge, focused the power from the wand on the loose spot among the rubble and chanted:

ridică-te și
rostogolește-te
înainte

The pile shuddered and started moving, pushing the rock and debris below into the arc of its slide.

The soldiers heard the rumbling and turned in time to see the mountainside coming down on them. They broke rank and tried to run, but for most of them, it was too late.

On my left, further down the valley, I could hear the clash of swords and the distinctive singing of Tessia's Voprian blade. She had engaged the enemy, and I was sure she was dealing out death and injury in ways the soldiers had never seen. There has never been a soldier or group of soldiers who could take on Tessia successfully.

Seeing the mountainside was stable again, I picked my way down the slope and was soon standing next to the river. To my right, there was a group of soldiers looking in my direction, startled to see a mage in full regalia standing on top of a pile of debris that had buried their fellows. To my left, Tessia was standing alone, the soldiers she had been fighting had fled or been killed by her sword. She lifted Agatha and waved to me, signaling all was well. I lifted my wand and waved back. If more soldiers were foolish enough to approach us, then we would deal with them. Otherwise, there was no need for more fighting on our part. In the air above the valley, I could see the dark cloud of dragons led by Nerdyn, Lord of the Skies, and from the western slope, Yvnede, Qayrgoin and Zeommarrelth were flying. Tyrmiss was zigzagging through the valley picking off stragglers. Any resistance from the remaining soldiers would be quickly dealt with. The Valley of the Dragons once again belonged to its rightful owners.

I walked along the river, looking at each dead dragon on the shore. Most of them I didn't know by name, but a few I did. Here lay Jogheosdarth, known as Eater of Bunnies for her peculiar culinary habits. And here lay Ughyrrynth, the Skinny One. And over there was the dragon-mother Gykurth, the Voiceless One who'd never learned to speak except through thoughts. Each dragon had had a precious life.

I looked up and saw Rozae, Tyrmiss's daughter, who'd survived the massacre by flying up the mountain and hiding when she saw the soldiers coming. Now she and her mother were braiding their necks together like snakes; Tyrmiss's relief was palpable. I felt a brief surge of joy before remembering I still hadn't found Ena or Adamu.

Tessia was sitting on a large rock outside the nursery cave, her face in her hands, weeping. Around her was the aftermath of battle, the bodies of soldiers who had been struck by lightning, others buried under boulders and gravel. I've seen Tessia slaughter whole armies and never shed a tear, so I knew what I was about to see was beyond comprehension. She looked at me and gestured at the cave entrance, not able to speak.

"Don't go in there," she managed to say between sobs. "Norbert, you don't want to see."

In front of the cave entrance, Adamu lay, his body sliced open in a dozen places. I realized the debris that killed the soldiers was thrown there by him. He must have stood his ground, throwing everything he could at the soldiers besieging them. Adamu died protecting what was inside the cave.

I was drawn like a man in a dream into the cave, not wanting to see what was there, but having to enter, nonetheless. My feet were leaden, my mind numb as I entered the half-light.

Oroz, the ten-year old dragon who'd showed us the cave on our first day, lay near the entrance, his lifeless eyes staring at the ceiling. I wondered if he had tried in his brave little boy way to protect whoever was in the cave. Inexperienced with dragon-fire, he hadn't stood a chance fighting soldiers with spears. I stepped over his body and walked into the half-light.

Ena was lying on her back on the floor of the cave, her eyes wide in death. She had been violated in countless ways I will not describe here. I fell to my knees in front of her. My first thought, may the Goddess forgive me, was of myself. I thought *I've killed her. I've killed my beautiful daughter. I brought her to this place to die. I left her to go to the parlay with Yvnede when I should have stayed here to protect her.* And then I thought, *what am I going to tell her mother? Idella will hate me forever.*

And then the Goddess spoke to me in my mind and said *Norbert, this is not your tragedy, but your daughter's. You must think of her, not of you.*

And somehow, I found the strength to look at the body of my daughter and think of how she'd suffered. It was clear the soldiers had abused and tormented her. My poor beautiful daughter. And the Voice came to me again and said, *See what else they have done. This crime was not just against your daughter but against Life itself.*

And then I realized where I was, what this cave was used

for. I rose and walked to the back of the nursery and saw dozens of dragon eggs. Each one had been smashed open. And when the dragonling was viable, it had been stabbed to death. This was the future of dragons, and it had been taken away.

Why?

I walked out of the cave and saw Tessia. She held out her arms and I went to her and sobbed and sobbed and sobbed. There was nothing left but grief and horror. The entire world had fallen into the hole opening inside me.

Chapter Fourteen

"I have called this council of the elders in order to decide what we should do now," Yvnede was saying.

I looked around the cave and there were less than half as many elders as at the last meeting. Evidently, most of the older dragons had been in the village when the soldiers attacked.

"I have asked our friend and ally Queen Tessia, who is a renowned general, to explain to us what happened with the attack. What mistakes we made," Yvnede looked at the floor and amended, "that is… what mistakes I made… So, we can understand where we stand now. And then, based on her explanation, this council can discuss our options. Tessia, I invite you to speak."

Tessia stood up, bringing her face level with the faces of the dragons. "King Beyazit must have ordered his soldiers to infiltrate the mountains behind us. The soldiers moved in small bands, disguised as hunting parties or perhaps as shepherds moving their flocks into the mountains. They must have dismantled their ballistas and carried them into the mountainsides above the valley. The invitation to parlay was obviously a diversionary move by King Beyazit. He correctly guessed we would be afraid of an ambush and would bring our best warriors as protection at the parlay. Having successfully lured away most of our fighters, he ordered the surprise attack on the village. Most of the dragons were killed before they even realized they were under attack, but many managed to defend themselves for a while. There are a number of dead soldiers who are either burned to death or who were mangled by dragon claws. You can be proud of your friends and family members. They died heroically.

"The two mages, Adamu and Ena, and the child-dragon Oroz," Tessia glanced at me, "positioned themselves in front of the nursery to protect the eggs. The two mages and the young dragon fought valiantly. There are a number of lightning scorch marks on the ground where Ena fought back against the soldiers, and there are piles of rocks and debris that Adamu threw at them, but the soldiers overwhelmed them. Adamu and Oroz died in front of the cavern, and Ena died in the cavern itself where she must have retreated to defend the eggs. Once the mages were dead, the soldiers smashed the eggs and killed any dragonlings who crawled out."

A dragon-mother let out a cry of pain. Other dragons were weeping.

"But why?" the dragon-mother wailed. "Why would they kill our babies?"

"Sometimes," Tessia answered quietly, "wars are not fought over wealth or territory or personal grudges between kings, but rather… a war is fought because one race wants to eradicate another race."

"Why?" the dragon-mother asked again. "Why would they want to eradicate us? Dragons have never done anything to harm humans. In fact, we have tried to avoid humans as much as possible. For centuries, we have hidden in these mountains. And now that they know we exist, they want to kill us? All of us? This makes no sense."

"I don't know," Tessia said. I could see this conversation was affecting her deeply. As a woman whose chosen profession had been the making of war, she was having to look at her life in a new way. She'd grown close to these dragons, and now she could see that warriors much like herself were threatening the very existence of her friends.

While Tessia struggled with her newly discovered revulsion toward her profession, I spoke up, trying to help the dragons understand humans. "In human history, it has happened a number of times that one nation tries to completely wipe out another nation, killing virtually everyone. This kind of war goes beyond a struggle for power; instead, it is something that exists as pure hatred of the other."

Everyone in the room was silent as we tried to accept this strange evil that humans are capable of. The image of Ena lying on the cave floor, staring at the ceiling from her ruined face, rushed into my mind, taking over my thoughts.

"I think we should wipe them out before they wipe you out," I said, not knowing where the thought came from, but welcoming it, nevertheless.

Tessia and Tyrmiss looked at me, eyes wide with shock.

"This is not the dragon way, Norbert," Tyrmiss said quietly.

"It is the human way," I retorted.

"May we take a break, Yvnede?" Tessia suggested.

"Yes, of course," Yvnede replied. "Please everyone, go back to your caves. Eat and drink something, and we'll continue the council meeting this afternoon."

"May I speak to you?" Tessia said between her teeth, taking me by the arm and leading me outside. She, Tyrmiss, and I went a little way into the woods. She turned and confronted me.

"Norbert, I am so sorry that Ena is gone. I loved her. Everyone loved her. And I know you are suffering."

I said nothing, waiting for her to finish what she needed to say.

"But, genocide is not what you want..."

"Yes, it is," I said. "I want King Beyazit and every one of his subjects to die."

"Norbert, you are a good man. You have always hated war."

"Yes, I have hated war, haven't I? And yet, somehow, I've managed to kill dozens of people in my lifetime. How does a good man who hates war end up killing dozens of people? He doesn't. I am not a good man who hates war, or I wouldn't have joined you in your quests. I allowed my daughter to accompany me on this quest, and she… she…" I started sobbing, unable to finish my thought.

Tessia took me in her arms and Tyrmiss placed her large head on my shoulder, and my two friends let me weep for my daughter.

After Tessia brought me food and drink, I felt slightly better. At least, I was able to stop crying. We sat quietly on a log in the woods and watched the light come down through the branches, and eventually the birds started to sing again.

As we walked into the council chamber, the dragons turned to look at me. Some appeared puzzled, others curious, but most of them looked at me with great sadness and sympathy. I knew I wasn't alone in my grief. Everyone in the room, including Tyrmiss and Tessia, had lost loved ones.

Tessia rose to speak, "Dear friends, please understand that all of us are feeling devastated by the losses we've suffered. None more so than my dear friend and comrade-at-arms Norbert. But despite our terrible pain and sorrow, we need to make a decision on what to do about the treachery of King Beyazit. Should we retaliate? If so, how? And how much?"

Komroisder, the old dragon who had consistently said he didn't trust humans, raised his head above the others and Yvnede recognized him to speak. "You know I've never trusted humans, and I argued against having a parlay with them. But I need to point out that seeking revenge is not the way of dragons. Our entire sense of justice rests on our ability to forgive wrong-doing and thereby give the transgressor an opportunity to make amends. Striking back against King Beyazit and his followers will not bring back our loved ones. It will only create more death, destruction, and chaos. We should grieve our dead and try to avoid more conflict. More war will not solve anything."

After a respectful silence in which the dragons considered what Komroisder had said, Tyrmiss spoke. "I lived among humans for seven years as a guest at Windkeep, Queen Tessia's castle, and I have to tell you that this restraint which Komroisder argues for will not work with humans. They will see our reluctance to fight as weakness and will take the opportunity to attack us again. Clearly, they are not interested in living in peace beside us as neighbors. They are interested only in wiping us out. We must fight or die."

A few of the dragons nodded in agreement, but most were silent.

"If the men see our reluctance to fight as an invitation to attack," Komroisder said, "then we should consider moving further inland, away from men."

"But the valleys to the east are occupied by trolls and witches. Where would we go?" an old female said without the benefit of being recognized by Yvnede, an unusual break in etiquette which I interpreted as a sign of the increasing fear among the council members.

"Then we should move to the third valley to the east, or the fourth or fifth," Komroisder replied. "We need a peaceful place away from men where we can rebuild our tribe."

"But most of our females are too old to lay eggs. Our time has passed," the female said, again without being recognized to speak. A number of dragons began speaking at once, drowning each other out. Arguments started breaking out. Voices were getting louder.

"Friends, friends!" Yvnede shouted. "This is not the dragon way. We have always shown restraint and respect in council."

The dragons in the room calmed down. Some of them looked embarrassed at the outburst. A few others seemed to be still angry.

"It seems our options are clear," Yvnede said. "We cannot stay here without engaging in war with men. So, we must decide whether we will stay and fight, or move to a different valley. All those in favor of staying and fighting the humans, please raise your heads."

The only head rising above the others was that of Tyrmiss. She looked around and lowered her head slowly.

"All those in favor of moving to a different valley," Yvnede said, "please raise your heads."

All the dragons except Tyrmiss raised their heads.

Since no resolution could pass without unanimous consent among the elders, a number of dragons turned to look at Tyrmiss. The custom was that the minority, in this case a minority of one, would concede defeat and support the resolution. Tyrmiss turned to look at Tessia and me, then reluctantly raised her head, making approval of the resolution to move the tribe inland unanimous.

I woke in the half-light of the cave and found I could not get out of bed. My body felt so heavy, I could barely move my arms and legs, and sitting up was impossible. I lay staring at the dark ceiling, thinking of Ena. The image of her mangled body was mixed with memories of her as a child. I remembered I'd dreamed of discovering a live rat inside a wedding cake. I retched, but my stomach was empty, and nothing came up. I knew I was feverish and probably delusional. At one point, Ena came to me, felt my head, lifted me into a sitting position and removed my soiled shirt. I was so glad to see her.

"Thank you so much, Ena," I said, feeling relieved. "I dreamed you had died horribly."

"Norbert, it's not Ena. It's me—Tessia."

I recognized the voice, then the face, and I realized I wasn't dreaming. Ena truly was dead.

"You must drink some water, Norbert. You are burning up."

"No, no, no," I wailed, turning my head away from the cup she offered. "I want to die. My daughter is dead. How will I ever return home and tell her mother what I have done?"

"Norbert, it wasn't your fault. Ena was a grown woman who chose this quest. You didn't want her to come. Remember? She chose to fight for the dragons, and she was killed in battle valiantly defending the dragonlings. She is a hero."

"I don't want my daughter to be a hero. I want her to be alive. I want her to bear me grandchildren and grow old and have her own grandchildren."

"I know, Norbert. I wish she were still alive as well. But we must accept the way things are."

A rush of anger rose up inside me. "YOU!" I shouted at Tessia. "You convinced her to come with us. If it weren't for you, Ena would still be alive!"

My anger startled Tessia. She stepped back and said, "That's not true, Norbert. She volunteered for this quest just as you and I did. Just as Adamu did."

"Adamu," I realized I hadn't thought about him since I discovered my daughter's body. *Poor Adamu,* I thought. *The boy died a hero's death. He should be honored.*

Tessia, having read my thoughts as she often did, said, "The funeral for Ena and Adamu was yesterday."

"Yesterday?" I asked, confused. "How long have I been lying here?"

"Five days. We waited with the funeral as long as we could, but the bodies..." Her voice trailed off.

The cup of water she'd brought was sitting beside the bed. I lifted it and took a sip. It tasted good. I drained the cup.

"Five days," I repeated. "You've been taking care of me?"

"Yes. I didn't know what to do. I've brought you water and made sure you drank it."

"I haven't eaten in five days?"

"Nothing at all in five days. I've brought some fruit for you if you want it."

Tessia took a few red berries from a platter on the floor and handed them to me. They tasted sweet and sour at the same time. I realized I'd never truly tasted berries before this moment. A great yawning emptiness opened inside me. I was ravenous.

"Do you have any more of those berries?" I asked.

Tessia gave a large smile and held the platter in front of me. It was full of various fruits and greens. I picked up a few more berries and slowly chewed them, savoring each one.

"How did you know I would want to eat today?" I asked.

"I didn't. I've been bringing you food every day, hoping you would eat, but it was all I could do to get a few sips of water down your throat."

I noticed a bedroll against the wall. Agatha and other possessions were neatly lined up beside it. "You've been sleeping here?" I asked.

"Yes, I didn't want to leave you alone," she said. "Norbert, I've been so frightened. I thought you were going to die… of grief."

"It sounds like I would have if you hadn't been here," I said. "Thank you."

"You would have done the same for me, Norbert," she said. And it was true. I would have.

I ate more fruit and Tessia brought me more water, and gradually I began to feel alive again. By the end of the day, I was able to walk down to the river and bathe.

"What happened to the… bodies?" I asked, gesturing up and down the river.

Tessia lowered her voice. "The dragons didn't know what to do with all their dead. It's so rare that a dragon dies they had to think back to the old rituals. In the past, they carried their dead over the sea and dropped them in the water, but this time, they had hundreds of bodies. It wasn't possible to carry so many to the sea because they would have had to pass over the land of men. So, the dragons carried their dead up into the mountains and used their breath to carve out great caverns out of the glaciers. There they placed their dead and sang songs over them."

"What happened to the bodies of Ena and Adamu?"

"Yvnede asked me about our customs, and I explained we usually bury our dead in the ground with a stone marker above the grave. I can take you to their graves if you like."

After I finished bathing, I put on a clean shirt Tessia had found in my kit, and she led me into the woods. The dragons, or perhaps Tessia, had chosen a lovely meadow for the gravesite. There were oak and elm trees shading the spot, and I saw signs of deer and elk on the path. Inscribed on one stone was "Adamu, The Tender Warrior." And on the other stone "Ena, Brave Defender of Dragons."

I kneeled on my daughter's grave and wept while Tessia, my true friend, kept her hand on my shoulder.

Chapter Fifteen

The dragons were preparing their migration inland. Nerdyn, Lord of the Skies, and his brigade had scouted the territory and found a suitable valley deep in the mountains. Tessia had pointed out that the dragons would be most vulnerable as they were starting their journey, and she'd volunteered to cover their retreat. Yvnede had gratefully accepted.

The best route was through the southern pass, so Yvnede stationed Tyrmiss, Tessia and me on a mountainside where we could look down on Nerdyn and his brigade accompanying the more vulnerable dragons. Yvnede, Tyrmiss and Nerdyn coordinated the operation by linking their thoughts.

Tyrmiss and I had not had much chance to talk since I had awakened from my grief-wrung sleep, so I asked her, "What do you think of the move to the inlands? Will the dragons be safe there?"

"They will be safe for a while, I'm sure," she answered. "But humans keep expanding eastward into the mountains, using up the trees, the animals, the water, and the soil. Your kind is insatiable. So, it will be only a matter of time, perhaps a few hundred years, perhaps less, before they discover the new valley. What then? Do we fight them again? Dragons reproduce very slowly. It will be thousands of years before we have a clutch of eggs like the ones they destroyed. We cannot keep retreating, or eventually we'll be close to the men of Osterbo on the east coast."

"The dragons will always be welcome in the Kingdom of Dragonja and Bekla," Tessia said.

"Thank you, my friend," Tyrmiss said. "I appreciate your

gesture. But you will live only another fifty years at best. What happens with the next monarch of your kingdom? Even if she's friendly toward dragons, will she be able to restrain the instincts of her people to dominate and control nature? Humans have an instinct to destroy whatever they cannot control."

"So, what's the answer?" I asked. "How can dragons be safe from humans?"

"I'm not sure," Tyrmiss answered, speaking slowly. "But we need more than just a delaying action—which is what this move inland is."

There was a long silence as each of us pondered the problem of protecting the dragons. Then I thought of Ena and again felt a rush of anger. I knew it was a violation of my vows to the Goddess, but I wanted to enact revenge for her horrible death. Tyrmiss was looking at me with knowing eyes, and I thought she may have picked up what I was thinking.

"Norbert, when Rilla was killed, I spun into a blind rage and went on a killing spree, slaughtering Ludek's soldiers wherever I could find them."

"I remember."

"The problem was that no amount of bloodletting could satisfy me," Tyrmiss said. "The more I killed, the more I needed to kill. It wasn't until I met you and Tessia that I began to regain my sanity. Your mission to overthrow Ludek became my mission, and there was a purpose to the killing. And when the war was over and Ludek had been dispatched by you, and the kingdom was in the rightful hands of the Wise Queen Varvara, then I felt satisfied."

"So, your point is that my killing soldiers will bring me no peace, but serving a higher purpose will?"

"You're a smart boy, Norbert," Tyrmiss said.

"Something is happening down there," Tessia said.

I looked where she was pointing. I didn't see anything, but her eyes were much sharper than mine.

"Beyazit's army has moved from their camp, and they're marching across the plain in this direction," Tessia said. "You can't see the men yet, but you can see the dust they are stirring up."

"They are planning to finish off the dragons," I said, suddenly feeling ashamed to be human.

Tessia turned to Tyrmiss. "Can you send a message to Nerdyn? Tell him to bring his brigade here, and we'll make a defense strategy."

In midafternoon, the dragon brigade arrived. As they flew toward us from the east, they split into three groups, one flying toward the opposite mountainside looking down at the pass, the second behind us, landing on a peak, covering our left flank, and one joining us on our perch.

As the dragons settled onto the ground around us, I saw how fit and strong they were. They were a mixed group of males and females, each of them at least 2,000 years old, the age of maturity for dragons. I saw the muscles rippling across their chests, and the skin of their wings taut across strong bones. These young dragons had been training together for months, and now they'd fought in two battles. They'd drawn human blood, and they'd seen comrades die. They were disciplined and ready for what was to come.

"You see where their ballistas are?" Tessia asked Nerdyn.

"Yes, they are mostly in the front of the army," Nerdyn replied. "Are they planning to set up their machinery in the northern pass to provide cover for the main force?"

"That would be my guess," Tessia said. "Their strategy is to establish a battery of ballistas, so they can pick us off as we fly toward them."

Tessia shaded her eyes with her palm and looked down at the Valley of the Dragons where the most vulnerable members of the tribe—the very young and the very old—were slowly flying toward us, stopping frequently. "Is it possible for the tribe of dragons to escape through a different route? Staying in the valley makes them easy targets for the ballistas."

"I don't think so," Nerdyn said. "The mountains are too high for some of the old ones to fly over. The tribe needs to come to this end of the valley and then turn east where the mountains are lower."

"How soon will they be passing through this end of the valley, Nerdyn?"

"Tomorrow. Perhaps in late morning."

"The army is traveling fast. If they keep moving all night, then they will have their ballistas set up by morning," Tessia thought for a moment. "So, we need to stop the army of men from setting up their ballistas in this pass, or it will be a bloodbath for the dragons tomorrow."

"It appears so, Queen Tessia."

"Is there a moon tonight, Nerdyn?"

"Yes, a full moon."

"A full moon would give them the advantage. They could see us flying overhead and could pick us off." She turned to Nerdyn and said, "We need to attack now before the sun sets."

"Why now, my queen?"

"Their ballistas are in forward positions, so we fly around their army and attack them from the rear. We'll be coming in from the west with the setting sun behind us. If we spread out the dragons, the ballistas will not be able to hit us."

"We will have to fly very quickly to get behind the army before sunset."

"Take two of your squadrons north, then west, staying out of range of the ballistas," Tessia said, pointing. "Tyrmiss, Norbert and I will lead another squadron south, then west. Once we are behind the army with the sun at our backs, we swoop in, using fire and talon to wreak havoc on the army."

"And what is our goal, my queen?" I asked.

"Our goal is to cause enough damage and confusion to the enemy army to stop its advance. They will have to reorganize to engage us. Once it is ready to engage us, we disengage, fly around the army and return here."

"Once the army has stopped its advance, it will take time for it to reorganize its march up to this pass? So, we are trying to delay the advance of the army long enough so the old and young dragons can get away?" Nerdyn considered the strategy and said, "This could work, but we must leave now."

He called over his communications officer, a young dragon with a talent for thought messaging, and dictated his orders, phrased as suggestions, to each of his squadron commanders.

Tessia climbed on Tyrmiss and I scrambled up to sit behind her. She had her bow ready in her left hand, and I had my wand unsheathed. I grabbed the back of Tessia's belt, and Tyrmiss lifted us in the air and turned toward the south where the squadron that would accompany us was already taking off in a widely spaced formation.

We flew with seventy dragons around the right flank of the army of men, staying out of ballista range, then turned to approach their rear with the sun at our backs. I could see the two squadrons led by Nerdyn mirroring our flanking operation. Before the army of men understood what had happened, we were descending on them, over two hundred dragons breathing fire and raking their ranks with their talons. A few bolts from their ballistas flew in our direction but went over us harmlessly. Tessia was shooting her bow to our left, picking off officers with deadly accuracy while I shot fist sized fireballs at the ranks of men, causing them to panic and run. Tyrmiss swooped low to the ground, her talons open and dangerous, ripping flesh wherever they touched. Faced with this surprise attack from their rear, the army of men roiled in chaos and confusion. Before we came to the ballistas, the dragons turned as one and went back over the army, tearing apart their ranks.

When we were back at the point where we started the attack, we retreated, banking and arcing wide before turning east again to return to the mountains. Tyrmiss landed on the mountainside where we started, and Tessia looked at Nerdyn who was listening to his communication officer.

"No casualties! We didn't lose a single dragon," he said with what passed for a dragon grin. "Thanks to your brilliant strategy, my queen," he added, graciously.

"Oh, it was a sound strategy alright," Tessia said. "But no strategy can be better than its execution. All the credit for this victory goes to you, Nerdyn, Lord of the Skies. Thank you."

Suddenly, Nerdyn looked very concerned. "Wait, I'm receiving a message." He listened for a moment and said, "Something is happening in the harbor! One of our scouts spotted a flotilla of war ships headed to the city."

"Beyazit must be using his navy to bring reinforcements," Tessia growled. "All we can do is to delay them long enough so the dragon tribe can escape through the pass."

"Shall I send a squadron to attack the ships at sea?" Nerdyn asked.

"No, you and your cohort are needed here. The soldiers may be able to reorganize and launch another attack." Tessia looked at me and Tyrmiss.

"What are you waiting for?" Tyrmiss asked, spreading her wings.

Tyrmiss carried Tessia and me high over the battlefield, over the city, and past the harbor where we could make out a dozen white sails heading toward us. But as we came closer, we saw two small figures on brooms flying back and forth between the ships. Below the figures, the water was roiling, tossing the ships back and forth.

"It's the Blue Witches!" Tessia shouted over her shoulder. "They're stirring up the wind and waves to slow down the ships!" And it was working, the ships could not sail in a straight line with the erratically shifting wind and the waves battering their prows. The storm was causing the ships to collide, damaging their hulls.

"Fly lower, Tyrmiss!" Tessia yelled. "Let's light their sails on fire!"

We swooped down over the wave-tossed ships, Tyrmiss breathing fire on their sails. Tessia picked off sailors on the decks, and I threw a few fireballs for good measure. Zamarrra noticed us and waved a greeting. As we drew closer, I could see her head was thrown back, her long silver hair whipping behind her like lightning, and she was laughing wildly.

As we pulled away from the burning ships, Zamarrra and Evanora joined us, following us back to the mountain pass where the dragon squadron waited.

"Thank you, Witches!" Tessia exclaimed, climbing off Tyrmiss.

"Not at all, Your Majesty," Zamarrra said. "We heard about the slaughter of the dragonlings." She met Tyrmiss's eyes in sympathy, then she looked at me. "And we were sorry to hear about your loss, Mage."

She and Evanora hugged Tyrmiss and me.

"When we heard about the slaughter of innocents, we realized we bore some responsibility, so we thought we could help by slowing down King Beyazit's reinforcements."

"And so you did," Tessia said. "What are your plans now?"

"We will return to your kingdom, Your Majesty," Evanora said. "There is still much work to do in reforesting the Dry Hills. We need to fly now before the cold winds come."

As the two witches disappeared into the misty air, I turned and looked down at the field of battle. Thousands of men lay dead or bleeding. Some of the soldiers were still running away, so frightened by the dragon's attack they hadn't yet realized the battle was over. It would be quite a while before Beyazit's army could reorganize for another advance. For the time being, the dragon tribe was safe.

Chapter Sixteen

"You know, Norbert, at some point we need to start our journey home," Tessia said, looking off to the east, her dark hair catching the sunlight.

We were sitting on a ledge above a lake whose waters were so clear I could see trout under the surface. The sky had a few wisps of clouds above the snowcapped peaks. This New Valley of the Dragons was the most beautiful place I had ever seen. On the other side of the lake, dragons were using their talons to dig holes in the ground which would eventually be caves in which they would live. It was late summer, a week after the last battle with the army of men and a month since we had left home.

"Home?" I asked.

"Yes, home. You know. Dragonja City? That place where we have jobs and family. Remember the School for Mages?"

Yes, I thought, *The School for Mages. Ena and Adamu. I remember.*

"Norbert, Idella needs to know what happened to Ena."

Yes, I thought, *Idella. My wife. Ena's mother.* My previous life seemed like a pleasant dream.

"You know what I want?" I asked.

"You want to stay here, so you don't have to tell Idella?"

"No, I want to kill King Beyazit."

Tessia laughed grimly. "I'm sure a lot of people want to kill him, but his crimes are no longer our business."

"No, really. I've been thinking about it. Remember the invisibility spell I used in the last war?"

"Yeah. It worked pretty well until a clumsy soldier bumped into you!"

We both laughed at the vagaries of well-laid plans.

"I want Tyrmiss to drop me off on the balcony outside Beyazit's royal chambers. I'll slip into the room, point my wand at him and kill him in his bed. He'll die in his sleep, seemingly of natural causes."

"Norbert, speaking as someone who is familiar with military tactics, I have to tell you that assassination is one of the most difficult tasks to pull off. Things rarely go as planned. You have to get close enough to kill the target, but also have an escape route. You need to have an insider who can tell you when and where the target is. There's the likelihood of being betrayed by the insider…"

"No one deserves to die more than Beyazit," I asserted.

"No doubt. But I worry about what this will do to you."

"I've killed people before!" I was starting to feel defensive. Tessia was treating me as if I were a boy pretending to go to war, instead of a seasoned fighter.

"Of course, you've killed people, Norbert, as have I. And no one is more effective than you are when you're defending people—or dragons—you love. In the heat of battle, with your heart pumping and people charging at you, killing comes easily after the first time. But killing someone who is asleep, unarmed, unaware of what's going to happen… that is a different thing altogether. When you're fighting for love, Norbert, you are magnificent in battle. But a cold-blooded assassination? That will change you. Please don't do it."

"Tyrmiss," I said the next day when we were alone. She was digging a cave in the side of a hill and the mud kept sliding down, filling the entrance.

"I don't think dragons were meant to be tunnellers," she said, stopping to catch her breath. She looked down at her talons which had become large balls of mud, then looked up the mountain to the snow at the top of the peak. "Our ancestors carved palaces out of glaciers, and here I am digging a hole in the mud like a muskrat. How far our race has fallen."

"Tyrmiss," I repeated.

"Norbert, I know what you are going to ask me, and the answer is no. Emphatically, no. I will not help you assassinate King Beyazit."

"But he deserves it."

"Well, don't we all? Oh, don't get me wrong. I would love for the earth to suffer no longer the presence of that flea on the furry neck of a rat, but as Tessia said, killing the king will irrevocably change you, and I like the way you are."

"Did Tessia tell you that I asked her first?"

"No, Tessia did not tell me about your insane desire to murder a king. You told me."

"Me?"

"Yes, you. Your dreams have been screaming at all the dragons. You've become the subject of gossip around here. I knew that sooner or later you would get around to asking me to help you, so I've had some time to think about it." Tyrmiss turned to look at me with her bright blue eyes. "Norbert, don't do this. It will not bring back Ena, and it will make you hate yourself."

That evening when I was laying out my bedroll next to the fire which had effectively been Tessia's and my home under the stars for the last week, Nerdyn landed some paces away.

"Norbert, come with me, please," and he led me to his newly dug cave.

As my eyes adjusted, I saw Nerdyn and two young males sitting in the dark, their blue eyes shining with excitement. I was glad to see that most of the young dragons had given up sniffing moon bark.

"Mage," Nerdyn said, "We want to help you kill King Beyazit. All three of us have lost our families by his treachery. We feel it is only by his death we can hope to live our lives."

"Alright," I said, after a long pause. "What's the plan?"

"Tomorrow night, Ciosyt and Iedreg," Nerdyn said gesturing to his two companions, "will accompany us to the castle and stand guard while I fly you to the balcony of King Beyazit's sleeping chambers. You will enter his room, kill him while he sleeps, and escape on my back."

"When do we leave?" I asked, and all three of the dragons smiled at me.

There was a new moon that night, making it a perfect time to fly. We would take shelter during the day on a peak overlooking Hoclav City, and after dark fly down to the castle to do the deed.

I went to my cave to get my kit. Tessia was there waiting for me.

"Norbert," she implored. "Please don't do this."

"How did you know..." Then I realized that Tyrmiss must have told her. In a place where everyone could hear each other's thoughts, there were no secrets.

"I have to do it, Tessia. I think of Ena constantly. She is in my dreams. I see her everywhere. I hear her voice..." I felt my throat closing and couldn't say anymore.

"So, you are going to kill a man to rid yourself of a ghost?"

"Something like that." I picked up my kit and walked out of the cave with her following me.

"Don't try to stop me, Tessia."

"I'm not going to stop you. You're a grown man and can do what you please."

"Then why are you following me?"

"Because I'm going with you."

I noticed she was carrying her kit and Agatha hung at her side.

"Tessia, you don't need to come with me. You've already said that this mission is a bad idea."

"I still think it's a bad idea, Norbert. But you've followed me when I had bad ideas, some of them worse than this one. So, I think I owe you. Besides, you may need me to cover your back."

When we approached Nerdyn, he looked at Tessia, but didn't seem surprised.

"Can you carry two humans?" Tessia asked.

"Easily," Nerdyn said. "But I don't think I'll need to, at least not tonight." He cocked his head behind him, and I noticed that there were not two dragons with us, but three.

"Good evening, Norbert." Tyrmiss's distinctive voice said. "Do you mind if I tag along to try to keep you and Tessia out of trouble?"

Shortly before dawn, we arrived at the top of the peak closest to Hoclav City.

"We'll rest here all day," Nerdyn announced. "And late tonight, after the city is quiet and most of the residents are asleep, we'll fly down to the castle."

I set down my kit in the snow and walked around, stretching my legs. We had flown all night without stopping. Tessia was stretching her legs as well, and the four dragons were arching their backs like cats, then curling up in the snow to rest. I brushed the snow from the ground and laid out my bedroll, where I curled up and tried to sleep, but I kept thinking about the mission. I wasn't worried about the danger—we would be in and out before the guards knew what was happening. I was worried about the act itself. I had never killed a man as he lay sleeping and wondered whether it would, as Tessia and Tyrmiss claimed, change me.

I woke in the freezing dark. The dragons were moving around the camp, and Tessia was sitting on a boulder a few feet from me. I got up, put on a second layer of clothing, packed my bedroll in my kit, and took out a bag of nuts and dried berries.

"Are we going soon?" I asked Tessia as I sat beside her, offering her food.

"It appears we are," she said, taking a handful of nuts and berries. "I'll be glad to get moving. It's freezing on this mountain."

Nerdyn, speaking only to Tessia and me because the dragons had already discussed the plan silently, said out loud, "The two of you will fly on my back to the balcony of the king's sleeping chamber. The other three dragons will stay high above the city. There's no moon tonight, so the dragons will be invisible to the soldiers standing guard on the walls. If we need back-up, our friends can easily fly down and hit the guards. But we are hoping that this will be easy. Just in and out."

Tessia swung onto Nerdyn's back and extended her hand to me. I swung my leg over the dragon's back and settled behind my queen. Before the previous night, I had never ridden any dragon but Tyrmiss, and I was surprised that being on Nerdyn felt quite different. He was bonier and leaner than Tyrmiss, and now as he took a few steps, lifted off, dived through the air to pick up speed, I felt jostled, but gradually settled in for the ride.

So, this is what it feels like to be an assassin.

We flew high above the castle, and as our three friends maintained altitude, Nerdyn wheeled around an imaginary hub directly over the target, carrying Tessia and me down to the High Tower. His landing on the balcony was surprisingly soft and almost soundless.

I opened the door of the king's chamber. The room was dark, but the fireplace had a few glowing coals, so I waved my wand and made the flames grow. In the bed was the sleeping king. He was snoring softly, his face turned to me, a bit of drool had pooled beneath the corner of his mouth as if he were a young child. Beside him was a woman about his age. I could hear their breath rising and falling together, the way two people who have slept together for decades have the same heartbeat, the same rhythm, like a wave carrying them together toward shore. The intimacy of their sleep caught me off guard. Somehow, I had never considered that Beyazit might have a wife, someone he'd slept with for many years, someone who cared about him and was growing old with him.

The sheet covered the bottom half of the King's body, so I couldn't see his squid-like tentacles, only the chest, neck and head of a man. I had thought it would be easy to kill the monster, but he appeared in this half-light to be nothing more than a husband sleeping beside his wife.

I steeled myself to do the deed I had come to do. With a quick flick of my wand, I could stop his breath. I could stop his wife's breath as well, but to kill them both as easily as swatting a fly seemed wrong. I should wake him first, I thought. He needs to know why he's being killed. I even thought of killing his wife in front of him. Make her die slowly as he watched, powerless to help her.

Suddenly I felt disgusted with myself. Nausea roiled my stomach and I felt dizzy. Then a calm came over me, and I stepped out onto the balcony.

"Did you do it?" Tessia whispered.

I shook my head.

She leaned her head close to mine and said quietly, "Do you want me to do it for you?"

I turned and looked at her with horror, and I finally realized what I'd done. I had used the loyalty of my friends against them. I had perverted love to serve evil.

What kind of creature am I?

"I'm sorry, Tessia," I whispered. "I'm sorry I brought all of you here for no purpose."

"Oh, I think there was a purpose. An important purpose," she said. "Let's go home."

I looked at Nerdyn, and I could see in his eyes he knew what I'd done, what I'd failed to do, what I refused to do, but in his eyes was not disgust or condemnation, but love. I felt confused by the reaction of the two of them. I had failed to do what I set out to do, and I had perverted the love and devotion of those who followed me.

Tessia and I climbed on Nerdyn's back and he lifted off. Silently we flew up to join our friends who were wheeling in the sky like stars.

Chapter Seventeen

We flew all night and when we landed in the New Valley of the Dragons, I noticed that all the residents, mostly young warriors since so many of the old ones and the dragonlings had been killed in the slaughter carried out by King Beyazit's soldiers, were lined up outside the village.

We landed in front of them, and as I dismounted from Nerdyn's back, all the dragons bowed their heads. I was startled and looked at Tessia who shrugged her shoulders, as mystified as I was by the behavior of the dragons. Then, I looked at Tyrmiss who was smiling at me, showing all her saber-like teeth.

"Norbert," she said. "They are honoring you."

"Honoring me?" I asked. "Why? I failed to complete my mission. I had the chance to kill their enemy, my enemy, but I lost my nerve. Why would they be honoring me?"

"You did not lose your nerve, Norbert. You lost your need for revenge. You had the opportunity to kill your enemy, but you showed him mercy. Among dragons, mercy and forgiveness are the highest virtues," Tyrmiss explained.

Yvnede raised her head, as the other dragons continued to bow. "It is the custom of dragons that when one of us has had a significant event, then the dragon is given a new name to mark the occasion. And so, in honor of your recent act of heroism, your name will no longer be Norbert Oldfoot the Mage. From now on, you will be known as Norbert Dragonheart, known as The Merciful."

I could feel my face blushing. Somehow, one of the most humiliating incidents of my life had turned me into a hero.

I went back to my cave and fell into bed. I was so exhausted I slept like the dead. In the middle of the night, Ena came into the cave. She was wearing her favorite blue dress. Her hair which was not quite as curly as her mother's, fell in ringlets on her shoulders. And her skin, which was not quite as dark as her mother's, shone like copper. She sat on the bed beside me and took my hand.

"I'm sorry," I said. "I am so sorry."

She smiled and put her finger to my lips. And I slept. The next morning, I woke knowing what I had to do.

"Well, Norbert," Tyrmiss was saying. "I don't understand why you are suddenly in such a hurry to leave. A few weeks ago, all you wanted to do was sleep, and a few days ago, all you wanted was to assassinate a tyrant, and now all you want is to go home."

We said our goodbyes to the dragons, and I was ready to go. Tessia seemed to be flirting with a couple of the female dragons, and I was getting impatient.

"I thought perhaps we could take a different route back," Tyrmiss mused. "Nygren told me about a shortcut through the southern mountains..."

"No, no," I said, starting to grow angry. "We have to go back the same way we came. I need to go to Zygmunt's island."

"Very well, Norbert," Tyrmiss said, sounding hurt. "Why are you angry? I just made a suggestion."

"I'm sorry, Tyrmiss," I apologized. "There's something I need to do on the Blessed Isle."

We flew west to the edge of the mountains, went through the pass where we launched the attack against the army of men and turned south, following the edge of the mountains. Once we were far from Hoclav City, we followed the coast. Late at night, we made camp next to the sea, drank the fresh water and dried fruit we'd brought, and slept. The next morning, we woke at dawn and continued down the coast. Late on the third day, we saw our destination ahead of us, the wooded isle in a blue sea.

"Welcome!" Zygmunt said, hugging his niece and smiling at Tyrmiss and me. "Wessel and I are very glad to see you again!" And indeed, Wessel stood beside his companion, smiling at us. Zygmunt glanced around, looking for Ena and Adamu, then looked at me with his head cocked.

"Ena and Adamu did not survive the war," I said. Zygmunt's face fell, and his shoulders sagged. He was an old warrior, and I wondered how many times he had heard news of this kind.

He went to me, his long arms stretched out and hugged me tightly. When he pulled away, I saw there were tears in his eyes. Wessel also wiped a tear from his cheek with the back of his hand.

"You can tell us what happened over dinner, my friend," Zygmunt said solemnly and made a sweeping gesture toward the keep. "We've kept your old rooms ready for you."

After Tessia and I got settled into our rooms and Tyrmiss made herself comfortable in the stable, we joined Zygmunt and Wessel at their table in the garden. As before, Tyrmiss had her own table close by, loaded with piles of fish and meat and a large silver tureen of spring water.

As we began to eat, Zygmunt said, "Please tell us everything that happened since we last saw you."

I told him about our flight north along the coast, our assessment of the defenses of Hoclav City and our flight inland to the Valley of the Dragons. Tyrmiss then summarized the history of dragons in that region and told of the ways they had tried to avoid contact with men. She told how despite the dragons' desire to be unmolested, once men had discovered them, conflict was inevitable. She went on to explain the responsibilities of the Council of Elders and their decision to declare war on King Beyazit's army. I noticed that Wessel was nodding as Tyrmiss spoke, clearly understanding everything she said. I wondered whether he could read the lips of dragons or whether Tyrmiss had connected her mind with him, as she did at times with me.

Tessia picked up the story and told about our participation in the three great battles between men and dragons: the first resulting in huge casualties on both sides, the second in a slaughter of dragons, and the third in a decisive win for the dragons.

"Tessia's brilliant strategies, inspired by you, played a decisive role in allowing the dragons to win the war, despite having a much smaller force than the men," I added.

Hearing this, Zygmunt wanted to know everything about Tessia's strategies. He was particularly interested in her invention of the feigned retreat in the first battle. He listened carefully to her detailed explanation, and said, "So you adapted the Grosur Maneuver?"

"The Grosur Maneuver?" I asked.

Zygmunt nodded, "Grosur was a legendary Drekavac general during the first war with men. In a famous battle, a Drekavac battalion engaged a much larger army of men, then retreated into the hills. The human general, whose name is no longer remembered, gave chase and had his men charge uphill at the Drekavacs. As you would guess, the main force of the Drekavacs had remained hidden. They charged downhill at the men, and being fresh and having the high ground, won a decisive battle."

Tessia smiled. She knew that only her uncle would be familiar with this historical example. "Yes, uncle," she said. "But in this case, we had to encourage the men to abandon their ballistas, something their generals would never have ordered them to do, and have the men charge in a disorderly way uphill."

"And so, you gave them a taste of victory and made them think that they could finish off the dragons if they charged... Brilliant!"

Zygmunt asked about the second battle, and Tessia glanced at me, and then summarized the events quickly, not mentioning the fact that the two young mages had lost their lives defending the baby dragons.

"Now," Zygmunt said. "The third battle interests me as well. You had a small force, not more than a brigade of dragons, and yet you managed to defeat a large well-trained army with ballistas which had proved deadly against the dragons in the past. Tell me again how you did that..."

Tessia recounted the battle slowly, including details about the range of the ballistas, the terrain and her intuition about the ways that the human soldiers would act in the face of direct attack from their rear.

"Ah, so you adapted the Vatnor charge in a way that took advantage of the dragons' ability to see each other over the battlefield?"

"What's the Vatnor charge?" I asked.

"Captain Vatnor was a cavalry commander known for flanking the enemy," Zygmunt explained. "He would have his horsemen go around both ends of the enemy line and attack the enemy from the rear. The problem with the strategy, which had never been solved before, was that once his cavalry had engaged the enemy, the battle became a melee in which infantry has the advantage and the cavalrymen lost sight of each other. So, the charge worked only if the calvary had limited engagement, caused as much chaos as they could, and then retreated. The tactic worked only as a diversion. Tessia adapted the strategy for dragons who can not only do much more damage to the enemy than horse cavalry can, and the enemy infantry is virtually useless unless the dragons are brought down by ballistas, but also dragons can see each other over the battlefield and communicate by thought message. In this way, they can maintain their formation and coordinate their attack." Zygmunt turned and looked at this niece. "Brilliant!"

"You taught me well, uncle."

Zygmunt suggested that we have a last bottle of wine in the inner garden where there were more comfortable chairs. As we got up to move, Tessia pulled me aside.

"Norbert, we skipped over part of the story," she said.

"I know," I said feeling a familiar lump rising in my throat.

"My uncle has been very tactful, not asking what happened to Ena and Adamu. Don't you think we should tell him?"

"I suppose." I was having trouble breathing.

"If you want me to, I can tell him about how King Beyazit betrayed us with the parlay, luring our best fighters away and how he attacked the dragon village. You don't have to be there when I tell him. You can go to your room or take a walk. No one will think you're being rude by not wanting to relive what happened to Ena."

I nodded and turned away from Tessia. I walked a little way into the orchard and stopped. The lemon trees were no longer fruiting, but the scent of their leaves filled the night air. The moon shone down on the island, and I thought about what I needed to do.

I returned to my room and sat on the bed. Moonlight slanted through the window, elongating the shadows. I reached into my leather pouch and pulled out a bundle of leafy river creeper, a wax-sealed jar containing ground semoseed, and a small piece of parchment smeared with the spore of appeath mushroom. I tore off a piece of parchment, then using a copper spoon, I measured the proper proportions of leaf and seed in a cup, added the bit of parchment, poured in a splash of water, and stirred the mixture. I recognized the unpleasant odor.

I drank a double dose of the potion. It tasted bitter, then sweet, then salty, then sour. The room grew brighter, and I saw two young people sitting beneath a tree on a broad flat plain, mountains in the distance. They were playing a game of stones, and I could clearly see the path that led to them.

Chapter Eighteen

"Norbert," Tyrmiss was saying. "This idea is the stupidest and most dangerous thing you've ever thought of. It's infinitely worse than your plan to assassinate King Beyazit, which, thank the Goddess, you failed to do."

I had asked Tyrmiss to fly me to the other side of the island so we could have a private conversation because she knew many things humans were not aware of.

"Tyrmiss, you haven't even allowed me to explain what I have in mind, and you've already decided I shouldn't do it."

"You don't need to explain anything, Norbert. The idea is crazy, not so much a plan as a symptom of the way that grief has affected your mind."

"Will you at least satisfy my curiosity? In your long life, have you ever heard of a mortal doing something like this?

Tyrmiss looked at me, disgusted. After a long pause, she answered, "Yes, I have heard of such a thing. In fact, if the old stories are to be believed, it has happened a number of times."

"Really?" Now I was intrigued. "Tell me the stories."

"Well, to tell them right, I would need a lyre, and I would have to remember the meter." She looked at me curiously. "Norbert, why don't you go get your lyre and we'll see whether we can puzzle out the old songs?"

"Tyrmiss, just tell the stories, and stop trying to distract me."

"Very well, then. Let me think…" Then with a deep rumble, she cleared her throat and began:

"There was once a hero named Gurudutt who went off to war, and when he returned, he found that Death had taken his wife Aditi whom he loved. He knew of a witch named Kanaki who had studied the ways of Death. So, the hero went in search of the witch, and when he found her, she told Gurudutt that there was no hope of getting his wife back for no one returned from that far land once they had been taken. Gurudutt, who had often achieved more than men thought possible, demanded to know the way to the land of Death.

"The witch told him that each evening, a ship took on board all the people who had died that day, and then set sail to the east. Kanaki pointed the way to the place on the shore where the ship boarded passengers each evening. Gurudutt, being the bravest man in the world, set out in the direction she pointed.

"After traveling many days and fighting many monsters sent by Death to stop him, Gurudutt came to the place on the shore where the dead gathered to wait for the ship that would carry them from this life. Pulling the hood of his cloak down low over his face, Gurudutt climbed on board the ship with the newly dead, and they set sail. When they arrived at their destination, Death met Gurudutt at the shore in the form of… *ahem*… a dragon and attacked him with fire and talon. Gurudutt, who was the greatest hero the world has ever known, fought Death and killed him.

"Gurudutt found his wife Aditi who no longer remembered him, so he kidnapped her and put her on board the ship headed for the land of the

> living. Aditi did not want to return to her previous life, so she fought him fiercely on board the ship. She turned into a lion who killed and ate the ship's captain and crew.
>
> "And in this way, Gurudutt and Aditi became lost in the sea between Life and Death, and to this day they are traveling on the ship we know as the Evening Star which wanders through the sky without knowing whether it is part of day or of night."

"He killed Death?" I asked.

"Yes," Tyrmiss answered. "In some versions, Death's sons War, Illness, and Hunger inherited the Kingdom of the Dead."

After a pause, I said sarcastically, "Well, that's a lovely story, but not very helpful to me. Do you know other stories about people who went into the underworld to bring back people they loved?"

"Actually, I know quite a few now that I think of it. Here's another one..."

> "Iritis was a queen who was the greatest warrior of her age. Her favorite concubine was a woman named Pili who had long black hair that waved down her back like the sea at night. After many years of happiness together, Iritis returned from war to discover that Pili had died from illness. Iritis grieved for forty days and forty nights, and finally went to the temple and asked the priests where the soul of Pili had been taken after she died. The head priest told her that Pili was still on the shore of the

Sea of Forgetfulness, waiting for a ship to carry her to the afterlife.

"The priest pointed the way to the shore, and Iritis headed off on a fast horse. She arrived at the shore only to find a multitude of people waiting to be carried to the afterlife. So many people had died in Iritis's wars that there was not room on the ship to carry them all. A soldier carrying his head under his arm recognized Iritis as the one who had killed him in battle. Other shades recognized Iritis as well: some had been her soldiers who had followed her into battle; others were women and children killed by her soldiers. The shades surrounded her, touching her living flesh, pointing to their fatal wounds and asking why she had served Death instead of Life. She had caused them to be stranded on this shore between two worlds. Why would she do such a thing?

"Regretting how she had caused so much death, Iritis walked into the Sea of Forgetfulness and soon she no longer remembered who she was. She no longer knew that she was a great warrior, and she joined the people on the shore who were waiting for the ship to carry them into the next life. But Iritis was not dead so she could not board the ship, nor could she return to her life which she had forgotten, so she sat down on the shore where she remains to this day, neither dead nor alive."

After Tyrmiss ended the tale, I sat quietly thinking about it. Iritis sounded much like Tessia, a great woman-warrior who loved women. Is it true that the people Tessia and I had killed were waiting on the shore waiting to be taken to the next life?

"Norbert," Tyrmiss said, sensing my growing dread. "These are stories which contain the truth, but they are not the truth. No one in this life knows what happens after death. All we have are stories that tell us how to live and how to die. No one knows what comes next."

"Tyrmiss," I said. "I want to go to the underworld, find my daughter and bring her back to this life. I cannot go home and face her mother. Idella will never forgive me for having let her daughter be killed."

"I know you are in pain over Ena's death, Norbert. And despite our many squabbles, I think you know that I love you, as I love Tessia. The two of you saved my life after Rilla was killed. You helped me find a use for my murderous rage at Ludek's Drekavac soldiers, and when the war was over you gave a home to my children and me. You have been a true friend, so I must tell you the truth. Ena is gone. Her *soul*, or whatever you want to call the essence that's left after we die, has gone on to find another form. Even if you were able to enter the domain of Death, find your daughter and bring her back, there would be no place for her in this life. You must go to Idella and tell her this."

I bowed my head and my tears fell on the dirt in front of my feet. "I can't, Tyrmiss. I cannot tell Idella that mistakes I made caused our daughter's death. It would kill Idella, and it would make her hate me which would kill me." I looked up at my friend, this ten-thousand-year-old dragon who had carried Tessia and me into battle again and again. "Are there stories where a man goes into the Kingdom of Death, finds someone he loves, and they return together to this life?"

"Yes, there are stories like that, but keep in mind that these old stories are not intended to give us maps for navigating the magical realms. The stories are meant to teach us lessons about how to live our lives."

"I know, but right now, I need to have some hint of how I can find my daughter and bring her home to her mother."

Tyrmiss gave a long sigh. "Very well, here's a very old story which has a happy ending:

> "There was once a poet named Entana whose songs were so beautiful that as he walked through the forest, flowers sprang up around his feet and larks followed him through the fields imitating the music of his lyre. Entana fell in love with a young man named Kaveh who was fair of form. Entana sang to Kaveh every evening until Kaveh fell in love with the poet as well. They had many happy days and nights together.
>
> "However, Lord Death had heard Entana's songs praising Kaveh's beauty and over time, the songs won the heart of Death. One night, as the two lovers slept, Death came and took Kaveh. Entana woke beside the lifeless body of the youth, and he was stricken by grief. Entana wandered the fields and forests lamenting the loss of his lover, and the songs were so beautiful that all of nature fell into mourning. Trees died and birds stopped singing until finally the Goddess of All Life came to Entana and asked him to stop creating so much sadness. Entana said that he could not stop lamenting because he missed Kaveh so much that everywhere he looked he saw the absence of his love.
>
> "So, in order to save the world from dying of grief, the Goddess gave Entana directions to the underworld and told him to go to Death, who was her brother,

> and give him a single pomegranate blossom as a message from her.
>
> "Entana, following her directions exactly, went to the shore where the ship carries dead souls across the Sea of Forgetfulness. On the far shore, Entana entered the palace of Death and approached the mighty king who owns the larger half of creation. Entana played his lyre and sang of his love for his friend and his sadness at losing him. Death, who has a love of poets because like him they know both darkness and light, wept inconsolably and felt shame at having taken this young man before his time.
>
> "Death released Kaveh, saying that Entana could go back with his beloved to the world of the living. However, there was one condition. He could not look at Kaveh until his youthful beauty had faded. Entana agreed to the condition, and he took Kaveh by the hand and without looking at him, led him back into the land of the living.
>
> "The poet took Kaveh to his home and left him, not returning for forty years when they were both old. Only then was the poet able to see beauty, not in youthful vitality, but in quiet wisdom. They spent their final years together, dying within days of each other, and willingly went together into the Land of the Dead."

"Then there is hope of bringing back someone from death?" I asked.

"So the story would seem to indicate," Tyrmiss said, sadly. "Norbert, I beg you not to do this. I told you one of the few stories which has a happy ending. Most of them end with terrible unforeseen consequences."

"Thanks for the warning, Tyrmiss, but I have to try. How should I start?"

"I think you know whom you need to talk to. She's the reason why you brought us back to this island, isn't she?"

Part Five:
The Kingdom of Death

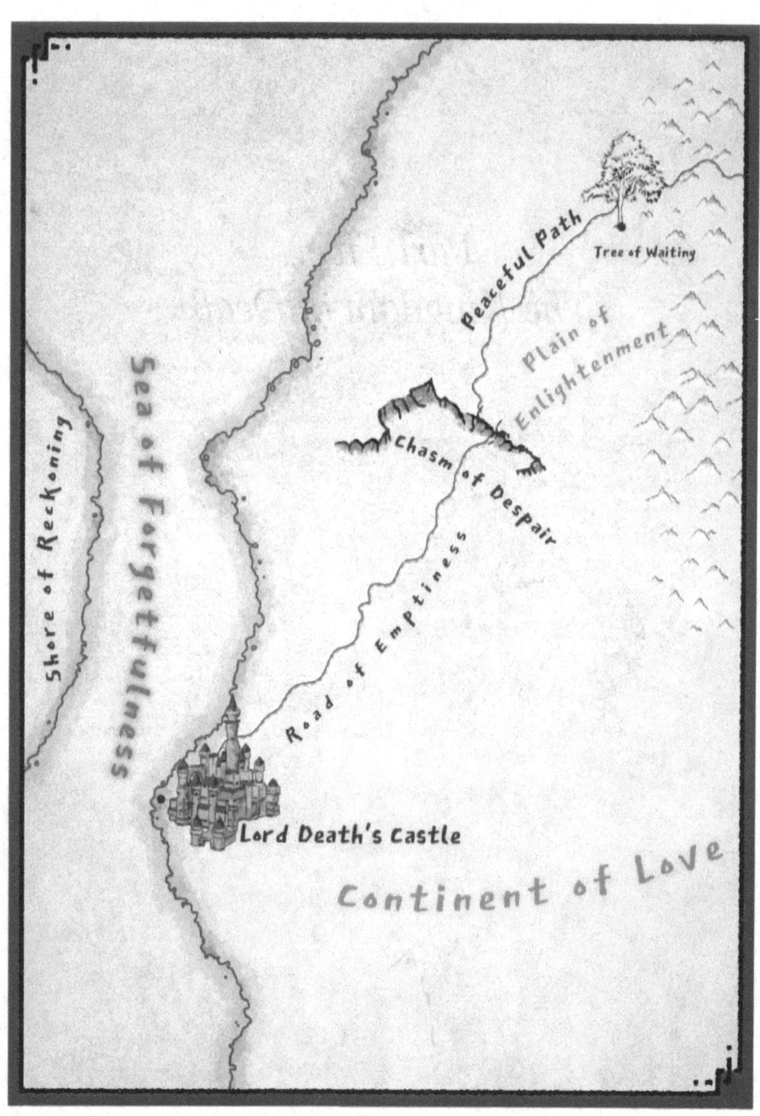

Map showing the Kingdom of Death

Chapter Nineteen

After dinner, I pulled Zygmunt aside and asked him to help me contact Liatris the Elemental.

Zygmunt looked at me curiously, "Why would you want to talk with her?"

"Just a professional interest," I said evasively. "I'm a mage after all, and she's an elemental spirit. She can teach me a great deal..."

Zygmunt obviously didn't believe my lie. I realized it was foolish to try to mislead someone as intelligent and perceptive as the general. If he had not been able to spot a lie quickly, he would have died many times in his long history of leading rebel forces. He looked at me patiently, and I noticed the dark circles under his eyes. Since the end of the revolution twenty years before, he had grown old. I felt ashamed of myself for lying to him when he'd always been kind and generous to me.

"I want her to help me enter the underworld," I confessed, knowing how preposterous the idea sounded.

To his credit, Zygmunt didn't scoff. Instead, he looked me in the eye intensely and responded, "You are in terrible pain over your daughter's passing, aren't you?"

I nodded, feeling the familiar lump rising in my throat.

After a decent silence in which he let me compose myself, he said, "I never had children, so I can't imagine what it's like to lose one's daughter. But in the war, I lost many friends, including one friend I killed, or rather I had Wessel execute..." His voice trailed off.

I remembered my friend Anja, Zygmunt's lover, who confessed to spying on us for Ludek. Anja's execution was still a painful memory for all of us.

"That was a necessary action on your part," I said. "Anja betrayed us all."

"Doing what is necessary…" Zygmunt said, with a slight edge of bitterness in his voice. Then, shaking off the past, he turned to me, "Are you sure you want to go into the underworld, my friend? I can't see how this could turn out well."

I nodded my head.

"Let's go then," he said. "It is dark enough now for Liatris not to object to our company."

As we walked through the long rows of lemon trees lit by moonlight, Tessia suddenly appeared beside me.

"You thought you could sneak off on an adventure without me, Mage?" She asked, mockingly.

"Tyrmiss told you what I planned to do and sent you to stop me," I said. It wasn't a question, and I'd expected this development.

"Of course," she answered, matching her stride to mine. "Zygmunt," she asked her uncle. "Are you actually helping this fool who wants to negotiate with Death?"

Zygmunt shrugged, "It is what he feels he has to do."

"Well then, I'm coming with you," she said.

"I don't want you to come, Tessia. This is something I have to do."

"And you really think that after all the quests we've gone on together, you are going to leave me behind when you embark on the greatest of them all? I don't need your permission, Mage. I am your queen."

I felt very grateful for her stubborn loyalty to me. I had no idea what we might encounter, and her courage and intelligence would, no doubt, be exactly what was needed.

"Tyrmiss told me you are planning to talk to an elemental who lives on this island," Tessia said.

Zygmunt nodded.

"I've heard of elementals, but I'm not sure exactly what they are."

Zygmunt said, "They are very old, some believe they are older than the Gods, older than Death itself. They are the original inhabitants of the earth, perhaps they are the earth. According to what I've been told by Liatris, there are five elements—earth, water, air, fire, and plant, and each of these elements takes many appearances, including that of human, but their actual being is invisible and pure."

"And this elemental that we are visiting… Liatris, what is she?" Tessia asked.

"She's a plant elemental."

"A plant elemental? You mean she lives in the forest?" Tessia asked, puzzled.

"No, no. She doesn't live in the forest," Zygmunt insisted. "She *is* the forest."

The solidity of the stone cairn was strangely comforting. It was exactly the way I remembered—my height and covered in acanthus vines. I realized it had probably been in this very spot for many millennia. Zygmunt, Tessia, and I kneeled before the cairn, and the general gave a short prayer of gratitude. As before, a woman walked out of the forest and stood in front of us. Again, Liatris appeared to me in the form of my Idella, and I wondered what she looked like to Tessia and Zygmunt.

"Thank you, Liatris, for coming to us in answer to my prayer."

"Zygmunt, I know why you've brought this mage again," she said inclining her dark head toward me. "He wishes to enter the underworld to find his daughter."

Still kneeling, I asked, "Is this possible, My Lady?"

Instead of answering my question, Liatris looked at Tessia,

kneeling beside me. "So, this is the Dragonqueen. Even in the spirit world, your name is becoming known."

Tessia gave a look of surprise but said nothing.

"Do you wish to enter the underworld, as well?"

"Yes, my lady," Tessia answered. "I wish to accompany my friend Norbert."

"Norbert," Liatris said, finally addressing me. "Your devotion to your daughter is admirable, but your grief represents a misunderstanding of life's many forms. Ena's death was not the end of her, but rather the end of one phase of her existence. For the time being, her essence has taken residence in the underworld. There it will wait until it is called to take another form. She may come back as a woman or a man, a tree or a rock, a stream or a blizzard. Perhaps her essence will divide and become many things. Or perhaps nothing at all."

"How will I know her if she comes back?"

Liatris shook her head. "The paths by which humans know things are very limited. If you cannot perceive something with your five senses, then you think it does not exist. But there are ways to know things without knowing them, to see things without seeing them. For example, Norbert, how do I appear to you?"

"You have the appearance of my wife Idella."

Liatris looked at Zygmunt. "And how do I appear to you?"

"You are a bright figure that I cannot look upon for fear that the brightness would blind me."

"And you, Dragonqueen?"

"You have no form, only a presence, like a breeze blowing from the forest."

"You see, each of you has chosen to see me as you wish, giving me the form that most pleases you."

"And your true form is the forest?" I asked.

"Yes, I am the forest, but not the forest you know. You think of the forest as being trunk, stem and leaf, but most of my form is underground—the roots and soil. I am the invisible creatures that digest the soil and feed the plants. I am the water flowing in the veins of the forest. I am the sunlight falling through the leaves, and the rotting leaves that feed the trees. I am the termite and the thrush, the mouse in the belly of the owl. I am the cycle of life in the forest."

Liatris looked at me with pity. "You suffer the absence of your daughter, and you fear the loss of her will hurt, perhaps even kill, your wife. Your son Alaric will suffer the loss as well. Your intention to bring back Ena from the kingdom of death is admirable, but I cannot grant your wish."

"And why not?" I asked impertinently. At this point, I felt I had nothing to lose, so why not challenge the forest to show me the way to bring back Ena? "Does an elemental go back on her promises?"

The eyes of the woman in front of me flashed anger, a look I knew well in my wife. Then her eyes softened, a look I also knew.

"The last time I was here, you granted me a boon in exchange for the gold which your sister had stolen from me."

"So I did, but I was thinking of something simple, easy to grant: a safe voyage home; a prosperous business; the love of a woman or man. I was not thinking of this... this abomination. Showing a man the way into the underworld in order to bring back his daughter? This is an ugly thing. It breaks all the rules."

"Hasn't it been done many times before?" I asked. "What about the warriors Gurudutt and Iritis? What about the poet Entana? Didn't they sail the Sea of Forgetfulness and find the ones they love? Didn't Entana bring Kaveh back from the Kingdom of Death? Why can't I?"

The being wearing Idella's form crossed her arms and looked at me with narrowed eyes. "So, you know the old poems forgotten by men? The dragon must have told you."

She tapped her foot twice, and I knew she was leaning

toward granting my wish despite her better judgment. I stayed silent and waited for her to decide.

"Very well, my children," Liatris said. "I will help you gain entrance to the underworld, and I will tell you some of what to expect while you're there, but I cannot help you once you enter the Kingdom of Death. I have no power there."

She looked at Tessia and me and sighed, "Your corporeal bodies cannot go into the underworld, only your souls. Your bodies will remain here. Zygmunt, I need for you to stay with them while their souls are traveling. We don't want any wild animals to think they have found an easy meal."

"Of course," Zygmunt said, putting his hand on the dagger in his belt and nodding to the elemental. "I will stand by them and guard their bodies while their souls are elsewhere."

"Norbert and Tessia," Liatris explained. "You will lie down here and go to sleep, and you will experience the journey as a dream. First, you will go down a long dark tunnel and then you will emerge into a gray light. There will be a shore, and on the shore will be the shades of people, all of them still bearing the wounds or decrepitude that took them from this life. You may recognize some of the shades because they are the ones who represent your sins against Life, and these people have been chosen to travel with you. Many of them have waited for you for years.

"Remember, you are pretending to be dead. If these shades believe you are still alive, then they will not allow you on the ship. So, I will slash your foreheads, and you will bleed profusely, the blood running down over your face and body.

"You will board the ship with your companions and sail across the Sea of Forgetfulness. The water is sweet, not salty, and the journey is long. You will see your companions cupping their hands in the water and drinking. You must not drink the water for it will cause you to lose all memory of your past life.

Instead, I will give you each a flagon of dew. When you grow thirsty, sip on the flagon and it will refresh your mind. You will remember everything that has ever happened in your life, and you will weep, for human life is full of loss. You will also laugh, for human life is full of joy.

"On the far shore of the Sea of Forgetfulness, you will see a castle. This is the home of Death. You must go to him and petition for the release of your daughter. Death hates to give up his subjects once they have entered his kingdom, so he will refuse you. You must bribe him with gifts, things that only you can give and which you know he wants. If you are successful in convincing Death to release your daughter, then you must go to her and convince her to come with you. This will not be easy because she will remember nothing of her previous life, not even you or her mother. Once she has agreed, then both of you will be allowed to return to this life. You will wake and your daughter will be beside you. Or not. The decision is hers."

Liatris waited, letting us think about her instructions. "Do you have any questions?"

"What dangers will we face on the journey?" Tessia asked, touching the pommel of Agatha.

"The dangers are not of a kind that can be faced with a sword, Dragonqueen," Liatris said. "They are dangers of mind and of will."

"What do you mean, my lady?" I asked.

"You may lose your way, forgetting who you are, where you come from, and why you are traveling through the underworld. You may forget that you are traveling through the land of shadow and forget that there is a land of life. You may think that the monsters you face are real and try to fight them, rather than ignoring them and continuing on your journey. You may come to realize who you really are and how your life has been misspent and become discouraged. You may see things that drive you mad. There are a thousand ways your mind can lead you astray, and only one way it can lead you to your goal. You must consider these thousand ways and choose the one right path."

Liatris stood before us, and seeing we were determined to go through with our plan, she drew her finger across my forehead. Blood rushed down into my eyes, soaking my clothes and running down my arms until I was completely covered. Liatris did the same thing to Tessia who was soon covered with blood as well.

She had us lie down in the grass next to each other and waved her hand over my face. I instantly fell into a deep sleep.

Chapter Twenty

I found myself walking beside Tessia down a long dark tunnel. It seemed endless, but eventually we saw a pale dot of light ahead. We emerged onto a rocky shore where hundreds of people, mostly men, were standing. Like us, they were covered in blood. Some of the men were holding their severed heads under their arms and were watching us from their blood-encrusted eyes. Many held their severed arms or the ropes of their entrails. Many were scorched with blackened skin and red boils. Many had their hair singed or their fingers burned off. And every single one of them was watching us approach.

"Who are you?" Tessia asked.

"We are your companions who have waited for you," said a man clutching his severed leg to his chest.

"And how have you been chosen for this task?" Tessia asked.

"Oh, Dragonqueen, don't you know? You murdered all of us."

"Don't forget that some of us were killed by the Mage!" a woman at the back said. The crowd of mutilated men parted like an incarnadine sea and I saw a woman holding a baby in her arms. Both mother and child had been horribly burned.

"I never killed any women or children," I cried. "You must be mistaken."

"Oh, there are no mistakes here, Mage," she said. "I was in the city of Osterbo with my newborn. We were leaving the house for the first time when you emerged from the keep shooting fireballs in every direction. I knew you weren't aiming for me, but that fact hardly matters, does it? You killed me and my precious baby and never even noticed."

I looked around at the burned and mutilated faces. Although the faces were not familiar, I did recognize some of the injuries: a soldier with the side of his face crushed from a stone I'd thrown at him with an atlatl spell; a man with a crumpled body I'd pushed off a parapet when I was invisible; a boy with a hole burned straight through the middle of his body. And I saw the Drekavac sergeant Zrul, his right eye blinded by me. He had been my comrade at arms, but in the heat of battle he had attacked my wife. I blinded him easily and hardly thought about him again. Later, Zamarrra and I had changed him into a mastiff as punishment for his crimes. The transformation had killed his man-essence, I supposed, so he was here as one of my accusers.

And then, my brother Ludek appeared in the crowd. His skull was partially crushed, and his body was mangled, but I would have recognized the crooked smile and the remaining bright blue eye anywhere, even here on the shore of Death's kingdom.

I turned to Tessia. Her eyes were wide open in horror at what she was seeing. She looked from one ruined face to the next, and I realized that most of the shades here had died on the edge of her blade.

We spent what felt like an eternity on the Shore of Reckoning, but it was impossible to know how long we were really there, because there was nothing to mark the passage of time. We were never hungry, so there were no meals. We were never tired, so there was no sleep. The gray light never changed, nor the sea which had no storms or tides, only the constant lap of small waves against the pebbled shore where we were trapped with the shades of the people we had killed.

One at a time, the shades came to us and told us their tales. There was the boy who'd grown up on a farm in the Bekla Valley. He had volunteered for Ludek's army, thinking he would get to travel. Tessia had sliced open his chest as he stood bewildered on the parapet of Dragonja City during the revolution. There was the woman, desperate to escape an abusive husband, who had disguised herself as a man to join the Osterbo guard. Tessia had cut off her arm, and she bled to death on the stone steps of the king's keep. Tessia had never known she was killing a woman, not that it would have made any difference.

Most of the dead, however, were Drekavacs who had never particularly wanted to join the army or fight for kings. Drekavacs, having grown up in poverty, were not allowed to take any other kind of work, and so they had to don a uniform or starve to death. As soldiers, their wages were low, so they couldn't marry and most of them didn't know their own children. Their lives consisted of standing guard, marching in drills, and drinking and whoring on leave. Nevertheless, their lives were their own, the only thing they had, and Tessia and I had taken their lives for no reason other than they were standing between us and what we wanted.

Finally, Sergeant Zrul, a Drekavac whom I once thought of as a friend, stood before me. He appeared less mangled than most of the shades: his scaly white skin and his sparse hair were much as I remembered. Only the empty socket of his right eye told the story of his death. Tessia and I had returned to Dragonja after a quest to find the city in chaos. Her consort and the finance minister had been having an affair for years, and they used Tessia's absence as an opportunity to plunder the treasury and flee to another city. In the anarchy that ensued, Sergeant Zrul and his men had looted the city. I found him in the Silver Pony Inn where he was trying to kidnap Idella. I shot him in the eye with a single lentil propelled by a burrowing spell. To spare him execution as a traitor, Tessia asked me and Zamarrra to transform him into a mastiff.

Zrul lived as a mastiff for a few more years but was killed by a wild boar Tessia was hunting. I hadn't ever felt guilt over blinding him because I was protecting Idella, but now I realized that despite my calling him my friend when we served together in General Zygmunt's rebel force, I knew almost nothing about Zrul. In fact, until now, sitting on the Shore of Reckoning, I had never known much about any Drekavac's life. They had simply been part of the landscape of the city, useful as guards and soldiers but never having identities of their own. Now, I was about to learn what it meant to be an invisible inhabitant of one's own native country.

Zrul's story began much like that of other Drekavacs—no father, a mother who raised him on scraps of food she scavenged in the alleys of Dragonja, the boy learning to fight and survive while avoiding jail. As soon as he was old enough, he joined the king's army, then commanded by the evil wizard Ludek. I listened to his story, trying not to be distracted by the bloody fluid trickling down from his withered eye.

"I loved the army," he said in his hoarse voice. "For the first time in my life I didn't have to wonder where I'd find food that day or where I'd sleep that night. I was actually able to have friends I could trust not to steal from my plate or knife me in the back. I had clothes on my back and money in my pocket. And all I had to do was to follow the rules and obey my commanders. I'd always known how to fight to survive, but now I learned to fight as part of a unit and as part of a higher calling. I was serving the king! I was protecting the nation!

"Over time, I was promoted, then promoted again until I became a sergeant. But I wasn't a fool. I could see we weren't protecting the nation at all. We were pillaging it. Our commander, the wizard Ludek, was inflicting evil on the land. We marched into villages, stole everything they had, killed the men, abused the girls and women and left them with nothing, no way to survive the winter. We did this again and again, destroying the Bekla Valley which we were sworn to protect.

"Then, one day my unit was on patrol in the Dry Hills chasing bandits when we were attacked by the dragon Tyrmiss. I saw my comrades engulfed by flames, their skin blackening and their fingers burning to stumps. I dodged the flames, but the dragon raked through our formation, killing the rest of my comrades. The flesh of my thigh was torn open, so I wrapped it in the cloak of one of my dead comrades to stop the bleeding. All of them were dead, and I was a week's march from the city. It was clear that without help, I would die soon.

"The day after the attack from the dragon, a party of men approached. At first, I thought they were the bandits we'd been chasing, but it didn't take long for me to realize from their bearing and discipline these were no bandits, but soldiers. They were a rebel patrol, part of Zygmunt's army trying to overthrow the king and his regent Ludek. They looked at the dead men around me, then approached me. I was armed with a sword and planned to take a few of them with me when they sent me to the underworld, but the leader, a deaf-mute I later learned was named Wessel, laughed and knocked the sword out of my hand. He gave a signal to his men, and they improvised a litter, lay me on it gently, and headed off to the mountains.

"On the second day, we headed up the switchback trail up to the pass between the Two Thumbs of the Giant. One of the men put a blindfold on me. He said they were taking me to the rebel camp, and if I removed the blindfold, he would have to kill me.

"'Choose to live,' he said, 'Keep the blindfold.'

After two more days, they set down my litter and removed the blindfold. I was in a tent, and there was a young woman who said her name was Mina. She cleaned my wound, and she was very kind, each day bringing me soup and changing my dressing. I've always healed quickly, a great advantage for someone in my profession. In a few days, I was able to walk and was summoned to talk to the leader—in those days, he wasn't called General, but simply Zygmunt or Commandant. His exploits in fighting Ludek's forces were already legendary, and I had gotten the impression the men and women under his command held him in awe.

"Wessel held back the flap and I entered the commandant's tent. Zygmunt rose to greet me, giving me a hug, and holding both of my shoulders, he looked into my eyes and asked how I was recovering. This was the first time I'd ever been treated as an equal by a man. It was clear he didn't see a Drekavac standing in front of him, but a military man much like himself, a professional soldier who deserved respect even if he were fighting for the opposing army. He had me sit at his table and Wessel brought us bread and ale, and Zygmunt asked about my background, nothing of a military nature, only personal.

"He seemed very interested to know how I had survived in the alleys of Dragonja where so many children die of starvation and neglect. He revealed that his companion Wessel, the same one who saved me in the Dry Hills, had also grown up in those alleys, and now Wessel was Zygmunt's adjutant, as well as their best captain. Not only was I pleased that this great rebel leader seemed genuinely interested in me, but also, I appreciated the fact he didn't try to extract any military secrets from me. He intuitively knew that betraying my comrades would be impossible for me.

"He said it was dinner time, and although he usually took his meals in his tent, he would be honored to accompany me to the mess tent where I could meet some of the men. As we walked across the camp, men and women did not salute Zygmunt. Instead, they greeted him in a friendly but respectful way, like younger brothers and sisters greeting their older brother. Later, I found that this informal comradery existed only in the camp.

When they went into battle, Zygmunt expected his orders to be carried out unquestioningly. And they were.

"In the mess tent, I sat at a long table with men and women. I was surprised to see Drekavacs like myself among them. They didn't seem to be treated any differently than the humans. They all greeted me with hearty cheer, immediately accepting me as one of them. Not wanting to give the wrong impression, I told them that I was actually a sergeant in the King's Army who'd been captured by Wessel in the Dry Hills, but they waved off that revelation, treating it no differently than if I'd said I was a farmer or carpenter. I later realized that most of them, and all of the Drekavacs, had served in the King's Army and now fought for the rebels.

"I was impressed by the quality of the food, always an important factor in recruiting soldiers. It was better than any food I'd eaten in the army, and there was plenty of it. By the end of the evening, I was swapping ribald tales and exaggerated stories of heroics, and we were laughing like old friends. I was given a bunk in the men's barracks. There was no guard making sure I didn't leave, and despite the blindfold, I knew pretty much where we were—close to the pass north of the copper mine—and I could have escaped at any time. Instead, I decided to stay and join the rebels.

"I was given the rank of sergeant and assigned as a drillmaster for new recruits, a mixed group of male and female humans and Drekavacs. After a few weeks, Zygmunt called me to his tent for a special assignment. He asked me to volunteer to contact my most trusted friend in the King's Army and turn him to the rebel cause. Over time, we would have a whole platoon on our side, an invaluable asset when it came time to attack the city.

"You know the rest, Norbert..."

Indeed, I did. The fifth column had opened the gates for Zygmunt's army, and the turncoats had been among the first to storm the keep. Zygmunt offered Zrul a promotion to captain, but he refused, saying the officers he'd known had been donkeys, while the enlisted men had been lions. He preferred to remain a lion. Zygmunt had laughed and kept his high regard for the sergeant. The sergeant became the Wise Queen Varvara's most trusted military advisor, and he continued in that role when Tessia became queen. So, it was natural that when Tessia and I went on a quest to save Tyrmiss's dragonlings which had been kidnapped by a witch, Tessia left Zrul in charge of the defense of the kingdom. Tessia had also left the governing of the kingdom to her wife Princess Taja and First Minister Caz. Little did we know that the two were having an affair. As the two regents pillaged the kingdom, morale among the troops fell. Abuse of citizens became commonplace, including the abuse of girls and women by soldiers.

Thinking back to that time, I felt I had to ask Zrul, "Sergeant, you were Queen Tessia's most trusted warrior. She left the defense of the kingdom to you when she left to help Tyrmiss. How could you turn against her by allowing chaos to take over the city?"

"Laddie," Zrul said, and even though I was now middle-aged, I felt a wisp of pleasure at hearing again his nickname for me. "I didn't turn against the queen, I simply reverted to my true nature. You have to understand that where I grew up in the alleys of Dragonja, every scrap of food had to be defended. If someone wanted to take something from you, you had to fight them, perhaps even kill them because to show weakness in such a place is to invite other attacks. And if someone had something you wanted or needed, you took it from them if you could. The only love I ever experienced was from my mother, and she taught me to use a knife when I was a small child, no more than five summers old. And later, when I felt desire for girls, I had to find one and force her, and it wasn't easy because they were fierce as the boys. Soldiering gave me a way to survive, and in

Ludek's army, we were expected to steal and rape. Ludek was counting on our viciousness.

"It wasn't until I joined up with Zygmunt's rebels that I learned a different way to be a soldier. Zygmunt taught us we were fighting for a higher cause, and when the revolution came, Drekavacs and men would be equal, and no child would have to grow up in desperate poverty and violence the way I did. In the rebel army, I proudly fought beside people like you and Tessia and Wessel. And all of you treated me with dignity, and you respected my skills as a soldier. And after the revolution, I proudly served Zygmunt, then Queen Varvara and finally Queen Tessia. They were honorable and generous rulers who served the people well. They always made sure that Drekavacs such as me were judged on what we could do, not how we looked. For the first time in my life, having white scaly skin and gray eyes did not count against me. I could go anywhere—an inn, a shop, a farm, even the royal court itself—and know I would be treated fairly. I saw that things had changed for Drekavacs.

"But this kind of morality needs to come from the leaders of a country. When ordinary people see their leaders have tolerance for Drekavacs and treat them with love and kindness, then the ordinary people start practicing that morality as well. The leaders of a country must act decently because their subjects imitate them. When Queen Tessia left Princess Taja and Minister Caz in charge, she made a terrible mistake. No sooner had the queen passed through the city gate, than those two villains began extorting money from merchants, stealing from the treasury, and using the castle guard to settle old scores. It was bad enough they'd been carrying on behind the queen's back—everyone knew about that but the queen herself—but it was the violation of the trust people had in the throne that did the most harm. Since they were stealing and abusing their authority, it didn't take long for me and the soldiers I commanded to do it as well. At first, we were just taking food and ale without paying.

Next, we were robbing travelers. And then we were grabbing girls off the streets or even out of their beds to take them back to the barracks."

"So, you're saying people act no better than their leaders?"

"That's right, Laddie," Zrul nodded his head and looked out over the misty sea. "I've had a chance to think about this subject a lot. They don't call this the Shore of Reckoning for nothing."

The Shore of Reckoning. Now I understood why I was here, why I was being detained before sailing off. Each soul must have a reckoning before sailing the Sea of Forgetfulness.

I looked around for Tessia and saw her down the strand, talking to a boy no older than ten summers. Tessia was weeping. She had many more shades to talk to than I did. It must have been terrible to realize how much harm she had done.

"I'm sorry I blinded you, Sergeant," I said. "I always admired you."

"Don't be sorry, Captain," Zrul said, using my military title. I'd been the Chief Healer in the rebel army—one of his commanding officers—and, I suppose, one of the officers Zrul thought of as donkeys.

"You were right to attack me," Zrul went on. "I was trying to take your wife away, and I don't need to explain what I had planned for her."

"Why Idella?" I asked. "Why did you choose her? There were thousands of girls and women in the city."

"Ah, Captain," he said meeting my eye with his good left one, as gray and opaque as the sky in this forsaken place. "I had always fancied her. And I was envious of you. You had a pretty wife, children who loved you and a farm of your own. What did I have but barracks, orders, and whores? I thought I could take what you had and make it mine."

"You were reverting to the Code of the Alleys?"

"Exactly, Captain. I was acting the way I'd learned as a child."

After Zrul walked away, a large group of men, women and children approached me. Their faces looked familiar, but I couldn't recall how I knew them. Surprisingly, none of them had visible wounds. After having talked to dozens of maimed soldiers, I wondered who this group of healthy wholesome people could be.

Standing in front of me, a woman holding a baby in her arms said, "Don't you recognize us, Healer? My name is Nusa."

"Oh, yes, now I remember you," I said, looking at her round freckled face. "You died in childbirth. I am so sorry. Please forgive me. I did everything I could to help you."

"Yes, you did," Nusa said, smiling at me. "You stayed with me all night through the difficult birth of my son. He was premature and stillborn." She looked down and smiled at the baby in her arms who gurgled happily. "And after the birth, I bled profusely and died two days later. You sat beside me through the whole ordeal."

"Are you here to blame me for your death?" I asked, looking down at my feet on the sandy shore. I didn't know how much more blame I could accept.

"Oh no," she said quickly. "I am here to thank you for trying to save my baby and me. The fact that you cared about us made my passing much easier."

I looked over her shoulder and suddenly recognized dozens of people whom I'd treated in my years as a healer. Some had recovered from their illnesses and injuries. Others had been too far gone for me to help them. All these people were smiling and nodding at me, and I realized this group of people that I had healed or tried to heal was much larger than the group of people I had killed. I sat on a boulder on the Shore of Reckoning while each of my former patients approached me and recounted how I had mended their broken bones, nursed their fevers, or eased their dying. Listening to them made me realize my life was much more than quests and battles. In fact, the most important part of my life had been helping people through their difficulties. I felt my soul being refreshed by their gratitude.

Finally, I understood why Tessia and I were on this Shore of Reckoning. Here, we had time to let everything go.

Chapter Twenty-One

My brother Ludek, known as the Evil Wizard, King Ottolo's commandant and the secret regent of the kingdom in the horrible days before the revolution, stood at the edge of the sea. His ruined head was turned slightly, so he could watch me out of the corner of his good eye. Half his skull was crushed from the attack by Tayra, the she-bear my wife had sent to defend me, and his body was twisted from a broken spine. The way he smirked made me think he knew something about me, and I wondered whether he had overheard what was recounted by the shades of the people I had murdered. Or perhaps he was amused by my pride in having helped people as a healer. In either case, I had no desire to talk to him.

After a while, it must have become clear I wasn't going to approach him, so he moved toward me, walking casually, despite having to drag his left foot. Ludek was the only shade in this dismal place I hadn't talked to, at least among the ones I'd murdered. My feeling was that he had been waiting until I'd heard from all the others because he wanted me to know who I was and how I had hurt others before he approached me. It was true I felt beaten down by my conversations with the dead, and I could see he was sizing me up as he approached.

"Hello, little brother," he said. There was no affection in his voice, but no animosity either. Whatever soul searching required of him was long past. This was my moment to embrace my evil nature, not his.

"Hello, Ludek," I replied.

"I can see, Norbert, you're not dead. You can fool the others with your dramatic smear of blood covering your face, but you are definitely still alive. What are you doing here? Wait," he said peering into my face intently. "Don't tell me you are one of those fools who come to the underworld to fetch their wives."

I winced, realizing this was going to be a difficult conversation.

"You *are* one of those fools! You've come to find… who is it? Not your wife, someone else…" He peered again into my face with his one good eye. "It's your daughter, isn't it? What is her name… Eda, Eva, Ena…? That's it! I'm right, aren't I? Your daughter Ena was killed defending baby dragons. I'm sorry. She must have been a complete idiot."

He laughed. I felt my hand going for the wand at my belt, but I stopped myself. I wasn't here to fight again with Ludek. Besides, I wasn't sure whether my magic would work in the underworld.

"Oh, your magic works here, Norbert." Ludek assured me, reading my mind. "But mine does as well. Shall we have a rematch? I can't allow you to kill me and get away with it. What do you say? A little duel between two wizards? Oh, I'm sorry. You never became a wizard, did you? Poor little Norbert. Never more than just a village mage. Have you tended any sick cows today, Healer?"

He laughed, knowing I had chosen not to embrace white and black magic and become a wizard because I did not want to become like him.

"This is the Shore of Reckoning, Ludek. The other shades came and told their stories to me. This enabled me to see the effect I had on their lives and to see the damage I had done in killing them. Are you also here for that purpose? Are you here to help me face a reckoning?"

"Our relationship has always been complicated, hasn't it, Norbert? What you are doing here is not a true reckoning because you are not dead. You still have lots of damage left to do in your life. You have talked your way into the underworld under false pretenses. And, unlike the other shades, I know I am not actually here. In fact, the essence that was me has moved on to another life. Right now, I am probably some fat charwoman stirring a pot while yelling at her children. Or maybe, I am a nightingale singing a song to two lovers who have met in a glade…"

"Or a cockroach eating manure in a sheep pen," I interjected.

The flash of anger in his good eye gave me pleasure. Then I thought, why am I still feuding with my brother?

"Why indeed?" Ludek asked, having read my mind. "Surely you realize that all the shades here, including me, are not actually here?"

"Then what am I seeing?" I asked.

"You are seeing your own feelings of guilt and regret played out. This place is a stage and you are one of the actors. You are also the writer, the director, and the audience."

"What are you talking about?"

"My dear Norbert, you are not arguing with me. You are arguing with yourself."

I considered what he was saying. The last thing I remembered was lying down in the meadow while listening to Liatris. Was this all a dream? Was any of this real?

"The question, Norbert, is not whether any of this is real, but whether anything in your life is real."

"I can't be bothered with metaphysics right now, Ludek. I am here to accomplish a task, something good."

"Something good?" Ludek laughed. "In what way is bringing back the dead something good? Little brother, Ena is better off where she is."

"And where is that?"

"Oh, now you want directions? Let's see… Sail over the Sea of Forgetfulness and enter the Castle of Death. There you should ask for the Lord. Give him your gift—"

"Gift? What do you mean?"

"A gift. You know, something you present to a king when you ask him to grant you a favor."

"I'm afraid I didn't bring a gift."

"Oh, I am sorry. You are going to have to go back to the meadow where you started and find a gift for the king. It would be very rude not to give him anything."

"I'm getting tired of your games and tricks, Ludek. I'm going to go now."

"Oh, but you can't go until you've finished reckoning with me, dear brother."

"I've had enough." I turned to walk toward the sea, but there was still no ship in sight.

"Don't you want to hear about my life?" Ludek's tone had changed. He was almost pleading to be heard.

I suddenly felt sorry for him. Whether this was a timeless dream I was having as I lay in the meadow beside Tessia, the two of us guarded by the valiant Zygmunt, or whether this was a real place in the nether of the universe, Ludek was still my brother, and I owed him my attention.

"Very well then," I said. "But no more tricks or word games."

He nodded, and I waved my hand, signaling him to start his story.

"As you remember, we grew up in a small village in the Bekla Valley. Our father was a traveling mage who made his living following a route up and down the river road, selling kitchenware—pots, pans, knives, and the occasional treat for children. He was always welcome among the farmers because he brought news from the neighboring villages, and he knew many of the old songs and stories which the villagers never grew tired of."

"I know all of this," I said. "For years after our mother was killed and you were taken, I accompanied Dad on his travels, and when he died, I took over the route."

"Yes, yes. I was just giving the backstory for anyone else who was listening," Ludek said, glancing upward at the swirling gray sky.

I looked up at the sky. There was nothing up there, and I wondered who could be listening to this story.

"What you didn't know, little brother, was that dear old Dad had tremendous magical powers which he rarely used. He was actually a powerful mage but had refused to advance in the profession and become a wizard because he was afraid of having to confront evil."

Ludek looked at me with his one good eye. "Does this sound familiar, little brother?"

"I'm happy being a mage," I said defensively. "I never wanted to be like..."

"Like me? You never wanted to be an evil wizard like your older brother?"

I looked down at the ground which I noticed for the first time was crawling with insects.

"Well, dear old Dad felt the same way you do, Norbert. He was happy being a village mage. He assisted midwives with difficult births—humans, Drekavacs, calves—it was all the same to him. He blessed fields for a larger harvest, he waved his wand over streams so the nets bulged with fish, he softened the earth so miners would have an easier time digging the tunnels. But he never charged anything for his charms and spells, claiming the Goddess had gifted him with magic, and he had no right to charge for Her gifts."

"He was much loved by the people."

"Indeed, he was. And despite having lost his wife and his first son years before, he was reasonably happy with his life."

"I don't think so, Ludek. I always thought of him as being sad. He..."

"Of course, he was sad, Norbert. His wife had been murdered and his first son, the gifted one, had been kidnapped by an evil wizard. And his second son was somewhat dimwitted, not much good for anything but leading a donkey up and down the valley."

I felt a rush of shame come over me, but then I realized that this was a mental trick that Ludek was playing on me. Somehow, he knew this was my longstanding fear—that my father didn't love me because I was a disappointment to him.

Ludek was smiling at me, his one eye full of mockery.

"I told you, Ludek. No more tricks or I'm leaving."

"Sorry, little brother, it's just that you are such an easy mark. I can't help myself. Getting back to the story... You may remember that one day you and Dad came across a boy who told you that his father, a woodcutter, was trapped under a tree that had fallen on him."

"Yes, I do remember that... We rushed into the woods and Dad used a spell to lift the tree off the woodcutter." I met Ludek's eye and said, "It was the same spell I used to drop a ceiling timber on you fifteen years later."

"It's funny how things come full circle, isn't it?" Ludek said, ruefully. "What you didn't know was that boy was no ordinary boy and that man was no ordinary woodcutter. The boy was an essence of the forest named Spyte which means *shadow*. And the man was an essence named Turve which means *dirt*. The two spirit beings had a wager to test the mettle of Dad. The loser would grant three wishes to the mage. Spyte claimed that the mage was of poor character and didn't perform higher level magic because he was afraid. Turve, on the other hand, believed that Dad was of strong character and refused higher level magic because it was not in keeping with his faith in the Goddess. When they tested Dad and he used magic to lift a large tree off Turve to save him, it was established that Dad had both a gift for magic and also was a man who would break his own rules in order to save the life of a stranger. So, Spyte later came to Dad in a vision and granted him three wishes."

"Wait a moment," I protested. "I've heard a version of this story before. Something about making a wish that brings about his own death?"

Ludek laughed, showing the crumbling ruins of his teeth. "Bard, you know better than anyone there are only a few stories in all the world, and they are relived and retold again and again."

Bard, I thought. It had been a very long time since anyone had called me by that name. Like my father, I'd entertained villagers with my lyre and my poems. Later, I'd made my living singing in the Silver Pony, and one of my first titles in Wise Queen Varvara's court was "Royal Bard." And, most significantly, I'd won Tyrmiss's friendship by improvising elegies about her wife Rilla who was killed by Ludek's soldiers. I started to tell Ludek about all of these accomplishments as a poet, but I realized he seemed already to know everything about me. However, I knew little about him, so I prompted him to continue the story.

"So, three wishes, huh?" I said, realizing how much of a dullard I sounded.

"Yes, Dad was given three wishes by Spyte. Dad spent weeks thinking about the three wishes. He knew about the danger of wishes coming true—how often they lead to tragedy. So, it is especially important to be careful when wishing for good things to happen to the people we love."

Ludek gave me a sly look and said, "His first wish was for you."

"Me?" I said, startled.

"That's right, Norbert. As much as I hate to admit it, Dad loved you with all his heart. If he seemed disappointed in you at times, it was caused by his fear of any harm coming to you. He wanted, above all else, for you to be safe, so his first wish was for your health and safety."

"You mean I've been living a charmed life?"

"Of course, you've been living a charmed life, you fool.

Think about it. As a healer, you've nursed hundreds of people through fevers. Have you ever once been ill?"

"No, but I thought I just had a healthy constitution."

"So you do, and you can thank the old man for that gift. And you've been on half a dozen quests with Tessia, you've flown thousands of leagues on Tyrmiss's back, you've fought in five major battles and dozens of skirmishes, and you've defeated the greatest wizard of your time—that would be me—with a simple timber-lifting spell."

"I always thought I was just lucky."

"And so you have been, Norbert. You have been extremely lucky."

"And Ena?"

"What about Ena?"

"You know what I'm asking."

"Ena carries my blood, not yours. She is my daughter. But you've known the answer to that question for a long time. Ena has, or I should say *had* an amazing gift for magic, far surpassing yours. She inherited that gift from me. And she loved performing magic. She was devoted to the idea that magic could help people, even save them. And Norbert, that goodness of hers, that full heart and clear mind, that moral radiance, she inherited from you and Idella. Let's face it, I was pure evil. Whatever good that was in me had been twisted and perverted by Imazz."

"Imazz was the wizard who killed our mother and kidnapped you?"

"Yes, he took me from my mother's arms and put me in a cave deep underground for a whole year. There he taught me the dark arts. He was planning to use me as his heir, but he taught me too well. As soon as I was strong enough, I killed him. It is the only murder I haven't repented in the afterlife."

"What was Dad's second wish?"

"For his second wish, Dad asked for peace of mind, not realizing that no one has peace of mind except in death. He'd been tormented with guilt for not protecting his wife and son, and nothing he did gave him pleasure. He hoped he could gain a sense of contentment. His third wish was to know my whereabouts. When Imazz kidnapped me, I disappeared from Dad's life, and of course he wanted to know what happened to me. Spyte told Dad where I was, no doubt knowing what would happen. When Dad came to me in the mountain fast I'd inherited from Imazz, I didn't recognize him because grief had aged him."

"What did you do to him?"

"I killed him with a rockslide as he was climbing up the mountain. By the time I got to him, he was dead. I didn't know it was him until I saw his wand."

Tears ran down Ludek's cheek. I took him in my arms and said, "Brother, brother, I forgive you. Please forgive me." And we sat together on the shore and wept for all the pain and all the wasted years.

Chapter Twenty-Two

The Sea of Forgetting was gray under a gray sky, and our black ship sailed over still water. Tessia and I huddled on the deck, shoulder to shoulder with the maimed victims of our ambition. In the Land of the Living, we had rationalized our killing, but now, in the Land of the Dead, we could see the suffering we had caused. We had harmed many people, most of them innocent, and we had foolishly felt we were justified in our violence.

On the Shore of Reckoning, we had heard the tales of ordinary people and how they had gotten caught up in war, how they had lost their children to hunger and disease, how they had tried to navigate the few choices available in their lives. It was too much for me to comprehend, and for Tessia who had killed far more people than I, the feelings of guilt must have been overwhelming.

The other passengers were cupping their hands in the water and lifting it to their lips. I resisted my thirst, an action that felt almost unholy. During my entire time in the underworld, I had not once been thirsty or hungry or tired. I was, it seemed, pure memory, capable of recalling and feeling, but having no corporeal presence. Now, finally, I could feel my hands, my feet, my belly. My throat dry as the sands of a desert, I craved the water around us, but remembered Liatris warning us not to drink from the Sea of Forgetting. If I did, I would lose all knowledge of my life in the Land of the Living. I pulled out the flask that Liatris had given me and took a long draught. It tasted of honey and lemons. I passed the flask to Tessia and she drank as well.

"I'm tempted to drink from the sea, so I can forget my life," she said. "I've done such horrible things, killing children, burning families in their homes, slaughtering whole regiments of men who were fathers, husbands, and sons. Their faces and their wounds are in front of me. How I wish I hadn't come."

I had known Tessia most of her life, and I'd never seen her like this. She had always shown admirable courage and resilience in the face of danger, yet here she was shaking with fear and moaning with self-pity. Nevertheless, I could not let her drink from the sea, or she would never be able to return to her life. I had always known she and I were very different from one another. I always went into battle reluctantly, and only when there seemed no other way to save my family, my friends, or my country. Tessia, on the other hand, had always loved the thrill of battle. Every day since she was a child, she had practiced with her weapons and trained for every exigency. She was an artist, and the battlefield was her canvas. I don't think she had ever given the morality of war a second thought. For her, war was an implacable fact of life like the weather. Useful at times, regrettable at other times, but inevitable, and it was necessary for warriors like her to fight to protect their native lands. Fighting was her profession, and she had a passion for the work. Now she was having to look beyond the art of war and see the mayhem it brought to ordinary people.

"Is that it?" one of our soulmates asked, pointing. "Is that the Continent of Love?"

All our companions were standing now, watching as we approached a white beach, and beyond there were green fields, and in the far distance mountains rose beneath a blue sky. We felt the bottom of the ship scrape on sand, and we clambered down and waded to shore. As each of our companions walked over the warm sand, their wounds healed. Ludek's crushed skull and disfigured face were restored. However, the blood on Tessia and me was not removed. We still looked like the walking wounded, which I suppose we were.

As our companions started walking toward the distant mountains, a soldier approached Tessia and me. "The king wishes to speak to you. Please come with me." And he turned and started walking down the strand with Tessia and me following.

We walked a long time, and the white sand gave way to a rocky shore, much like the one we had left at the Shore of Reckoning. Eventually, we came to a large castle perched on the edge of a stone cliff. The waves crashed below, and black clouds swirled above the tall towers.

"What is this place?" I asked the soldier who had not spoken since we left the ship.

"It is the Palace of Death," he replied. "The residence of our king."

"Honored guests," a man murmured as he descended the wide staircase in the foyer of the palace. He was handsome, clean shaven with blonde hair tied back, a simple gold diadem crossing his forehead. He was simply but elegantly dressed in a white woolen tunic embroidered with a scene of a battle stitched in red and black. As he drew closer, the pattern of the embroidery became clearer, and I recognized Tessia brandishing Agatha on the back of Tyrmiss breathing fire. I was astonished to see me sitting behind Tessia waving my wand at the crowd of soldiers below, several of whom seemed to be on fire.

"My friends!" The man said as he approached us. "It is such an honor to meet you at last! Is this Tessia, the Dragonqueen, the hero of the Battle of Hoclav Plain and so many other great feats?" The man approached Tessia with wide arms and gave her an enthusiastic hug. Her eyes were wide in surprise.

"And you must be Norbert, the Green Mage of Dragonja, the one who engineered this visit to my humble kingdom." He bowed to me. Not knowing what else to do, I returned the bow, dipping my head slightly lower than his. If this man was indeed Death, I certainly didn't want to offend him.

"Your Majesty," I said.

"Oh, please," he said. "Call me Mannie. It's short for Mnuurluth, named for my uncle who passed a long time ago and left me this pile." He looked around at the exquisitely carved marble, the golden door fixtures, the hundreds of white candles on the giant chandelier above our heads. "Isn't it hideous?" he said, waving at the furnishings dismissively. "So overdone. Completely over the top. Well, I suppose appearances must be maintained. I am, after all," he said with a boyish giggle, "Lord Death."

Tessia and I exchanged a quick glance of baffled amazement.

"Oh, I've been looking forward to meeting you both," Mannie said, his gray eyes shining. "You've made my job so much easier, all that slaughtering you did. Beautiful work! And it's especially wonderful you have arrived here with your memories intact. I want to hear all about the Battle of Hoclav Plain. I've been given all the credit for that one, but really, my part in it was small. The two of you did all the heavy lifting."

"Lord Death… I mean Mannie," Tessia said, going down on one knee. "We offer a gift."

Her gambit surprised me. Even though Ludek reminded me, I'd forgotten Liatris had said we should bring a gift for Death.

"A gift? For me?" The god said, clapping his hands. "How generous."

"In my kingdom, we will build a temple to you, so people will know your greatness."

"Oh, really? I am familiar with your kingdom. Tell me where my temple shall be."

I could see that Tessia was caught off guard. "Next to the Dragonja River, My Lord," she improvised.

His eyes narrowed. "My sister Nilene has a temple in the city itself, doesn't she?"

"Well, yes, My Lord," Tessia said, her eyes moving side to side as she tried to think of a way to salvage the situation.

"If I may, My Lord," I interjected. "The spot where your temple will be built is quite lovely. It is at the foot of the tallest mountain in the kingdom and all traders and travelers going south will walk by it."

Lord Death seemed to grow by a few inches until he was taller than Tessia and me. He raised his chin, looked down at us and said in a rumbling voice that made the furnishings tremble, "Very well, I am honored. I shall visit my temple when it is finished."

Then, he slowly shrank until he was eye to eye with us. He regained his hospitable manner, noticed our torn clothes and bloody faces, and said, "Oh, you must go to your rooms, get cleaned up and refresh yourselves. And then we'll have dinner. My chef has made you something special."

We were shown to our separate quarters. My room had a large bathing area with two beautiful attendants holding towels. One of the attendants, a young man with black skin and the countenance of an angel, helped me remove my filthy clothes. Another, an equally beautiful young woman who may have been the young man's twin sister, scrubbed my back. The water was exactly the right temperature, and the walls were covered in frescoes. As I looked closer, I realized that each painting depicted one of the battles that Tyrmiss, Tessia, and I had engaged in. Here was the attack on the keep of Dragonja during the height of the rebellion, and over there, the second battle on the plain outside Hoclav City where we led the dragons in the slaughter of thousands of men. And in the middle of the opposite wall, in a place of honor, a scene from my fight with Zrul in which I blinded him with a well-aimed lentil in his right eye.

As I sat in the tub, thinking of the number of people I had killed or maimed in my life, I began to feel dizzy. As I stood, the two beautiful attendants helped me from the bath, and the young man held a basin in which I vomited. Afterwards, the young woman cleaned my face with a cloth and helped me to dress in silken robes.

Mannie, as Lord Death insisted we call him, met us in the parlor, an elegant little room decorated with cherubim. I was relieved not to see another illustration of Tessia and me slaughtering draftees. Tessia's face was drawn and pale, and I surmised that she also had been ambushed with frescoes of her murderous deeds.

"My sister Nilene let me know you would be dropping by," Mannie was saying. "I'm so glad you did. I've been wanting to thank you for all you've done in service to me."

A servant handed us wineglasses filled with what looked like red wine. I sipped it, tasting something vaguely sweet and metallic. I set aside the glass, but seeing Mannie frown at me, I picked it up again and took another sip. The taste began to grow on me.

"The Goddess Nilene is your sister?" I asked, trying to make conversation. How do you make small talk with a god?

"Yes, of course," Mannie said, looking at me puzzled. "Since Nilene said you were one of her most trusted servants, I assumed you would know about her family."

At this point, Tessia stepped in, saving me from further embarrassment. "Oh, Norbert knows a great deal about the gods, of course, but I have to admit I know little. Could you explain the royal family tree?"

"I'd love to, Tessia," Mannie said, making flirty eyes at her.

"Let's see, where should I start? You met Liatris, the elemental, right? She is the one who showed you how to get here? Well, she is the… Let me count the generations… She is the great-great-great-great grandmother of Nilene and me."

"Really?" Tessia said. "She is so beautiful. I would never have guessed she was so ancient."

"Oh, don't be fooled by her looks, my dear. Grandmama Liatris has had a lot of work done on her face to restore her beauty. Her youthful look is merely an illusion. You should have seen her five thousand years ago. She was HIDEOUS, believe me. She is really ancient, and I think, perhaps a little senile. She hardly ever leaves that little island of hers. What's the name of it again?"

"The Blessed Isle," I said.

"That's right," Mannie said. "A pretty name for a pretty place. But really, Grandmama really should get out more. The world is changing, and she has lost touch."

"She was gracious to us when we were on the island as guests," Tessia said.

"Oh yes, her sister Purpura sets a lovely table. And those orchards on the island? To die for." Mannie took a sip of his drink and added, "But those old broads are getting pretty batty, aren't they? Did you meet her sister?"

"Liatris mentioned her," I said looking into the bottom of my glass.

"Well, if you ever do meet her, be careful. That old bitch is a kleptomaniac. If you have any gold around, she will steal it. I mean, *really.* What is she thinking? She is a semi-divine being, for Dark's sake. She could have anything she wants, and she steals gold from mortals? She has been an embarrassment to the family for millennia."

He looked at us, assessing our needs like a perfect host, "May I freshen your drinks?"

Tessia and I declined. I was starting to feel tipsy, drinking on an empty stomach. "What's in the drink?" I asked.

"Oh, a little of this, a little of that," Mannie answered, waving his hand dismissively. "Do you like it?"

Tessia and I nodded enthusiastically, scarce believing how well we were being treated.

"Now, Tessia, you asked about the family tree. Let's see… Liatris was the mother of Stelolas, who was a centaur. Grandmama always had a thing for horses," he said, winking. "Who was the father of Nimbus Pearshimmer—that wasn't her real name of course, but she became queen of the fairies and needed a flashy name to go with the job. Then there were a couple of old wankers whose names I can never remember. Then my grandfather Uatrus who somehow inherited this castle and became LORD DEATH, a title that comes with the estate. He loved the title, but I find it rather pretentious, don't you? I remember he kept hellhounds in the foyer, can you imagine? I was terrified of the beasts and even more terrified by my grandfather who had three heads. Mind you, he was a god and could have taken any appearance, and he chose *that* look? Forgive me for saying so, but my family is more than a little bonkers."

Mannie rolled his eyes. "Then there was my father, who was pretty useless. The kingdom went to hell under his management. All he was interested in was chasing the cherubim around the bath quarters, not that they minded being caught. And when he died, the castle and the title went to my Uncle Githoped, whom I knew as Uncle Ed. He was nice to me, but a real terror to everyone else. There was nothing he liked better than a good burning at the stake. 'Oh, how lovely,' he used to say. 'Everyone loves a barbecue.'

"Well," Mannie said. "To make a long story longer, I inherited the palace, the lands, the title, the whole shebang. And here we are! I try to do a good job managing the kingdom, and I have a wonderful staff who've been with us literally forever, but sometimes there are messes I need to clean up…" He looked up as a retainer appeared at the door. "Anyway, that's quite enough about me and my boring family. I believe it's time for dinner."

Mannie showed us into the dining room where a long table was set with golden platters piled high with cuts of meat, bowls of puddings, and more blood-red wine in sparkling crystal. The table was so long it disappeared into the distance. Wide platters heaped with rare steaks, a haunch of roasted meat bloody in the middle and charred on the outside, a dozen sauces of different colors, drumsticks piled high, small and large sausages, rectangular casseroles and round tureens filled with gravy, a great sculpture of a swan made of gelatin, fatty meat and headcheese on buns, gravies and soups, meat pies and puddings, loins, shoulders, ribs, sides, jowls, legs and flanks. There were fried chicken feet, fried fish filets, and piles of oysters and clams. There were live lobsters trying to crawl from the tank at one end of the table. And a few paces down, in the middle of the banquet table there was a large platter covered with a silver dome.

Seeing how much trouble Mannie had gone through in planning this feast, we politely sat down. The host was at the head of the table, Tessia on his right and me on the left. There were half a dozen footmen around us. With a graceful gesture, Lord Death waved his hand and the footmen served our plates. Starting with the gelatin swan, they removed her head and served it on our small plates on the right side of our settings. Imitating the king, we had just a taste of the swan before waving it away. Next, we tried a bite, no more, of the blood sausage, a bit of the casserole which tasted of cinnamon, a bite of steak, of roast, of venison, of hog-jowl. Each one with its own sauce or gravy. Although I'd never been a big meat eater, the food was quite delicious.

"I understand you enjoy the hunt, Your Majesty," Mannie asked Tessia.

"Yes, I do," she replied.

"And what is your favorite game animal to hunt?" He

seemed like the perfect host, engaging his guest, drawing her out and giving her a chance to talk about her interests.

"I suppose I like hunting wild boar." Tessia said, considering the question. "I enjoy the challenge. They are intelligent and by far the most dangerous of the game animals."

"I thought you would say that, Your Majesty," Mannie responded, smiling. "Here, please try some of this garlic roasted tenderloin." The king used silver tongs to lift a few pieces of meat from a platter held by a footman.

"It is actually from the huge boar you yourself killed in the mountains above the Dragonja River. Do you remember the animal? You planted your spear in the ground and he charged you? The point went into his throat, but he kept charging? You had to step aside, or he would have ripped your leg apart?"

She nodded, surprised and looked at me. I felt a sense of dread coming over me. I looked down the table at the mounds of meat on the table which stretched far into the distance.

"Mannie," I asked. "Is all of this meat from animals we killed?"

"Yes, of course," he said, chewing on a piece of tenderloin. "I'm sorry. I thought you understood that this was a banquet celebrating all you've done in service to me. Of course, on this one table we couldn't possibly fit all the meat from everything you've killed or maimed. What we have here is merely a sample. After all, isn't it considered a point of honor for hunters to eat what they kill?"

Mannie gave me a shy smile, glanced at one of the footmen and said, "I think it is time for the *pièce de resistance*, wouldn't you say?"

Two footmen brought the platter covered with a silver dome and placed it on the small serving table behind Mannie. One of them lifted off the cover with a flourish to display the severed head of a Drekavac with the top of his head cut neatly off. Inside the skull was a gray soup with swirls of red. I noticed that the Drekavac was missing one eye.

Tessia pointed her finger at the Drekavac's face and asked in horror, "Is that Sergeant Zrul?"

The sergeant's one good eye looked at me and I swear he winked. I felt dizzy.

"I'm so sorry that the dinner last night upset you," Mannie said. "I meant to celebrate the occasion of your visit. You have done so much for me, and I wanted to honor your work."

Tessia, Mannie, and I were sitting on marble steps in the courtyard of the palace. Despite the beauty of the garden with its blossoming pear trees and banks of azaleas, Tessia and I were uncomfortable in this palace, and sensing our discomfort, Mannie was obviously distressed by his social blunder of the dinner menu the night before.

"I really don't understand humans," he confessed. "How can they devote so much time and energy to killing each other, with entire industries and professions dedicated to this task and yet still claim they are disgusted with war? It seems to me that little boys with their war games are much more honest than adults on this subject. Boys are not ashamed to think of murder as a game while their parents pretend to be horrified by it."

Mannie shifted his position, not able to find a way to sit that felt right, or perhaps wanting us to understand the difficult position humans had put him in. "Do you know how much work it is for me to kill people by disease? It usually takes years of culturing illness before the person succumbs. How much more efficient war is. My goodness, the two of you have fomented so much fighting, and you rationalized it so brilliantly. Killing people was always about protecting the homeland or aspiring to be free or protecting the babies. Did you ever think about how many babies you killed in order to protect the babies? You always were fighting for some abstract ideal while ignoring the hard facts in front of you. Why, if you had stayed for dessert last night, we were going to have baby fingerlings baked in honey." His eyes grew dreamy as he thought about the delicacy. "You would have loved their crunchy sweetness."

Tessia blanched, and my queasiness returned. I didn't want to think about the meat we'd eaten the night before.

As we sat in the beautiful garden, my stomach settled, and my curiosity returned. Here we were talking with Death himself, and he wanted to be friends with us. "Mannie, may I ask you something?"

"Of course," he said, brightening.

"This land is called the Continent of Love, isn't it?"

"Yes, it is a very old name."

"And yet it is ruled by Lord Death?"

"Yes…" he looked at me with curiosity. "Oh, I see, you think that Love and Death are opposed to each other. You are suffering under the mistaken assumption that Death does not rule over Love, but rather Life rules over Love." He gave an indulgent chuckle. "Well, it's a common mistake."

I glanced at Tessia. The color was returning to her face, but her eyes still looked frightened and uncertain. I had seen this seasoned warrior face down entire armies and not be alarmed, so I realized she must have been changed by her experiences since we left The Blessed Isle.

"Well, let me think about how to explain how things are and how they came to be… I suppose I should start at the Beginning…

"There was once a very tiny dot, smaller than the tip of a needle, that was jammed with Everything. That is, everything we know—all the light and life and time and thought and feeling and belief and… everything else you can think of—was contained in this dot. And all around the dot was the infinity of Nothing. The two existed together with Everything taking up only a tiny portion of Nothing. Then one day—except there weren't any days in those days—the dot exploded, and

Everything came out, speeding through the Nothing, filling it with Everything. And that's how we got here, part of Everything."

Mannie smiled and looked at us, obviously satisfied he'd explained Everything.

"What?" Tessia said. "That makes no sense. How could everything be contained in a tiny dot?"

Mannie seemed disappointed she didn't see the perfectly elegant logic of his explanation. "Well, Your Majesty, it's just a theory. It's what we believe happened in the beginning."

"Who is 'we'?" Tessia asked, skeptically.

"You know, the gods and elementals and other beings..." Mannie was losing confidence in the explanation.

"It sounds like utter rubbish to me," Tessia said, always practical. I was glad to see she was regaining her confidence and, not for the first time in her life, standing up to Death.

"According to this theosophy," I asked Mannie. "Where did the gods come from?"

"Well, of course," Mannie answered, glancing nervously at Tessia. "It's all just theory, but I've been told that in that initial explosion, energy was spread unevenly. There were pockets of energy, maelstroms and eddies that were formed. These places where there was more energy became the gods, and the places where there was less energy became the mortals."

"I still don't understand why you are Lord Death, but you rule over the Continent of Love," I said.

"Oh well, that cleaving goes back to a decision that Time made right after the Big Explosion. Time divided her domain between her two children—her son Day and her daughter Night. Day in turn had his children: Life and Joy. And night had her children: Death and Love. Anyway, generations later, I eventually became Lord Death and ruled over the Continent of Love, and my sister Nilene became My Lady of Life and ruled over the World of Joy."

"And so, the world we know, it is Joy?" I asked.

"Yes, funny isn't it since your kind has pretty much turned the world into a place of misery, but that was your choice. Nilene has done everything She could to make the world beautiful, but you just can't have nice things anymore, can you?"

Tessia's face was flushed with anger. This was the kind of conversation she loathed. Talking about things that may or may not exist while ignoring the obvious things that needed to be done right away.

"Obviously, you know what you're talking about," Tessia said. "But it's of no help to us, so let's put aside all the cosmic theory and the history of your screwed-up family, and you tell us the things we need to know to accomplish our mission."

Mannie shrugged, realizing that even Death had to know his limits when faced with a woman who knew her own mind. "Very well, my dear, how can I help you?"

Tessia narrowed her eyes, and I was glad to see my old friend focusing on what she did best, developing a strategy to accomplish a mission.

"Norbert and I are here to fetch Ena and bring her back to her family. I personally feel outraged you took her at such a young age."

"Tessia, my dear," Mannie said, for the first time calling her by her name. "First, I took Ena at the exact time she was supposed to leave your world. And second, it is not within the rules of the Possible to take someone from this kingdom and return her to her previous life. It is simply not done."

"Nonsense," Tessia said, firmly. "What about all those old stories about heroes like…" she looked at me for help.

"Entana, Iritis and Gurudutt," I murmured helpfully.

"Exactly, what about them?" Tessia asked, pointing her finger emphatically at our host. "They came into the underworld, found their loved ones and brought them back. Why can't we?"

I didn't mention that the three heroes who are said to have gone into the underworld had less than successful outcomes to their quests, but Mannie didn't seem to notice the flaw in Tessia's argument, so I let it pass.

Mannie looked Tessia in the eyes for a moment, then said, "It is highly irregular, and the other gods are going to criticize me for not following the rules of the Possible, but I've always thought of those rules as merely suggestions, not laws. So, I'll give you a map to the place where Ena, or rather her essence, is living these days. It's a long walk from here, but Time doesn't have as strong of a presence here as she has in your world. Once you get there, you can try to persuade Ena to accompany you back to your world, but I wouldn't expect her to want to go."

"Why wouldn't she want to have her life back?" I asked. It was the first time I'd considered the idea that Ena would not want to leave the underworld and come with me.

Mannie looked at me as if I had asked a completely absurd question. "Norbert, don't you realize that your world is Hell?"

"What?" Again, I felt dizzy.

"Surely, you've noticed that Life is suffering, right?" Mannie said to me, slowly, as if I were a backwards child. "Illness, war, hunger, injury and pain exist in your world, but they don't exist in mine. Think of childbirth. How you humans begin to suffer at the first moment you emerge into the world. My sister Nilene gives you continuous suffering and brief moments of joy. I give you love and endless serenity. Why is this process so hard to understand? Death is not evil. It is simply a different stage of being. The purpose of your existence is to keep moving forward. Why would Ena want to go backwards?"

Tessia looked furious. She was focused on our mission, and she'd had quite enough of Mannie's confusing rhetoric, cosmic theories and irrelevant explanations, and she was ready to explode.

"WHERE IS ENA?!" She shouted.

Mannie was startled at her outburst. He quickly reached into the large pocket of his tunic—a pocket which hadn't been there before—and withdrew a scroll which he gently unspooled, revealing a map.

"There's no need to shout, Tessia," he said, trying to placate her. He pointed at one end of the parchment. "You are here in the castle." His finger followed a line down the middle of the map. "You'll need to follow the Road of Emptiness into the Hills of Ecstasy and then climb the Mountain of Vision. You might want to stop and enjoy the view from there, quite something really."

Mannie saw Tessia starting to get irritated again, so he moved his finger further along the map. "Then you'll have to find a way over the Chasm of Despair. Be careful. If you fall into the chasm, you may have stay there for eternity. Once you are across the chasm, you'll need to find the Peaceful Path. Follow the path until you emerge on the Plain of Enlightenment. You'll find your daughter beneath a tree in the middle of the plain. I believe her partner … her *boyfriend* as you say… is with her now. They've actually been together for many lives."

Mannie handed me the map. Then unexpectedly, he gave me a hug, then Tessia a hug.

"I'm… I'm sorry I blew up at you, Mannie," she said, looking at the floor sheepishly. "I sometimes get angry. I'm grateful for all you've done for us."

"No need to apologize, my dear," our host said. "You are a young soul, and we gods must make allowances for youthfulness."

Then he turned to me and said, "On the other hand, Norbert, you are an old soul, so you should be embarrassed not to be more enlightened. When you get back to your world, you have a lot of work to do."

I nodded, realizing he was right.

Mannie walked us through the courtyard of the palace and stopped in front of the outer gate.

"This is the Gate of Acceptance. Once you leave here, you'll be on the Road of Emptiness. Keep following the road to the mountains."

Mannie's eyes filled with tears. "Farewell, my friends, I'll be seeing both of you soon," he said gently. And Tessia and I walked through the Gate of Acceptance and stepped onto the Road of Emptiness, turning to wave goodbye to Lord Death.

Chapter Twenty-Three

We followed the road, our thoughts and feelings flowing out of us the way water flows from a pitcher. There was no need to speak, for Tessia and I were one, breathing the sweet air and feeling the soles of our feet on the hard surface of the road. The gray light lifted, and the day became silver like a summer morning. We were neither happy nor sad, joyful nor afraid, but rather we were at peace. And the union between Tessia and me was extended and we became one with the hills which were covered in flowers. And as we walked down the road, we became, for the first time in either of our memories, ecstatic. This experience was much larger than happiness. It was a feeling of being absorbed by the landscape around us. Our individual identities disappeared, and we departed from any thoughts of ourselves. We did not *look* at the flowers. We *were* the flowers. And the dirt. And the sky. As we followed the road through the hills, we became the hills.

The road became steeper and narrower. We followed the path until it ended, and we found ourselves standing in front of a steep cliff that seemed to rise into the clouds. I had no idea how we could climb such a cliff, but I knew we had to if we were ever to find Ena. I wished I'd been able to somehow bring my flying broom into this underworld. Suddenly, it occurred to me that if this journey was a dream, then I should be able to control, or at least influence what happened here. I waved my hand and murmured a spell, trying to conjure a broom to appear, but nothing happened.

Tessia was standing a dozen paces from the cliff, looking

upward. I could see her studying the contours, tracing a route up the cliff. Finally, she said, "Norbert, follow me." And she started climbing the cliff, zigging this way and that, working her way upward. I followed her lead, putting my feet where hers had been, grasping the small outcroppings she had. We made our way upward, higher and higher, until the Hills of Ecstasy were far below, and we were climbing through mists and clouds, following the route that became clearer with each new ledge or handhold. Who could tell how long we climbed? It seemed a lifetime or more, but time had become something different, swirling around us, lifting us as we rose into the air.

When we reached the top of the mountain, we rested. Tessia and I lay in each other's arms, not as lovers or friends, but as one being who'd traveled far to arrive at the place we didn't know existed but had yearned for through our many lives. We woke and walked between the boulders to the other side of the mountain and looked down at the chasm below us. And beyond was a large verdant plain where I knew Ena was.

"It seems to me," Tessia said, looking down into the darkness below, "that there are only two ways across the chasm. We can climb down the side of the mountain, all the way to the bottom of the chasm, then we climb up the other side until we reach the top."

"But we don't know how deep the chasm is," I pointed out. "Nor do we know what is at the bottom. And we don't know whether we can climb up the other side."

"We climbed up the cliff to get here," she pointed out, optimistically. "I'm sure we could climb up the other side of the chasm."

"Since we don't know how deep the chasm is, then we don't know how far we'd have to climb," I said.

"The other way across the chasm is to build a bridge," Tessia said.

I looked around. "Build a bridge out of what?" I asked. "There's nothing on this mountain but rock and lichen."

Tessia scowled at me. She hated pessimism. "So, what's your solution, Norbert?"

"I don't know yet. I need to think about it. In the meantime, can't we just enjoy the view, as Mannie suggested?"

She looked at me, disgusted. "I'm in no mood for sightseeing, Norbert. We have a mission to accomplish."

"Well, my friend, maybe enjoying the view is part of the mission."

Tessia rolled her eyes and walked away. A little way off, she stopped at the edge of the cliff, looking beyond the Plain of Enlightenment to the far horizon. There were clouds there in the distance, beyond where we were going, tinged with golden light. I wondered what that land was called.

Sometime later—a day, a year, a century—Tessia stood on the edge of the cliff, her gaze measuring the distance across the chasm to the other side which was somewhat lower than this side. Then she walked back across the mountain top and paced the distance to the edge above the chasm.

"What are you doing?" I asked.

"I count forty-two paces across the top of this mountain, and I estimate a distance of one hundred paces across the chasm to the other side. The other side is lower, so we have the advantage of height."

I looked at her skeptically. "You plan to fly across the chasm?"

"Not fly. Leap."

"Leap? You think you can leap over the chasm? Tessia, please don't do this. It's impossible. No one has ever leaped that far in the history of the world."

She walked across the mountaintop and lowered herself into a sprinter's crouch.

"It's going to be a Leap of Faith, Norbert. It's the only way to get over the Chasm of Despair. Don't you see? This whole journey has been leading to this test. Do we have enough faith to emerge onto the Plain of Enlightenment? Strength, skill, intelligence, and magic are not enough. In the end, we have to have faith, or we fall into despair."

"Tessia, if you successfully make this leap, it will be a miracle and not one likely to be repeated. I will not be able to go with you. You'll have to leave me here."

"Yes, you can, Norbert. If you see me make the leap, then you'll know it's possible, and it will be much easier for you."

Tessia closed her eyes and concentrated on building up her courage for the impossible leap in front of her. I also closed my eyes and concentrated on all the love I felt for my daughter Ena, my wife Idella, my son Alaric and my friend Tessia. I thought of all the beauty and wonder I'd experienced in my life. Then I opened my eyes and saw Tessia sprinting toward the Chasm of Despair. At the edge of the mountain, she left the solid ground and flew across the chasm, landing in a rolling fall on the other side.

She stood up and waved her arms at me. "It's your turn now, Norbert!" She yelled, smiling.

After a long hike across a green pasture, we found Ena sitting under a giant oak. Beside her was Adamu. They were playing some kind of game that involved taking turns moving stones around a board. From what I could tell, Ena moved the white stones and Adamu moved the black. The two young people looked exactly the way I'd seen them in my vision.

Ena lifted her head and looked first at Tessia and then at me. It was obvious she didn't recognize either of us.

"Hello, Ena," I said.

She tilted her head. "Sorry, do I know you?"

"Yes, I am your father, well, actually your stepfather. Your mother Idella and I raised you."

When she didn't respond, I said, "This is Tessia, your godmother, who is also the queen of the land where you lived."

"Do I know you as well?" Adamu asked.

"Yes, your name is Adamu, and you were my student in the School of Magic. You were also… Ena's lover."

Adamu and Ena looked at each other and laughed. "That's not possible," Ena said, shyly.

"Why is that not possible?" Tessia asked.

Adamu looked at Ena out of the corner of his eye, barely hiding his embarrassment. "It's not possible because Ena is my sister. It would be unnatural for us to be lovers."

Tessia and I sat down in the soft green grass beneath the oak. The sunlight was warm and gentle, and there was a pleasant breeze. Nearby, I could see other couples sitting in the wide shade of oaks as well. Some of the couples were men and women; but others were made up of a pair of men or a pair of women; and in one case, there was what appeared to be a mother and child. The oaks which sheltered pairs of people were scattered across the plain as far as the eye could see.

"What is this place?" Tessia asked.

"It is the Plain of Enlightenment, located on the Continent of Love," Adamu answered. Even in the underworld, he had an instinct for precision.

"Did you have a difficult journey to get here?" he asked, picking up the black and white stones from the board and dropping them in a silk bag.

"It was challenging," Tessia answered. "But we learned a great deal about ourselves and about the gods along the way."

"The gods?" Ena asked, curiously. Noticing how dark her eyebrows were, I felt a pang in my heart, so many small things make up the memory of a person you love.

"Yes," Tessia said. "We met Lord Death, Mannie as he likes to be called."

Ena and Adamu looked at each other, shrugging. "Lord

Death is named Mannie?" Ena asked me, raising her eyebrows.

"That's right," I said. "What's the first thing you remember?"

"I remember being in a boat with a lot of people and dipping my cupped hands in the fresh water of the river. Then Adamu and I followed the road with a crowd of souls. The road led through hills covered with flowers. Most of our companions chose to stay in the hills. We climbed a cliff to the top of a mountain which had a beautiful view of these plains. We were the only ones who crossed the chasm to get here," Ena responded, a faraway look in her eyes.

"Did you jump over the chasm?" Tessia asked.

"Oh, my goodness, no," Ena answered. "There was an old bridge over the chasm. It looked unsafe, so most of our companions stayed on the mountain. But Adamu examined the bridge, and he told me it was safe, and I trusted him." She smiled at him. "I have faith in my brother's intelligence about such things."

"And I have faith in Ena's love," Adamu said, reaching for his sister's hand. They were obviously very close.

"Have the two of you been together long?" I asked.

"Since we don't remember our previous lives, then we can't answer your question specifically," Adamu said. "But I have a sense we've always been together. I think perhaps in some lives we're brother and sister. Other lives we're mother and son, or father and daughter. Other lives we're close friends."

"And in some lives, you are lovers?"

Ena covered her mouth with her hand and laughed. "If you say so..."

"And why are you here," Tessia asked, "on this plain?"

"We're waiting," Ena said.

"Waiting for what?" I asked, looking around at all the couples who seemed to be content, sitting in the shade. Were they all waiting, as well?

"Waiting for our next assignment, of course," Adamu said, as if the answer to my question should be obvious.

"Are you hungry? Or thirsty?" Ena asked, reaching into a hollow in the old oak, pulling out a platter of bread, fruit and nuts and handing it to me. She reached into the hollow again and pulled out a wineskin. "Please help yourselves."

It seemed an eternity had passed since our disastrous meal with Mannie. I picked up the loaf of bread and tore off a small piece. It was warm and fresh. Since I was married to a baker, my standards for bread were high, and this was the best I had ever tasted. There were also grapes, plums, apples, citron and papaya, as well as a variety of nuts. Tessia watched me try the food, and when I seemed to be enjoying it, she selected a grape and put it in her mouth. Soon, we were both eating heartily and lifting the wineskin to our mouths.

"Aren't you eating?" I asked, noting that Ena and Adamu were just watching us. They seemed to be finding pleasure in our appetites.

"No, we rarely get hungry, and when we do, it is just for the pleasure of the taste and textures of a specific food. Since we don't have corporeal bodies, we don't actually need nourishment."

"How did you get here?" Adamu asked. "I didn't know that a soul could enter the underworld without the body dying first. But the two of you experience hunger and fatigue, experiences which are just vague memories to us."

"Liatris, the ancient elemental, allowed us to come because she felt she owed us a favor," Tessia said, taking a bite of an apple.

"And why are you here?" Adamu asked, his eyes narrowing. It was clear he was beginning to suspect that our journey had a purpose he might not approve of.

I stalled for time to think while I chewed the bread and washed it down with wine. From the beginning, I had foolishly assumed that once I showed up, Ena would recognize me and be pleased to return to her life.

Tessia broke the awkward silence. "We are here to take Ena back to her life."

Ena's jaw dropped and her eyes grew wide. "You *what*?"

I started talking rapidly, wanting to help her understand why it was imperative she come with me back to the life she had. "Ena, I love you so much. Your death was horrible. The soldiers… they did things to you no one should have to endure. I can't return to your mother and tell her that you died when I was supposed to protect you…"

Ena and Adamu were looking at me with disgust.

"Let me see if I understand what you are saying," Ena said slowly and deliberately. "You, whose name I don't know and whom I don't remember at all, say you were my stepfather in my most recent life."

I nodded and glanced at Tessia who had picked up a blade of grass and was examining it closely as if the conversation in front of her were not happening.

"And you're saying there was some kind of terrible war in which I was violated by soldiers and then killed?"

I nodded.

"And was Adamu with me?"

"Yes, he was killed at the same time. The two of you were protecting dragonlings."

"What are dragonlings?" Adamu asked.

"Baby dragons," Tessia said, suddenly interested. "There are no dragons in the underworld?"

"From what I gather, each species has its own underworld, that is, each kind of consciousness has a separate and distinct experience of death," Adamu said. Strange, I thought, he's a philosopher even in the afterlife. I would love to discuss with him the manifestations of reality—which was turning out to be something quite different than I expected. But, we would have to forego that conversation, at least for now.

Meanwhile, Ena was still trying to grasp what I wanted from her. "And you want me to return to this ghastly life where I was violated and murdered while trying to protect babies?"

I nodded, beginning to understand how ridiculous I must look to these two wise souls.

"And why would I do this?" she asked.

"Because it will break your mother's heart if you don't."

"Well, it's very nice that hearing of my death will break my mother's heart. She must have loved me very much." She turned to Adamu. "Isn't that nice? To be loved so much?"

"It's very nice," Adamu agreed. "But it doesn't change anything."

"What do you mean, it doesn't change anything? Love changes everything," I pleaded.

"No, no…" She looked at me, puzzled. "What is your name again? Norbert? You have a misunderstanding. Love is a constant in the universe. Love doesn't change anything. It is the basis of all things. The very continent you are standing on, the entire underworld, is love. The world you come from is love. It is only when we forget that fact and think that other things, such as truth or death, exist as entities separate from love, that we do evil things. Evil is not a substance in itself, it is merely the absence of love." Again, she turned to Adamu. "Am I right about this, brother?"

"Yes, you are right, sister," he answered. "But it has taken us many lives to understand this principle. You can't expect a young soul like Norbert's to understand."

"Actually, Lord Death told me I have an old soul," I answered defensively.

Ena and Adamu looked at the ground. "If it's true that you have an old soul, then you really should know this stuff, Norbert," Ena said.

Even Tessia, who hated philosophy, shrugged, embarrassed for me.

"Actually, Lord Death said the same thing… for an old soul, I am remarkably unenlightened," I admitted sheepishly.

"Well then," Adamu said. "You know what you have to do,

don't you? Return to your life, console Ena's mother, and get started learning what you are supposed to learn…"

"And so, the two of you will not come back with me?" I asked in a small voice.

"Oh, was I invited as well?" Adamu said mirthfully as if he just realized he'd been invited to a boring party. "I thought you were talking only Ena."

He and Ena laughed, and I could see that they truly were soulmates.

"Norbert," she said. "I'm very pleased you loved me when I was in your life, but I have to decline your invitation. You will have to live without me. But please say goodbye to my mother for me. She sounds like a wonderful woman."

Tessia and I stood up and turned to go. Adamu stood up as well.

"Wait a moment," Adamu said. "Now I know why you're here. I'm supposed to go back with you."

Chapter Twenty-Four

I opened my eyes and saw Liatris and Zygmunt standing in moonlight beside the stone shrine. I turned my head and saw Tessia lying on her back, her eyes open, staring at the stars spread like spilled milk across the sky. She blinked and turned to me. She stretched out her hand and I grasped it, reassuring myself that I was back in the world we knew.

"How long have we been asleep?" I asked.

"Not long," Zygmunt answered. "It's not dawn yet."

"I had a dream in which I saw Ena and Adamu," I said.

"Are you sure it was a dream?" Liatris asked, glancing to my left.

I turned my head and saw Adamu, sleeping beside me. I reached over to wake him, but Liatris grasped my arm.

"Let him sleep, Norbert," she said. "He needs a little time to let his soul migrate into his body. He'll wake up later and meet you for dinner in the garden."

"Now I'm very confused, Liatris. Did I dream that Ena and Adamu died? Is Ena still alive?" I asked, my hope starting to rise.

"Ena is gone from this world," Liatris said. "Adamu is here. You can explain his presence beside you any way you wish."

"What happened, Norbert? Where did we go? Did we have the same dream?" Tessia asked, trying to regain her sense of reality.

"We went through a long tunnel and came out on the shore of a lake. Waiting for us there were the… the…" A lump came into my throat.

"Waiting for us were the souls of the people we have killed," Tessia said, without feeling.

"Yes, then we took a boat across the Sea of Forgetfulness..."

"And came to the opposite shore where a soldier took us to a castle..."

"And Lord Death invited us to a feast..."

"Where there were piles of meat..."

"The flesh of all those we've killed. The pigs, the chickens, the cows, the fish..."

"The flesh of our enemies as well." Tessia said, turning to me in awe. "Norbert, we had the same exact dream."

"It doesn't sound like a dream to me," Zygmunt said. "It sounds like a vision quest. What happened next?"

"We joined a crowd of people, pilgrims I suppose, who were following a road into hills covered in flowers," I related. "Most of the pilgrims fell in love with the beauty of the place and decided to stay. But we continued until the road became a path which led to a mountain. We climbed the mountain and could see a long way. There was a chasm on the other side of the mountain. We had to cross the chasm to reach the plain where we knew we had to go. Tessia, my brave friend, made an impossible leap across the chasm, and once she made the leap, I knew I could as well."

I paused, thinking about our journey and how I could never have accomplished it without Tessia.

Tessia picked up the tale: "We found Ena and Adamu playing a game of stones beneath a tree. They didn't recognize us. Norbert tried to convince them to come back with us to this life, but they laughed at us, saying it sounded like a terrible world where we lived, and they certainly would not want to go back to it. Besides, they said, they were waiting for their next assignment."

"Assignment?" Her uncle asked. "What kind of assignment?"

"Their next life, I suppose," Tessia said, sounding less assured. "Surely it was a dream, don't you think, Norbert?"

"It must have been a dream," I concluded. "Our journey took weeks and weeks, but you say we were sleeping here for only part of the night. How could we take such a long journey in such a short time?" I looked at Liatris, hoping she could unravel this paradox.

"Mage," she said, gently. "You are wiser than most men, but there is still much you do not understand."

"So I have been told, My Lady. Can you give me at least a glimpse of the Truth?"

"Very well," Liatris said. "Let me use an analogy. You, like all humans, think of time as a long piece of twine you are following in a straight line. But imagine the twine is not stretched out in a straight line, but rather it is wound in a ball. In this *dream* as you call it, you crossed from the part you've been following to another part which touches yours. You followed that part of the twine until it came back to where you started."

Tessia looked at the ground and shook her head.

"Your Majesty," Liatris said. "I know you hate to think about such things. You are a person of action. You would much rather take a Leap of Faith than think about what Faith is, but Norbert needs to understand that Faith is the willingness to accept the Unknown and to trust it is Good. Please be patient with Norbert. He needs you to act, and you need him to question."

Tessia looked at me, smiled and said nothing. We knew that Liatris was right. Tessia and I needed each other. Without me, she never would have attempted the vision quest, and without her, I never would have completed it.

I looked around, suddenly aware of where I was. "My Lady," I asked. "What is this place? According to Mannie, you are extremely powerful, as old as the cosmos, and the ancestor of the Gods. Why are you in this place and nowhere else?"

"Ah, this place is the Blessed Isle, my place of refuge. This was what the world was like before I gave birth to the gods, and then they gave birth to more gods and they proliferated. I grew so tired of their lying, bickering and fighting with each other. I grew to despise their selfish greed. Their pretentious bragging. My descendants, I'm afraid, are very tiresome. Can you believe that the gods actually went to war against each other repeatedly? All their violent feuds with their lightning, floods and volcanoes. I was so sad to see them kill each other. And finally, there were only two left: Nilene, who is my favorite although far too idealistic, and Mannie, who is a spoiled brat. But what can you do but tolerate your family even if they behave in ways you disapprove of? So, a few eons ago, after the Last Great War of the Gods, their father, immortally wounded, willed half the world to Nilene and half to Mannie. And ever since then, the world, this world, has been divided. Life and Death as they like to think of themselves. Light and Dark. Right and Left. Up and Down. Earth and Sky. Woman and Man. Peace and War. Knowledge and Ignorance. Fortunately, there are other worlds where these dichotomies don't exist."

"But this island, My Lady," I asked. "Why have you created this Blessed Isle, your refuge, to be perfect while the rest of the world is so wretched?"

"Yes, it is wretched, isn't it?" Liatris said. "War, poverty, disease… I don't know how things could have gone so wrong, but I suppose it is inevitable, given where humans came from."

Her voice trailed off, and the silence seemed disturbing.

"Where did humans come from?" Zygmunt finally asked. He had been listening intently to Liatris, and he seemed as disturbed as I was by the ways the ancient elemental had been describing the history of the gods.

"Yes, I'd like to know too," Tessia said, taking a sudden interest in impractical things.

"Oh, sorry," Liatris said, looking from Tessia to me. "Since you spent time talking with Mannie, I thought you knew."

"Knew what?" I asked.

"Humans came about when Mannie had sex with a monkey," Liatris said nonchalantly.

Now the silence was so thick you could have cut it with Tessia's Voprian blade.

"WHAT?" Tessia shouted, truly disturbed. "Humans are a cross between monkeys and Lord Death?"

"Well, yes, of course," Liatris said. "I would think your lineage would be obvious. Haven't you noticed your hands and faces are much like monkeys?"

"Of course, we're like monkeys," Tessia said. "It's the other part, that we are descended from Lord Death, I don't understand."

Liatris shrugged, "I would think that side of your lineage would be obvious as well. Monkeys don't usually kill each other, and they certainly don't spend a great deal of time developing weapons for that purpose. Just in the last few weeks, my dear, you personally have killed... how many people?"

"Sixty-six," Tessia said softly, looking down.

"And how many in your entire lifetime?"

"Four hundred and four," Tessia said, a tear coming down her cheek.

"And you, Mage, how many have you killed in your lifetime?"

"Eighty-one," I answered, barely audible.

"And how do you know this?"

"Because I talked to each of them in the underworld," I answered.

"And you talked to Lord Death in his castle. You were his guest?"

Tessia and I nodded.

"And how well did you get along with my descendent?"

"I actually liked Mannie a great deal," I said.

"He was charming until..." Tessia stopped herself.

"You found him charming until he served you the flesh of

your enemies?" Liatris asked. "Well, at least you have your standards. Mass murder is heroic, but cannibalism is revolting. I'm glad you draw the line somewhere."

Liatris looked at Zygmunt. "How many people have you killed, General?"

"I do not know, My Lady," he said in a soft voice, looking down.

"Make a guess," she suggested.

"Perhaps thirty or forty," he hazarded.

"Those are only the ones you killed with your own hand, General. How many others were killed as a result of your orders?"

"Thousands," he said, starting to weep.

"And have you grieved those thousands?" Liatris asked gently.

"Every day," Zygmunt whispered, falling to his knees and weeping.

She put her hand on his head and said, "There, there. You were merely doing what you were supposed to do in the Grand Scheme of Things."

"My Lady," I said, pulling myself out of my shame. "What is the Grand Scheme of Things?"

"I haven't a clue," she said. "But I have to believe there is one."

Walking back to the keep, Zygmunt, Tessia and I were silent. So much had been revealed to us in such a short time, we each needed to be alone for a while. We quietly greeted Wessel and Tyrmiss when we saw them, but they sensed we were not ready to talk about what had happened to us.

I went to my room, lay on the bed and stared at the ceiling. Huge mysteries had been revealed to me, and underneath those mysteries lay other, larger mysteries and underneath those still more mysteries, and finally we had come to mysteries even the gods themselves fail to understand. My small mind had been filled to bursting, and I knew I had to let go of the uncertainties and concentrate only on the things of this world.

It was obvious now that Ena would not be returning to us. She was gone from this life, and there was nothing I could do about this fact. No amount of denying or bargaining with death was going to bring her back and I would have to accept the loss.

I started tossing and turning, cursing and yelling, screaming with anger against the soldiers who killed her, the king who ordered it, the smiths who made the swords that cut her beautiful skin. Suddenly, Tessia was holding me, crying and screaming with me, soothing and comforting me until I was exhausted and couldn't cry anymore. I lay still as my friend took off my shoes, covered me with a blanket, put her hand on my forehead and soothed me like a mother whose child had woken only to find the horrible nightmare was true.

Later, when I came down to the garden, Adamu was explaining the metaphysics of death to Zygmunt, Wessel and Tyrmiss. Tessia sat at the end of the table ignoring them while she devoured a huge plate of fruit, nuts, bread and beans. She obviously had grown bored with all this talk of philosophy and was focusing on the practicalities of life.

As I sat down at the table, Adamu turned to me and said, "Mage, I need to tell you that I have been called back to this life by the Goddess Nilene to save the world of men and dragons. Evidently, she asked her brother Lord Death for a favor, and he granted my temporary release. Ena was not available—there are Big Plans for her, but my next assignment can wait."

I tried not to feel resentment that this skinny brainy kid had been granted a commutation from death while my beautiful Ena was needed elsewhere.

"And so, you have come back for a specific purpose?" I asked, spearing a pear slice on my knife and lifting it to my mouth.

Wessel and Zygmunt were heartily eating venison steaks. I noticed the bloody center of the cutlets and thought of the piles of meat in Mannie's castle. I doubted I could ever eat meat again.

"Yes," Adamu said, looking me in the eye. "I am supposed to go to Hoclav City and become a teacher."

"A teacher?" I asked, surprised. "Are you going to found a School for Mages?"

"No, I will be teaching young people Dragon Philosophy."

Tyrmiss looked up from the mound of fish she was devouring and asked, "What do you mean by 'Dragon Philosophy'?" she asked.

"Living with the dragons over the last month, I had a chance to listen to many of the Old Mothers," Adamu replied. "Once they realized I was serious about learning what they had to teach, they were very generous with their time. They sang the old songs and told the old tales. They explained to me the oneness of all things. *Interconnectivity*, they called it. How every action, no matter how small, ripples out through the world. I began to realize that most of the problems humans face are caused by our ignorance of this principle."

"I agree, Adamu," I said, nodding toward Tyrmiss. "Our kind can learn a great deal from dragons, but why do you think the king, or more importantly the citizens of Hoclav will listen to you?"

"I know it won't be easy to convince them," the young man, who now seemed much older than his eighteen years, replied. "I will have to earn their trust."

"And how will you do that?" Zygmunt asked.

"I will start by using my magical skills to help the citizens rebuild their city," Adamu replied speaking slowly, his eyes focused on the distant fields. "The war with dragons did a great deal of damage, and they could use a good engineer. Then we will need to undo the damage caused by generations of abusing the land. Forests need to be replanted. Rivers and streams need to be made pure again. They need to learn how to grow crops without depleting the land."

"And once you have their trust, what then?" Zygmunt asked.

"I will establish a School for Dragon Studies in which young people learn everything there is to know about respecting the gifts of the Goddess."

"And what about the men who hunt dragons?" Tyrmiss asked, her deep voice rumbling in anger.

"The Goddess has a plan for that problem as well," Adamu said, looking straight into the eyes of the dragon, an act most men were incapable of. "She will be visiting you tonight to discuss your assignment, my friend."

Looking at Adamu, I remembered that I always had had a feeling, even when he was my student, that the Goddess had chosen him to live a life beyond my comprehension.

The next morning after we saw Adamu fly off on my borrowed broom to return to Hoclav City, I was sitting on a stone bench in the courtyard garden when I heard a sound behind me that I recognized. Considering that Tyrmiss weighed as much as three horses, it had always amazed me how lightly she could land on the ground, as if a leopard had dropped from a tree behind you.

"Hello, Tyrmiss," I said glumly, not bothering to turn to look at her.

"Moping, are we?" She rumbled.

"As you well know, I have reasons to be sad, so please none of your taunts today, Tyrmiss."

"Oh, I'm not going to taunt you, Norbert. In fact, I'm here to invite you on a little jaunt."

"I'm not feeling up to a picnic today, Tyrmiss."

"Oh, it's something more than a picnic I have planned. It's more of an excursion to see the wonders of the world."

I turned to look at the expression on her face. She seemed to be serious, so I said, "Alright, I'll go find Tessia and ask her whether she wants to come."

"It would be best, Norbert, if you and I were to take this excursion alone and leave Tessia here."

I was surprised. Although Tessia often flew alone on Tyrmiss's back, I had always flown behind Tessia, holding onto her belt. I always had the impression Tyrmiss tolerated me only because I was Tessia's friend. Through the years, I'd gotten used to her verbal jabs, and they no longer bothered me. At least, not much.

"Have you mentioned this plan to Tessia?"

"In fact, it was Tessia who proposed it. She and I received a visit from the Goddess Nilene last night," Tyrmiss responded.

Intrigued, I asked, "Where would we go?"

"The Southern Islands."

"The Southern Islands? I've never heard of them."

"Very few humans know about the Southern Islands which, in itself, is a good reason for you to see them. There are a number of natural wonders there, as well as exotic animals and plants. You will find it a rewarding trip."

"How long will we be gone?"

"Just a day. As you know, I can travel very quickly when I want to, so we'll be back late tonight."

"Do I need to bring anything?"

"Just your wand."

Chapter Twenty-Five

It felt strange at first to be flying alone on Tyrmiss's back. I leaned forward and held onto the spines on her neck. Over her head, I could see the clouds rushing toward us. Turning to the right, I could see leagues of ocean, green then blue, and to my left, the Blessed Isle disappearing behind us. Also, without Tessia's body in front of me to shield the wind, I had to hold on tight, not to be blown off the dragon's back. It was exhilarating. I'd never realized how much I'd been missing by riding behind Tessia.

The ocean seemed to move endlessly below us. Eventually, we came in sight of a small island with a broad sandy beach which gave way to a low mountain covered with jungle. Tyrmiss landed on the beach, and I dropped to the ground and stretched my arms and legs. I saw a curious flash of red between the trees, and I started to walk in that direction.

"Wait, Norbert. Before you start exploring this island, you need to know where we are. I don't want you blundering into a situation without knowing the dangers."

"Dangers?" I asked, peering into the darkness between the trees and pulling out my wand. "What's the name of this island?"

"Melehune Island," Tyrmiss answered. "It is part of the Raskshas Archipelago. We'll visit a few of the islands in the archipelago. I just thought we would start here because of some of the exotic fungi."

"What kind of tree is that?" I asked, nodding toward the

edge of a jungle. "It has a green crown like an oak, but the leaves are so tightly packed together they look like a solid form."

"It is a solid form, Norbert. In fact, that's no tree, but a giant mushroom. Would you like to touch it? It's not poisonous. In fact, it's edible, at least to humans."

I walked over to the brown trunk of the mushroom and placed my hand on it, soft with the texture of linen. I pushed my fingers into the trunk and pulled out a handful of spongy meat. Lifting it to my mouth, I bit off a small piece. The taste was bland, but not unpleasant.

"What do you think, Norbert?" Tyrmiss called from the beach where she lay, sunbathing.

"Not bad," I said. "It tastes sort of like boiled turnips."

"I've been told that the mushrooms have all the nourishment people need, and they grow very quickly. You could feed an entire human city from the mushrooms grown on this island."

I walked back to Tyrmiss and looked up and down the beach. The water was blue, slightly darker than the sky. It was a beautiful place.

"Who owns this island?" I asked.

Tyrmiss looked at me and laughed. "No one owns the island. The Goddess Nilene uses it as an experimental farm. She developed these mushrooms as a potential crop."

"How do you know this?"

"Norbert, you forget that I am ten thousand years old. I know all kinds of things."

I looked at the small mountain in the middle of the island. "Do you think I could explore the jungle? Find out what else is here?"

"I wouldn't do that if I were you, Norbert. You remember that flash of red you saw earlier?"

"Yes."

"It is a lure for seabirds. The birds see the color and come to investigate. Once they land, their feet are stuck in a glue that some of the mushrooms excrete."

"What are you saying, Tyrmiss?" I said, trying to suppress a laugh. "Are you saying there are carnivorous mushrooms on this island?"

"Exactly, Norbert. Another of the Goddess's experiments. I suggest you walk into the ocean and bathe in the salty water. It will kill any spores you've picked up. I don't think the goddess is ready for these experimental mushrooms to start taking root on other islands."

Across the wide sea, an island rose in shimmering violet light. As we drew closer, I could see the color came from the fronds of tall ferns that grew over the entire island. In the tops of the ferns, there was a flock of strange birds. Each had a bright yellow beak, and a single red feather grew from its head, pointing at the sky. And then the birds began singing a rich and complex symphony. One of the birds kept time by pecking a tree trunk, and others supplied counterpoint and bass lines. I sat down on a log and listened.

"What is this place?" I asked.

"This is Fiară." Tyrmiss answered. "It is an island where the Goddess Nilene comes to amuse herself. She whimsically changes animals and plants to suit her mood, then changes them back to their natural form before she leaves. It is, I suppose, a form of meditation for her."

As Tyrmiss and I sat on the beach, animals appeared. We saw a purple deer, a two- headed tiger and a six-footed horse.

"Since the animals are in whimsical form, does this mean that the goddess is here now?" I asked.

"Oh yes, she is on the island now."

"Is she visible?"

"Only if she chooses to be. She can take any form. She might be a tree, or a rock, or one of the whimsical animals in front of us. Or she may be invisible, taking the form of the wind."

"May I speak to her?"

"Of course."

I fell to my knees, closed my eyes and said, "Dear Goddess Nilene whom I've served my entire life, thank you for all your gifts. Please give me wisdom to understand what you require of me and patience to accept your will."

I sat in silence a while longer, feeling at peace. It was the first time I had felt serenity since I'd left my farm two months before.

On our way to the next island in the archipelago, Tyrmiss flew close to the water, grabbed a swordfish close to the surface and carried it to a rocky cliff. She lay the gasping fish on a large flat stone, killed it with a single talon to the brain and breathed fire. Soon the fins and gills were crispy. Other than the bite of mushroom on Melehune Island, I hadn't eaten since returning from the underworld the day before, and my stomach gurgled with anticipation. Tyrmiss sliced a filet from the side of the fish and gestured for me to help myself. I picked up the warm fish with my fingers and took a bite. I chewed and swallowed. Immediately, I thought of the piles of flesh Mannie had served us, and my stomach started boiling. I vomited up the fish and sat down, feeling dizzy.

Tyrmiss looked at me with concern. I could feel her probing my mind. "Ah," she said. "It may be quite a while before you can eat flesh again. Lord Death really made you face your own crimes, didn't he?"

"It wasn't just the banquet of flesh, Tyrmiss. The whole experience made me aware of how I've lived my life. I need to become a different person, I think."

"Perhaps not a different person, Norbert. Perhaps just a better person. Tessia has had a similar awakening."

"Has she?" I asked. "I haven't had a chance to talk with her since we got back."

"It's going to take a long time for both of you to learn how to live in a way that fits your new knowledge. In the meantime, you may want to walk over to the tall grass behind you. There are some lovely seaberries you will like, and they should settle your stomach as well. I'm going to finish the rest of this swordfish."

After we'd eaten, we sat for a while in silence, enjoying the cool breeze coming from the salty sea.

"What's the name of this island?" I asked, noticing the profusion of grasses that grew between the rocks. The island rose to a low hill, but I couldn't see anything here other than rocks and grass.

"It's called Magičen Stolb," answered Tyrmiss.

"Is this another of the goddess's experiments?" I asked.

"Not exactly," she answered. "You probably know that magical power exists in fields that emanate from the earth's core, right?"

"Yes, I'm familiar with the theory."

"Well, this island is the southern pole of the magical field. This spot is exactly opposite to the Northern Magical Pole."

"This is the location of the Southern Magical Pole?" I looked around at the nondescript island. "This place is a source of powerful magic? I imagined it to be spectacular like a snow-capped peak or a giant magical wand, or something."

"No, this is the place. Go ahead, pull out your wand and cast a spell. But be careful. Your magic will be increased by tenfold."

I pulled out my wand, pointed it at a stone the size of my fist and, using the atlatl spell, threw it toward the horizon. The stone sped away, throwing sparks behind it like a shooting star.

"I said to be careful, Norbert."

"What are the limits of this power?"

"Well, let's test... what's the most powerful spell you know?"

"Changing one species into another species," I said without hesitation.

"All right," Tyrmiss said looking around at the gulls in the air and the barnacles on the rocks. "As an experiment, try turning one species into another."

I looked at Tyrmiss skeptically.

"There's no spell I know of where I could turn one species of animal into another so easily. To achieve this feat, the animal would need to eat the flesh of another animal that had already been transformed from a different species, and then I would have to say a whole series of incantations while hitting the exact harmonic sequence on my lyre. It's complicated. I can't just wave my wand to achieve a transformation of this kind."

"Norbert, the rules of magic are much looser on this island. You really can do just about anything you want."

Not believing her, I pointed my finger at Tyrmiss as a joke and intoned in an exaggerated oratorical voice, "Now you are a goat." A moment later, I was looking at a goat where Tyrmiss had been standing.

Frightened by my own power, I again pointed my finger and said, "Now you are a dragon."

And Tyrmiss was again standing in front of me. "Don't you ever use your magic on me again, Norbert!" She said, her eyes blood-red.

"I am so sorry, Tyrmiss," I said, truly surprised at the vast increase in my magical power. Previously, I had to train for days or weeks to learn a new spell, but on this island, all I had to do was point my wand and mutter a few words.

I sat down on a rock. "By the Holy Hem, I never knew such a place as this island existed."

"No one does, Norbert. At least no human does."

"Imagine if an evil wizard such as Ludek knew about this place. The harm he could do."

"Exactly. And that is why you must never tell anyone about this island. And there is something else you need to know…"

"What?" I dreaded hearing what the dragon was about to say.

"Now that you have been here, you have become part of the magical field that emanates from the earth. Your powers have been increased exponentially, Norbert, even after you leave this island."

A great fear started to rise in me like bile. "I don't want this power. I just want to live my life, love my woman, and serve my queen. I've witnessed the obscene horrors magic can cause. Why have you done this to me, Tyrmiss?"

"Because the Goddess has plans for you, Norbert. And great power can be trusted only to those who do not want it."

After I had time to adjust to my new power and try a few experiments to find out how it—and I—had changed, we were ready to leave the unremarkable-looking piece of rock in the bright blue sea and fly to our next destination which Tyrmiss said was not an island, but a place on the southern continent.

As we approached the coast, Tyrmiss raised her voice above the sound of the wind and shouted, "The people below have never encountered dragons and I don't want to alert them to my presence, so I'm flying high, just below the clouds."

From this height, people resembled fleas, and a huge city spread out below looked like a sandcastle built by children. It was the largest city I had ever seen, probably twenty times the size of Dragonja City. Tall buildings were topped by golden spires catching the sunlight. The streets were wide and crowded with people and wagons. Children played in the green open areas, and markets were filled with food and trade goods. And on the hill, a great castle rose, gates open wide and silver turrets topped by pennants. Beyond the city walls, orchards, fields and green pastures spread for leagues, and fishing boats and trading vessels dotted the sea.

"What is this place?" I shouted to Tyrmiss.

"It is called the city of Eolbiasor!" Tyrmiss shouted.

We flew in a circle high above the city, getting a good look, then flew to a rocky islet far off the coast where only seagulls lived.

"I wanted to show you Eolbiasor because it is what the Goddess Nilene wants Dragonja City to become, a place of peace and prosperity where people live in balance with nature and with each other. There is no poverty, no violence and no oppression."

"How do you know the Goddess wishes this?" I asked.

"Because She told me."

"You talked to her directly?"

"She visited me the other night when you were on your vision quest to the underworld, and then again last night when Tessia and I received our assignments."

I thought about what Tyrmiss had said for a moment and remembered the beautiful woman I had spoken to in my orchard months ago. "In what form did she come to you?"

"As I said before, the Goddess can take any form she pleases, but yesterday she came to me as a beautiful dragon with silver scales."

"Were you frightened when you saw Her?"

"Oh no, I felt completely at peace."

"What did She say to you?"

"She... explained things to me. Why I am here and what I must do."

"And what must you do, Tyrmiss? I ask because I feel baffled by my own life. I know I must return to Dragonja to tell Idella about Ena's death, but beyond that terrible duty I don't have the slightest idea of what I should do."

Tyrmiss was silent for what seemed a long time while I waited, listening to the waves lapping against the rocks at our feet. I looked at the far horizon and thought how the sea seemed infinitely large and inhospitable, and yet there were blessed isles where men and women lived their lives and found happiness.

Finally Tyrmiss said, "I don't know what the Goddess requires of you, Norbert. All I know is that She asked me to take you to see the three islands and the city of Eolbiasor. Perhaps She wanted you to see the possibilities that lay in front of you. The fact that your magical power has been greatly increased seems to indicate that She will be requiring large labors from you, but I don't know what they would be."

Baffled by all that I had seen and how little I understood, I sat on a seaweed-covered rock in the middle of the ocean, watching the seagulls wheel over my head, screeching in a language I was beginning to understand.

"There's one more thing we must do before we fly home, Norbert, so climb on my back."

We flew inland past the city of Eolbiasor and into the mountains. Far from any sign of human settlement, we landed on a ledge on the side of a peak. I pulled my cloak around me against the cold as a few snowflakes blew onto my face.

"This looks like the place the Goddess spoke of," Tyrmiss said, looking around. She seemed to be triangulating between this peak and two others nearby. She broke the crust of the snow with her talons and began to dig. Soon she uncovered the entrance to a cave, and when she had cleared a large enough space, she crawled into the opening. Since she was blocking the opening with her body, I waited, stepping away from her twitching tail for fear of being knocked off the ledge. Soon she emerged with an object held in her mouth which she gently laid at my feet. A dragon egg. She went into the cave and returned with another egg which she also gently placed in front of me.

"Norbert, if I brought you a small log, do you think you could carve it into a box with a lid?"

I nodded, struck dumb with the enormity of what lay in front of us. If these eggs were viable, then they represented the future of her species.

Tyrmiss flew off, spiraling down the cliff to the forest below.

She quickly returned with a pine log. I used a carving spell to hollow out the wood until I had a serviceable cradle the length of my arm. I brushed aside snow and filled the cradle with sand and gravel. I then carefully placed the two eggs in the box, closed it with a tight-fitting lid, and tied it shut with the tough vines that grew on the cliff.

"Tie the box on my back where Tessia usually sits, and you can sit behind it, making sure it doesn't fall," Tyrmiss said. "Let's go back to the Blessed Isle and show Tessia what we found."

Chapter Twenty-Six

After saying tearful goodbyes to Zygmunt and Wessel, we climbed on Tyrmiss's back. It was crowded with the cradle strapped where Tessia usually sat, Tessia where I usually was, and me on Tyrmiss's shoulders where I could feel the muscles beating below me in a rhythmic motion. But as long as Tyrmiss flew slowly, we could manage. We rose through the air and headed north over the mountains and into the valley. I looked back at the Blessed Isle slowly vanishing in the mist. After traveling hundreds of leagues by myself on Tyrmiss, it felt strange at first to be in this crowded arrangement, but I soon grew used to it. We followed the Iskar River between the mountain ridges and landed in late afternoon at the Round Keep where our friend Narrra lived with the other mimic sheep. Tyrmiss landed downriver, not wanting to frighten the sheep, and Tessia and I walked through the field of tiny oaks.

"Oh, my friends," Narrra said. "What a pleasure to see you! I hope you'll stay the night?"

"Thank you, Narrra," Tessia said. "We could use a rest."

We sat in the pasture and talked with Narrra. She told us that a pack of two headed dogs, no larger than squirrels, had come to the pasture, barking and trying to scare the sheep, but Narrra convinced her friends not to be afraid of the small dogs, and the sheep had chased them off.

"That was very heroic of you," Tessia said. "Sheep are naturally afraid of dogs, so it must have taken courage to confront them."

"Yes," Narrra said, "We are learning courage, but it is a difficult attitude to master, isn't it?"

She looked around, "Where is your daughter Ena and her friend Adamu? Did they decide to stay with their new friends?"

"No, Narrra," Tessia said, taking a quick look at me. "I'm afraid that Ena was killed by soldiers."

"Oh, no," the kind ewe said. "I'm so sorry to hear that. She seemed like such a wonderful young woman."

"Yes, she was," Tessia said. "Adamu decided to stay in Hoclav City and become a philosophy teacher."

"Oh, that's wonderful," Narrra exclaimed. "Pardon me for saying so, but humans aren't very wise, are they? Teaching philosophy is a noble endeavor, don't you think?"

"Oh, yes, certainly it is," Tessia said, glancing at me. I wondered whether she was coming around to appreciating philosophy.

Tessia had to carry the conversation with Narrra because I couldn't speak at all to her. I kept thinking of the last time we were here, and how much Ena had enjoyed being with the sheep. Narrra didn't try to draw me out, but let me simply sit in this peaceful place. Since neither Tessia nor I had been able to eat any kind of meat since our experience in the underworld, we were content to eat sweet clover and ewe's milk, the way lambs do.

From the Round Keep, we followed the Iskar River north to the place where the human settlements began. Here we turned east, keeping the switchback trail that leads through the pass between the Two Thumbs of the Giant below us until we came to the meadow near the cave where Hamlin the Bear lives. Hamlin greeted us with a nod of his head as he lay beside the stream watching the moving water. Tyrmiss had brought him a salmon and we walked through the magical illusion of rock and brush that disguised the entrance to his lair. Tyrmiss laid the fish on the flat cooking stone and braised it with her fiery breath. She then sliced open the fish and gave a piece to Hamlin. Out of courtesy, she offered to slice pieces for Tessia and me, but she knew we'd decline. Tyrmiss picked up the remainder of the fish and swallowed it whole. Hamlin noticed his two human guests hadn't eaten any fish, so he signaled that we should follow him. He led us to a blackberry patch where we ate our fill and then came back to the cave where we settled comfortably.

The bear looked at the three of us, then focused on Tessia, tilting his head questioningly, silently asking why Ena and Adamu were not with us.

"Ena was killed by soldiers. Adamu stayed in Hoclav City to be a teacher," Tessia said simply. It was becoming clear to both of us that this simple-hearted bear did not need the explanations that a human would. The simple fact that Ena was gone, having passed into the next life whatever it may be, was enough. I realized, as perhaps Tessia had as well, that the whole story was too much and not enough. A life is gone. Another begins. Such is the way of all things. But humans need, or at least want to know the progression of events that led to the passing. For us, words are necessary, but for bears fewer words are needed.

I caught Tessia's eye, and we left the cave together. We sat on a flat rock beside a stream, the very one where Rilla, Tyrmiss's wife for thousands of years, was speared through the heart by one of Ludek's Drekavac soldiers twenty years before. The evening light slanted through the trees, and the coolness of the air was pleasant on our faces. I sat and waited for Tessia to speak.

"Norbert," she began. "Yesterday when you and Tyrmiss were visiting the Southern Archipelago, the Goddess Nilene visited me again."

I sat up, suddenly alert. The numbness I'd felt all day was gone, and I was ready to listen.

"What form did she take?" I asked.

"She appeared to me as a warrior-woman, wearing a breast plate, greaves, and a helmet with a plume. She had a sword in a sheath on her belt, and she carried a spear. At first, I thought she was an assassin sent by my enemies, so I drew Agatha, but the Goddess held up Her hand, and said, 'Queen Tessia, rest assured I am not your enemy. Put your sword away. I am the Goddess Nilene,' she said. 'I have come to tell you what you need to know about the coming years and what you must do to save your people.'

"'Are my people in danger?' I asked.

"'Only from themselves,' she answered. 'The people of the Dragonja and Bekla valleys, the very ones you've been chosen to lead, have forgotten the Old Ways. They no longer burn incense in the temples. They no longer speak the truth to each other. Husbands strike their wives. Wives diminish their husbands. Children do not respect their elders. Shepherds let their sheep destroy the pastures. Farmers do not cart dung to their fields but use up the nourishment from past years. Fishermen catch more than the sea and rivers can sustain. People let their waste pollute the waters. No one has respect for the Old Ways of doing things, the habits and customs that allowed people to live without destroying what they hold in common.'

"'What must I do?' I asked.

"'You must be a queen to them,' she answered. 'In peacetime, you must lead by example, just as you do in war.'

"And then she left."

"What do you think she meant by 'lead by example' in peacetime?" I asked.

"I'm not sure, Norbert. But I know what it means to lead by example in war. It means I'm at the front of the attack. I'm the first over the wall, the first through the door, the first to engage. I'm the best warrior, showing the men how to fight. I never say 'Charge!' Instead, I say 'Follow me!'"

"And in peacetime, what does it mean to lead from the front?"

"It means I need to do what I expect the citizens to do. I need to provide an example for them to follow."

"And what is it that you expect the citizens to do, Tessia?"

"I'm not sure yet, but I want to turn Dragonja into a place like Eolbiasor, the city on the southern continent that Tyrmiss showed you. She explained to me it is a place of peace and prosperity." Tessia turned to me and added, "I asked Tyrmiss why she showed the city of Eolbiasor to you and not me. Why not both of us?"

"I wondered the same thing. What did Tyrmiss say?"

"She said that you were the one of vision and I was the one of action. You learn from dreaming while I learn from doing. She said I would need your imagination to build the new city."

She looked at me expectantly.

I laughed. "It's difficult to be imaginative on demand, Tessia."

"I know, Norbert," she said, smiling. "What does our city, our nation need?"

"The biggest problem in the city is poverty," I ventured. "Our nation is wealthy with rich farmlands up and down the Dragonja and Bekla river valleys, mines in the mountains producing copper. We have timberlands, fisheries and gamelands. Moreover, merchants bring gold, gems, purple earth and luxury items from other lands, trading them for our resources, making many of our citizens wealthy. Our metalsmiths, weavers and leather workers are the best in the world. And yet, despite all this wealth, many of our people—especially the Drekavacs—barely get by. Children go hungry and die of diseases that come from bad water and rotten food. Women die in childbirth. Men become desperate and turn to robbery to survive. The Drekavacs, in particular, are shut out of most trades, and landowners will not sell houses or farms to them. Most of the soldiers and guards are Drekavacs who have no other way to make a living, but they don't make enough money in the military to support a family."

"Are you saying I am trying to keep my subjects poor?" Tessia asked, her voice beginning to rise in anger.

"No, no," I hurriedly said, not wanting to offend my friend, but after I thought about it, I decided to explore the truth with her. "Well, actually, yes. We're all trying to maintain the status quo. You and me, as well as Heikum, Femke, Alaric, Kana, Idella and every one of our race benefits from the way things are. Drekavacs scrub our floors, clean our latrines, raise our children, wash our dishes, guard our homes, businesses, and temples, and we take their essential labor for granted. In fact, we actually expect them to be grateful for having paid work, never mind that the work is worth far more than what we pay them. Meanwhile, in the alleys of Dragonja City, their children are living on the garbage they find behind the homes of the well-to-do. In the alley behind the Silver Pony, I've seen children fighting with dogs over scraps of food."

"Norbert, this is the way things have been for a very long time. What can I do about it? My position is largely ceremonial. I gave my power to the Citizens Council twelve years ago, remember?"

"You actually have a great deal of power, Tessia. You are the queen. People look to you to set the example. You might start by paying your guards and your staff a higher wage."

"And where would I get the money for the pay raise? The Council has the power of the purse. They have to approve every cent I spend."

"We will have to convince the Council they should raise taxes on wealthy merchants and spend the money to give the poor a reasonable wage."

She laughed, "Heikum and the other merchants are not going to like this idea."

"No, but we can persuade Femke it's the right thing to do, and she'll convince Heikum, and he'll bring around the other merchants. Femke has a big heart, and the thought of suffering children moves her. More than once, I've seen her pass a loaf of bread or a cup of soup out the back door of the inn. In fact, before I met her, Idella's husband was ill, and she was desperate to feed her baby Alaric. Femke invited her into the Silver Pony kitchen, fed her and gave her a kettle of soup every day for months to take home to her family. And what a wonderful investment that was for the inn! For the price of a hundred bowls of soup, Femke made a lifelong friend who has stood beside Femke and Heikum countless times. This is what people don't see yet. If you feed a hungry person, then that person will help you later. By giving the Drekavacs a decent wage, we will turn them from desperate outsiders into productive citizens. We need to convince the merchants that helping the Drekavacs is good business."

"The Citizens Council will never approve this, you know."

"Then we will change the Citizens Council, Tessia." I considered our options. "As queen, you have the power to appoint a certain number of council members each year, right?"

"Yes, I do. I can appoint up to ten members each year," she answered carefully, seeing where I was going with this argument.

"And this means that you effectively have the power to remove members of the council in order to make room for new members?"

She nodded reluctantly. "If you are saying I should remove merchants and farmers from the council to make room for Drekavac soldiers and housecleaners, then I have to object. This kind of change would be disastrous for me."

"Why would it be disastrous?"

"Because the rest of the council would punish me by not approving my household budget, or even worse, by removing me from the throne."

"Don't be ridiculous, Tessia. The council is not going to remove you from the throne. You're very popular with the people. Besides, you're barely halfway through your second ten-year term."

"All right, Norbert, let's think through your plan. I get to appoint five men and five women to the council. The other forty-five men and forty-five women are elected by the citizens. How am I going to influence the council with those numbers working against me?"

"You have to give Drekavacs the right to vote."

"They already have the right to vote, but they choose not to exercise their vote. It's their own fault there are no Drekavacs on the council."

"In the constitution, Drekavacs are given the right to vote, and they are given full equality under the law, but in practice they are shut out of participation in government. There are no Drekavac judges, no Drekavac military officers, no Drekavac council members and no Drekavac merchants."

"There are actually two Drekavac military officers, Norbert. Lieutenant Tyrnox and Captain Ogloq," she corrected me firmly.

"Two officers out of how many?"

"There are over two hundred officers in the military and twenty-five in the guard."

"You've just proved my point, Tessia. Drekavacs are not given a chance to make a living in Dragonja."

"Drekavacs *are* allowed to vote," she insisted stubbornly.

"Again, Drekavacs have the theoretical right to vote, but if they try to practice that right, then they may find themselves dismissed from their jobs or even beaten by humans as an example to other Drekavacs. This is why there are no Drekavac council members."

"What am I supposed to do?" she asked, throwing up her hands.

"Station your guards at every polling station to protect their fellow citizens' right to vote."

"Oh, this is going to make me popular," she grumbled sarcastically.

"It will make you very popular among Drekavacs. And also among men and women of good will, such as Femke and Idella… and me."

"Drekavacs will vote only for Drekavacs, you know. We'll end up with a city run by them."

"Drekavacs will vote their own interests, of course. At first, they will vote only for citizens who look like them, but after a while, they'll start to see that some men and women can represent their interests as well."

"What about the council members who make a lot of noise, stirring up the people who hate Drekavacs?"

"Every year, you have the power to remove five men and five women from the council and appoint new members. So, at those times, you'll remove ten demagogues and replace them with Drekavacs of good character. The other council members will get the message: either go along with the reforms or lose their place on the council."

"Reforming the council and giving every Drekavac who works under me a pay raise… Norbert, those are two huge undertakings," Tessia pointed out. "Isn't there something simpler that I could do to improve the city?"

"Of course."

"What is it?"

"We should stop calling half of the citizens of the city 'Drekavacs.' The name is demeaning to them. The name 'Drekavac' refers to mythical ghouls who live in the far north."

"What should we call them?"

"We should call them what they call themselves—Minmissian. They originally came from the far north, the Minmissian Ice Sheet. As you know from the old songs, the Minmissian people originally migrated here through the mountains until they came to the fertile valleys of the Iskar and Dragonja rivers. There was a war between them and our ancestors. We won. The Minmissians who were captured became slaves. Now they make up the bottom class of our society. It's time to accept them as full citizens and stop making them pay for the transgressions of their ancestors."

"Minmissians," Tessia said, trying out the word. "Alright, I can do that. As for fighting the Citizens Council..." She laughed. "You know I've never shied away from a fight."

We sat for a while, watching the braids of the stream as it flowed through the meadow.

"Are you afraid of bringing the news to Idella about Ena's death?" Tessia asked.

"Yes, I'm afraid the news will destroy her, and I'm afraid she will hate me for not protecting our daughter."

"At least she has you and Alaric to comfort her in grief."

"A husband and a son can do little to assuage a mother's grief, I'm afraid."

Chapter Twenty-Seven

When we got back to Hamlin's cave, I caught Tyrmiss's eye and realized she had been listening to the conversation between Tessia and me. I could hear Hamlin snoring in the back chamber.

"I like the fact that you've taken up the cause of the... *Minmissians,* Norbert," Tyrmiss said. "I've always found it puzzling that human society was divided into two classes, with one class getting almost all the benefits of society and the other class getting virtually nothing."

"People have become so accustomed to taking the Minmissians for granted that we don't question the justice of the situation," I replied, glancing at Tessia who was still settling into the idea we were going to try to make the kingdom fairer to the Minmissians.

After a while, Tessia said, "I hate politics."

Tyrmiss gave a deep chuckle and responded, "Of course you do, my dear. Any honest idealistic person hates politics because it is all about maneuvering and compromising. You like battle because it is straightforward: the best fighter wins the bout; the best tactician wins the battle, and the best strategist wins the war. Politics, on the other hand, is rarely straightforward. Words nudge and prod. People ignore you unless you appeal to their own interests which they rarely admit to. Politicians speak in lofty terms, but they're often lying about their motives. I'm afraid you and Norbert will have to educate yourselves quickly in the art of persuasion and the science of extortion." She laughed. "I'm glad I won't be here to see the many mistakes you make, but you'll learn how to make democracy work for all the people, not just the privileged."

"You're going back to the new dragon village in the mountains?" Tessia asked.

"Yes, I will first go back to deliver the eggs to the care of the mother-dragons."

"And then, you'll come back here?" Tessia asked hopefully.

"No, actually I'm going to Hoclav City," Tyrmiss responded.

"Hoclav City?" Tessia exclaimed. "You can't go back there. They'll kill you on sight."

"Perhaps they will at that," Tyrmiss said, smiling. "But only if they see me. I've learned a great deal about war from you, Tessia. Thank you for being my teacher."

"You want revenge for the death of the dragonlings," I said. It wasn't a question.

Tyrmiss thought for a moment and finally said, "When my beloved Rilla died at the hands of a soldier, I wanted revenge. Frankly, I went insane and started ambushing Ludek's Drek—sorry, *Minmissian*—soldiers. I loved swooping down on them at night when they were camped, frying them in their armor. I am ashamed to say I even nibbled the flesh of a few of them, tasting their blood. But later, when I learned more about the world of men, I realized individual soldiers were mostly innocent. I learned that humans are not like dragons. You remember when the dragons decided to go to war? Every adult had to agree before we could take action. Humans are different because they have leaders who make the important decisions, and then each individual in the tribe or kingdom has an obligation to obey. I find this quality of humans quite bizarre. You have a sophisticated brain, a mind capable of subtle thought, and many languages that can express beautiful sentiments; and yet, when it comes to politics, most humans give up their ability to think, to make distinctions, to weigh alternatives, and simply choose a leader and obey him or her."

"You plan to assassinate King Beyazit?" I asked.

"*Assassinate* is such an ugly word, Norbert. I prefer to think of it as *pest control*."

"What will be your strategy?" Tessia asked. I suspected that she wasn't just professionally curious but had an agenda.

Tyrmiss looked at her friend and smiled. There was no hiding anything from her. "No, Tessia, you will not be coming with me."

"But you will need my help," Tessia insisted.

"Yes, at times I will miss your proficiency with Agatha and your brilliant grasp of strategy," Tyrmiss replied. "As well as your skill with a wand, Norbert. But you both have your tasks to do. Bringing justice to your own kingdom is a noble quest, my friends. Perhaps practicing politics is not as much fun as slicing off heads and throwing fireballs, but nevertheless, you are needed in Dragonja. The two of you are destined to be remembered as the greatest monarch and the most revered wizard in the long history of the kingdom. And this greatness will not be achieved by slaughtering foreigners, but by bringing justice to your people and finding harmony with nature. You have much work to do."

"What will be your strategy, my friend?" Tessia asked again, her tone showing that she was not planning to fight beside Tyrmiss, but rather she was concerned about Tyrmiss's safety.

"Not to worry, Queen Tessia. My strategy is sound. I will hide in the mountains overlooking Hoclav City. King Beyazit will have to emerge from the keep at some point, and when he does, I will swoop down, snatch him and one of his retainers and fly back to the mountains. There I will make the retainer watch while I pull each tentacle off the king. It will be a long slow death. Then I will tell the retainer he will be allowed to return to the city to report to the citizens that the king was punished for ordering the attack on the dragons. From now on, humans will not molest dragons, and in return, dragons will not molest humans. If a human does harm a dragon, then the human will be killed and the monarch who let it happen will be tortured to death. They should tell their children and their children's children to stay away from dragons on pain of death, and the monarchs of Hoclav will be held responsible for enforcing this law."

"What about the Dragon Way?" I asked. "What will the Goddess Nilene think of your plan to slay kings and queens who harm dragons?"

"Actually, Norbert," Tyrmiss said quietly. "The Goddess came to me while you two were in the underworld. She was horrified by the attack on the dragonling nursery. She wants humans to understand they are not the only species on the earth, and they must respect her creation. Also, it seems that she and the other gods think Beyazit is an abomination. His mother the demi-god Thortia is a niece of Nilene's and the old she-crab has always been troublesome. It seems Thortia allowed herself to be seduced by a giant octopus renowned for his foreplay and, as a result, gave birth to Beyazit. She used her influence over the priests of Hoclav to give her son the crown, thinking it would keep him out of trouble. Humans need to learn they should *never* give a sadistic narcissist power over others. Nilene will be glad to be rid of Beyazit."

Tessia and I were silent for a few moments while we recalled Nilene and Mannie's extensive family and their odd appetites.

"What is a *narcissist*?" I asked, but the dragon simply rolled her blue eyes.

"Do you think the strategy will work?" Tessia asked, bringing our attention back to the issue at hand. "Will the dragons be safe from now on?"

"I imagine it will work for a few generations, and then some young fool who wants to prove himself a mighty warrior will search out the dragons and try to kill one of us."

"And what will you do then?" I asked.

"I will have to kill the young warrior, of course, and then I will have to search out the monarch, whoever he or she is at that time, and give the monarch a slow painful death like the one that Beyazit will receive."

"You're planning to hold leaders responsible for what their subjects do?" Tessia asked, obviously horrified at the thought that she might be punished for a foolish act by one of the citizens of Dragonja.

"Yes, my dear, I plan to hold leaders responsible. It has become clear to me that the only way humans will stop making war is if the leaders have to pay the consequences of their violent polices. As long as we have kings and queens who use their soldiers as playthings rather than as living beings, and who suffer no consequences for their horrific actions, then humans will have war. Let's punish a few monarchs for their soldiers' war crimes, and then we'll see a period of peace."

"Not many people will want to ascend the throne in that case," Tessia grumbled.

"Not true, my dear queen, not true," Tyrmiss responded. "Human ambition has no limits. Not even fear of a horrible death will keep people from wanting to rise to the top of society. You really are a strange species. Dragons have no political ambition. One of us might want to be leader because he or she has a vision, and the other dragons listen to the song and decide if they want to go in the direction the vision foretells. Dragons have no instinct that makes us want to rise above others. We become leaders not because we want to feel more important than others; instead, we become leaders because we feel a need to serve. Humans, on the other hand, have an instinct to dominate others; in human society, being a leader is not a chance to serve, but rather an opportunity to feel important."

Tyrmiss was silent a moment, then shook her head slowly and said, "I don't understand how your kind has survived as long as it has. You consume and destroy. You dominate and control. You deprive children of the basic necessities of life if they are the offspring of others. It is different with dragons. The young ones of the tribe are cared for and protected by all the adults, not just their parents. I feel…"

Tyrmiss grew silent, put her head down on her talons and wept. I knew she was grieving for the dragonlings killed by soldiers. After a while, she said, wearily, "The Goddess must have been having a very bad day when she created humans."

Tessia and I exchanged a look, both of us reluctant to tell our dragon friend what Liatris had revealed: humans are a cross between Lord Death and a monkey.

Epilogue: The Orchard

The next day, we packed our kits and said goodbye to Hamlin. Tessia hugged him around the thick ruff of his neck. He held up his wide paw to me, and I held it for a moment, and he and Tyrmiss nodded to each other. Tessia and I climbed on Tyrmiss's back behind the cradle. We lifted into the air, banked toward the city in the valley below and Tyrmiss shot like an arrow toward Dragonja. She landed on the flat roof of Windkeep, and Tessia and I clambered off, leaving the cradle with the precious eggs tied to Tyrmiss's neck. Tessa put her arms around the dragon's neck and held her a long time.

"I will never forget you, Tyrmiss," she said.

"And no one will ever forget you, Your Majesty," Tyrmiss replied. "I won't let them."

"Where will you go after you take care of your business with King Beyazit?" I asked.

"I'll return to the new dragon village. I hunger to be with my own kind. Rilla and I had a lovely life in the mountains above Dragonja, but without her, I've been very lonely. I need to raise my daughter among other dragons, so she can learn who she is and how she can serve the Old Way. Raising her among humans would do her a terrible injustice."

Tyrmiss's eyes filled with tears. "I'm grateful to both of you, Tessia and Norbert. You taught me that humans can be kind. Not all humans are greedy and murderous." Then, she added, "Only some of them."

I checked the cradle, making sure it was still securely tied, then nodded to Tyrmiss. She spread her wings, took a few steps, leaped off the roof of the keep, dropped a few feet and started climbing into the air. We watched her bank toward Hamlin's pass, and from there she would fly directly over the mountains to reach the new dragon village. The grandmother dragons would be thrilled to have two new dragon eggs to care for. I guessed Tyrmiss would rest a few days, spending time with her daughter Rozae, and then fly to the mountains above Hoclav City where she would wait for the king to make an appearance.

"Will we ever see her again?" I asked.

"I don't think so," Tessia answered. "She's had quite enough of the affairs of humans."

"Wait a moment," Tessia said as we stood at the top of the stone stairs on the outside of the keep. "What are we going to tell our friends and family?"

"What do you mean?"

"Well," Tessa looked out over the city. "If we tell people we went into the underworld and met Lord Death, people will think we're insane."

"Don't you think that Idella deserves to know where her daughter is?"

Tessia looked at the ground, shifting her feet. This was one of the few times, I had ever seen Tessia acting indecisive. "Norbert, I'm beginning to wonder whether it actually happened. Could it have been a dream?"

"A dream we shared?"

"We've joined our minds before through Tyrmiss. Couldn't the whole quest have been a shared hallucination?"

"Then how do you explain Adamu suddenly appearing, right as rain and ready to go to Hoclav to become a teacher?"

"I can't explain it," Tessia said. "I just don't want to tell a tale that makes me look foolish. As queen, I can't afford to appear..."

"Impractical? Silly? Irrational?"

"Exactly."

"Alright. We won't tell the tale right away, but someday I'll write a song about it."

"Thank you, Norbert."

I dreaded going home to tell Idella about Ena's death, so I gave in to my cowardice and stopped at the Silver Pony to see my old friends, vaguely thinking they could give me advice about how to break the news to my wife. Heikum was behind the bar, washing tankards and getting ready for the evening rush of customers.

"By the Holy Hem!" He shouted. "If it isn't the Green Mage himself!"

He came from behind the bar and gave me a bear hug, his salt and pepper beard brushing my cheek. "Femke!" He called to his wife. "See what the troll dragged in!"

Femke bustled out from the kitchen, wiping her hands on her apron. "Oh, thank the Goddess, we heard you were dead! Travelers brought news of great battles in the west. Dragons and flaming arrows and such. And two mighty wizards were killed." She looked around the room and looked back at me with a worried look in her eyes. "Where is Ena?" She asked, her eyes wide with concern.

When I looked down, unable to answer, she said, "Oh no, not dear Ena." And she grabbed the edge of the bar to steady herself. Heikum went to her, took his wife in his thick arms, and they stood together, her face on his shoulder as she sobbed. Heikum cast a sidelong look at me, his eyes filling with tears.

"And her friend Adamu? Did he make it back?" he asked. I told them that Adamu had decided to stay in Hoclav to work as a teacher.

Femke nodded, somewhat relieved but unable to speak.

"How did it happen?" Heikum asked in a hoarse voice.

"Soldiers were trying to wipe out the race of dragons," I said, quietly. "Ena died defending the nursery."

"Ena died defending baby dragons?" Femke asked. "Oh, how much like her that is."

"Ena is dead?" I heard a familiar voice from the stairway behind me. I turned, and my wife Idella was halfway down the stairs. She was still as a statue. Her beautiful black face was immobile. I went to her, held out my arms to her. But instead of hugging me as I expected, she punched me hard in the face, a roundhouse blow that knocked me down the stairs. I lay on the floor, shocked at her violence. I had never seen her strike anyone before.

"You didn't protect our daughter?" She snarled, her teeth showing. "You let Ena die? You promised you would protect her."

"I, I, I didn't know. I mean I tried, but…" I stammered.

Idella walked past me through the inn and out the front door. Heikum and Femke watched her leave, then turned to me in utter horror at our shattered lives.

Thinking Idella didn't want to see me, I stayed the night at the Silver Pony in my old room upstairs. I didn't sleep, but spent the night staring at the ceiling, thinking about my mistake of leaving Ena and Adamu in the dragon village. She should have been with me and Tessia where we could have protected her. Idella was right to hate me.

The next morning, I went downstairs and sat at a table. Femke gave me a cool wet rag to place on my black eye and placed a bowl of soup and a thick slice of bread in front of me.

"It's best you eat, Norbert," she said gently. "You'll be needing to go out to your house and talk with Idella today."

"It was pretty clear yesterday she never wants to see me again." I said. "And I don't blame her. I'm responsible for our daughter's death."

"Nonsense," Femke said, sitting down next to me and patting my hand. "Ena was a grown woman who knew she was going to fight in a war, and quite a vicious one from what we heard. You and Tessia could have been killed as well. You all took your chances. You're not responsible for what the soldiers did."

I had a flash of memory of seeing Ena's ravaged body, and I started sobbing. Femke sat with me, holding my hand and making soothing noises. After a while, I gained control of myself and took a few bites of bread and soup.

Tessia came into the inn, followed by her bodyguard, a Minmissian sergeant named Splunk who stationed himself at the back of the room with his hand on the pommel of his Voprian sword. Tessia hugged her old friend Femke, then sat beside me.

"I just want to let you know, Norbert, I visited Adamu's father and told him his son distinguished himself as a hero in the war, defending baby dragons from soldiers. And I told him Adamu had decided to stay in Hoclav to become a teacher. I doubt the old man will ever see his son again. So, I hope what I said gave him some solace."

She and I exchanged a conspiratorial look, having agreed not to tell anyone about our trip to the underworld. Who would believe us anyway? Tessia stared into space for a moment, thinking no doubt about all the things we couldn't tell our friends, and then coming back to herself, she noticed my eye was swollen.

"Did you tell Idella about Ena?"

I nodded. "She didn't take it well."

"She gave you that shiner?"

I raised my hand to my eye. It was starting to hurt, but I hadn't noticed. The deeper pain had distracted me.

"By the hem of the Goddess, she really slugged you, didn't she? Do you have a place to stay?" Tessia offered. "You can stay in Windkeep if you want to."

"No, I'm staying here at the inn until Idella takes me back—*if* she takes me back."

"Oh, Laddie," Heikum said from behind me, having returned to his customary position behind the bar. "She just needs time to get over it. Give her a few days, then you can go home."

Femke glared at her husband fiercely. "You men have no idea what is going on, do you?"

Heikum looked confused but was experienced enough to stay silent.

"Idella doesn't need to be alone. She needs to be with the people who love her," Femke said, nodding her head emphatically.

"But, but," I stammered. "She hit me. Hard. In the eye."

"Oh, you've had worse blows than that, I'm sure," Femke rolled her eyes. "You're just getting back from a war after all." She looked me up and down, sizing me up. "When did Ena die?"

"About five weeks ago," I said.

"Granted, you haven't had very long to grieve, but remember, for Idella the grief has barely begun. You need to be beside her now… And what about the two of you?" Femke said, looking from me to Tessia. "Were either of you wounded?"

Tessia said, "I had a wound on my thigh, but it's almost healed now."

"And you, Norbert?" Femke glanced up and down my body.

I shook my head—quickly, and perhaps wisely, deciding not to announce that I was under a charm from the forest essence Spyte, and I was also one of the favorites of Lord Death himself because I had sent so many souls to him. I knew I could never tell anyone, especially not Idella, that Ena had died in a war in which I was completely protected from injury. I felt ashamed I had accompanied two young people into a very dangerous situation while being immune to risk myself. But how could I have known? In fact, the worst wound I'd ever experienced was the black eye Idella had given me the day before. I realized then that the anger of a grieving mother represents a life force more powerful than even the strongest charm.

Femke got up and started packing a bag.

"Where are you going?" I asked.

"I'm going to your farmhouse, Norbert. And you and Tessia are coming with me. Heikum, you stay here and mind the inn." Femke looked at Tessia and said, "Please send one of your *Minmissian* guards to Windkeep to ask Princess Kana to come to Idella and Norbert's farm. Idella needs her. And tell the princess we're bringing food. She'll know what to do."

I'd been gone only a few months, but it seemed much longer, so I was surprised that almost nothing had changed since I last saw our farm. The grass in the pasture was taller; the apple and cherry orchards, in bloom when I left, now bore rich fruit, and the walnut and almond were almost ready for harvest, but it seemed a normal summer day, one of many I'd spent here. Our house, with its yellow thatched roof and wide windows with open shutters, had never looked more beautiful. But I was afraid I had lost this life, that my carelessness had brought an end to all this bounty.

Idella stood in the open doorway wearing a white dress that set off her flawless black skin. As I came closer, she opened her arms wide and pulled me close. She whispered in my ear, "I am so sorry."

Idella looked at my swollen eye, and said, "I didn't realize I hit you so hard, husband. Does it hurt?"

"Not anymore," I said, taking her hand. Her eyes were red and swollen from crying.

Tessia signaled Sergeant Splunk to stand outside while the rest of us came into the house where Princess Kana was setting the table with silverware.

"Can you tell me what happened to our daughter?" Idella asked quietly sitting beside me, her hand on my arm.

"We were betrayed. King Beyazit of Hoclav called for a

parlay, and we agreed to meet, but fearing an ambush we sent our best warriors, including Tyrmiss, Tessia and me, to meet with the enemy. While we were gone, his forces attacked the dragon village. Ena died defending the baby dragons."

"And Adamu?" She asked.

"Adamu was wounded badly and we thought he was dead, but he recovered and decided to stay in Hoclav City to be a teacher." Despite my promise to Tessia to stay silent about our dream quest, I felt a strong urge to tell my wife everything.

"So, Adamu was almost killed as well," Idella mused, shaking her head sadly. "It was so like the two of them to try to protect the babies." I realized this was the same thing that Femke had said. The two young people would be remembered as heroes—a small comfort, but right now in our deep grief it was all we had. Actually, this was not true, I thought, Idella and I had each other. And we had Alaric, our son. And we had our friends.

"I'm so sorry I allowed this to happen, Idella," I said. "We suspected the parlay was a trap, but we didn't realize what the ultimate goal of the king was."

"And what was his ultimate goal?" My wife asked.

"To exterminate dragons permanently," Tessia interjected. "You need to know that Norbert was in no way to blame. If anyone was to blame for Ena's death, it was me. I misjudged the situation and left the village vulnerable to attack. Don't blame Norbert. He was not in charge of strategy."

Idella looked at me with tears in her eyes and said, "I know it was not your fault. I'm so sorry my first response was to blame you. And striking you," she lifted her hand and gently touched my sore eye, "was a horrible thing to do. We have never intentionally hurt each other in the past. It is I who need forgiveness, not you, dear husband."

"Of course, my love," I said and bent forward to kiss her, tears of relief coming to my eyes.

"Are you two needing a bed now, or are you going to eat

first?" Femke asked, and we all laughed. She put the pot of stew on the table in front of us. "This is a vegetable stew," she said looking at me. Tessia must have told her we couldn't eat meat anymore. I wondered what she'd told Femke about why we no longer consumed flesh. My mind flashed back to the pile of butchered corpses on Lord Death's dining table.

"I was thinking—hoping actually—Norbert would come by today and bring friends—" Idella said.

"Well, actually, we're here as Norbert's bodyguards," Tessia said, in mock seriousness. "That roundhouse punch you gave him made me realize he was in serious danger coming back here."

"All those years of kneading bread has given Idella a pair of arms like a wrestler's," Femke said, pointing at Idella's muscular forearms.

We all laughed. Suddenly my eye stopped hurting, and I felt better than I'd felt since Ena died.

"Alright, stop it. You're embarrassing me," Idella said, rolling her eyes. "I promise not to attack anyone, or at least not until after we've eaten. The stew smells delicious, and I've baked loaves of fresh bread and a dessert of cherry pastry. And our dear friend the princess has brought lovely place settings."

Idella smiled at Princess Kana who was dressed in a cotton blouse and a long skirt like Femke and Idella. Unlike her predecessor, the princess was a woman of the people, but she wasn't above providing simple elegance when it was called for. Each place at the long table was set with a linen napkin, a finely carved wooden bowl, a bronze chalice and cutlery embossed with gold.

At our table, the balance between the elegant and the commonplace seemed right and natural.

Idella looked at the door. "Oh my, Tessia, is your guard still outside? Please invite him in. There's plenty of food for everyone."

I could see that Idella had put aside her grief for the moment.

Later, after everyone had left, she and I would hold each other and weep.

We feasted, and when we'd had our fill, Sergeant Splunk looked at Tessia with his gray eyes, and she signaled him with a tilt of her head to go outside and keep an eye on things. As the soldier stood, bowed to Tessia and Kana and walked out the door, I wondered how long it was going to take Tessia to feel safe again after many weeks of being alert. The few days of our last stay on the Blessed Isle had not been long enough for her to let down her fear of imminent attack.

I, on the other hand, was feeling relaxed if not quite happy. I'd had over a month, as well as a trip to the underworld, to grieve for Ena, but I knew it would take much longer for Idella. She always felt things more deeply than I. She had a heart as wide as a continent and as deep as an ocean. I knew it wouldn't be difficult to recruit Idella and Femke in the peaceful struggle to bring equality to the Minmissians. These tall, pale, strangely beautiful people would need our help at first, but later, they would carry on the struggle without us.

After we ate, we took our wine into the garden behind the house to sit on the stone benches where we entertained guests in fine weather. From there, in the shade of an ancient oak, we had a lovely view of the orchards and the distant hills. I noticed a tall familiar figure approaching.

"Alaric is coming," Tessia noted. She had probably noticed him before I did. As my stepson came closer, I could see a broad smile on his dark face, which was so much like his mother's, and like her, his eyes were clouded with sadness. He hugged his mother, then embraced me and welcomed me home. He bowed his head before his queen who acknowledged him, and he gave Femke, who was like an aunt to him, a big hug. He acknowledged the salute of Sergeant Splunk and bade him to be at ease.

"There's something I need to tell you, Alaric," I said.

He waved his hand in courteous dismissal. "I heard about

Ena," he acknowledged, trying to save me the pain of telling him the terrible news.

I thought, *of course he's heard.* My stepson is head of Tessia's guard, her first advisor on security and defense, and he's the former head of her intelligence service. Tessia would have briefed him on the death of Ena shortly after we arrived home. Sometimes I forget he's not the gangly adolescent I met over twenty years earlier when Tessia and I arrived in Dragonja City and his mother was struggling to get her bakery started.

His mother looked at him sharply. "You knew about Ena, and you didn't tell me?"

"Mother," he said, gently. "There were rumors a week ago about two mages being killed in the war between dragons and humans on the west coast, but I didn't know whether the travelers who related the rumors were reliable, and besides, I didn't know who might have been killed." Alaric glanced at me, and I realized he had assumed I was dead, just as Femke and Heikum had. I also realized that none of them wanted to repeat the rumor to Idella until they had more information.

There was a long awkward silence, and then Femke raised her glass and said, "We are glad to have Queen Tessia and Mage Norbert home. Long may they live!"

I raised my glass in the toast, but I thought for the thousandth time I would have infinitely preferred for Ena to have survived and for me to have died, but such things are not for mortals to decide.

Idella raised her glass and gave a big smile, then her face broke, and she dropped her wine glass which broke as it hit the bench beside her. Red wine splattered on her white dress. She looked down at the red stain and started sobbing. Femke and Kana went to her. Femke wrapped her arms around Idella and let her sob on her shoulder uncontrollably. Kana stroked Idella's back and murmured softly to her.

After a few moments, Idella calmed down and said she'd

like to walk in the orchard. "It's so pretty this time of year," she said, regaining her composure. The three women walked into the apple orchard, the branches over their heads crowded with fruit. Femke had her arm around Idella's shoulder, and Kana had her arm around Idella's waist.

"I feel I should go with them," Tessia said uncertainly.

"Go with them if you want to," I said. "But it looks like Femke and Kana are giving Idella what she needs."

Tessia looked at the three wise women walking away from us, light and shadow playing over their receding forms. "I've never been very good at comforting people," she said wistfully. "Just at killing them..." She bowed her head in shame. "Norbert, after all we've done and seen, what are we going to do? We are not the same people we were."

"Well, you know you did promise Mannie a temple in his honor," I said.

"Yes, I know, Norbert. I was thinking we could build the temple right here in this grove next to your house," she said, looking at me earnestly.

"Oh no, Tessia," I burst out. "No, no, no. Idella would never allow a temple to Lord Death on our farm, and if you went ahead and did it over her objections, she would find a way to blame me."

Tessia laughed. "Relax, Norbert, I was joking. Actually, I was thinking we'd build the temple half a day's walk south of here, a place between the road and the river. The soil is rocky there, so no one farms the land, and limestone and granite can be quarried nearby for building material. What do you think?"

Relieved, I said, "It sounds like a lovely spot." After a long pause, I took a slow deep breath and said, "Tessia, I think we need to tell Idella about Ena. It would give her comfort to know where she is."

I glanced at Alaric who was paying close attention to the two of us. "What about my sister? She's not dead? Where is she?" He asked, urgently.

Tessia took a deep breath and said, "We saw her. Your father and I went into the underworld and talked with her."

"What?" Alaric exclaimed. "You went into the underworld? How?"

"Son, let's wait until your mother is ready, and then we'll tell the whole story. Everything that happened. Perhaps you and the others can stay for dinner, and afterwards Queen Tessia and I can tell all of you at the same time."

Tessia and I had agreed never to tell anyone about our trip to the underworld, but now we'd blurted it out. At first, I regretted telling Alaric, then I settled back, resigned to the new course of action. Of course, we'd have to tell our friends and families what had happened to us. They needed to know Ena was still alive. How could we keep it from them?

Alaric, like the shrewd street kid he'd once been, nodded, sat back and waited. Tessia and I were the two most powerful people in the kingdom, and he must have been curious to see how our quest had changed us. Alaric was thirty-one now, and his gift for sizing up a situation quickly was gradually turning into a practical wisdom, much like his queen's.

"General," Tessia said, using Alaric's formal rank. "What is the state of the kingdom?"

Alaric looked out at the distant hills, formulating an answer. "Your Majesty," he said slowly. His voice was deeper now, more resonant. He was no longer speaking to his parents' friend Tessia, but to the Dragonqueen, his sovereign, and I had the impression he'd rehearsed this report and now delivered it with appropriate formality.

"Fourteen years ago, when you and my father returned from a campaign, you found the kingdom in chaos and rebellion, but the current welfare of the city could not be more different.

"Princess Kana has enacted her duties as regent with a gentle diligence that has made people love her, and all modesty aside, I've kept the soldiers trained and ready while making sure guards enforced the laws supported by just and efficient courts. The farms and pastures outside the city walls are green and productive. The roads are safe for travelers, and the Blue Witches have made progress in reforesting the Dry Hills. I send guards out on patrol, and they report that the kingdom seems peaceful and prosperous."

Tessia nodded with quiet satisfaction at Alaric's answer. However, having spent time with the Western Dragons and learning something of their philosophy, and having traveled to the underworld and facing my own violent past, and having seen the city of Eolbiasor and catching a glimpse of what our city could be, I felt an unease at the unfulfilled promise of Dragonja.

As we had walked through the city from the Silver Pony to my farm, I had noticed the alleys were still filled with the poor—mostly Minmissian children dressed in rags and thin as twigs. I thought of what the shade of Zrul had told me about the harsh and perverse lessons he'd learned growing up in desperate poverty. As if for the first time, I'd seen young Minmissian men standing around the marketplace with nothing to do but pass wineskins among themselves, avoiding the glances of disapproving citizens who hurried past them fearfully. And outside the city walls, there were encampments of refugees who had fled wars, droughts and floods only to discover they were unwelcome here. As we'd crossed the bridge outside the city, I saw a young mother and her small children drinking water from a river polluted by human and animal waste. I saw the tree stumps of denuded forests climbing the hills and mountain sides, and the smoke that hung over the city from cookstoves and fireplaces.

And now, Tessia, Alaric and I sat together, quietly waiting for Idella and her friends to return. But watching the three women standing under a walnut tree, talking earnestly, I realized it would take a while before they came back to us, so I decided to share what I'd been thinking since Tyrmiss had shown me the city of Eolbiasor.

"Your Majesty," I said. "You asked what we are going to do, having been changed by our experiences? Here's the answer. We will devote ourselves to the people of this kingdom. We are going give them what they need."

After an expectant pause, Alaric asked, "And what is it that the people need, Father?"

Tessia looked at me, "Tell me, Mage, where do we start?"

"We start by giving justice to the people. The Minmissian people have been treated as if they're guard dogs and beasts of burden for hundreds of years. We need to give them the opportunity to make a decent living and to be treated with equality under the law as our constitution guarantees," I answered.

"The native Beklans are not going to like it," Alaric said. "They'll resist reform, fearing that anything that the Drek—the *Minmissians* gain will come at the expense of the Beklans."

I noticed that my son, quick to pick up cues, had corrected himself and from now on would use the preferred name for the Minmissians.

"They certainly will, but if the Beklans see that new opportunities are being given on the basis of merit, with neither race being favored, then the Beklans will eventually accept the new policies. We can start with your purview, Alaric. You are head of both the military and the city guard. Are there Minmissians who are qualified to be officers, but have been passed over?"

Alaric nodded his head. "I've long thought that since the forces are staffed mostly by Minmissians, it doesn't make sense to have almost entirely Beklan officers. It would improve morale for the soldiers and guards to be led by Minmissian officers."

"How about promoting half a dozen of your best Minmissian soldiers and guards to the rank of lieutenant, and then all promotions afterwards are on the basis of merit without regard to race?"

Alaric looked at Tessia. When she nodded, he said, "I can start tomorrow looking at possible candidates."

"And we have to do something about the poor quality of water in the city," Tessia said. "People are getting sick."

"Weren't you, Ena and Adamu planning to build an aqueduct from the mountains?" Alaric asked.

"Yes," I answered. "The plans are completed, but the construction was going to be conducted by Ena and Adamu." I suddenly felt sad again, thinking of the two talented young mages. With the challenges that lay before us, our city could have used their talents.

"I can assign a couple of platoons to help you with construction if you need them," Alaric said, glancing at Tessia who again nodded.

"Thank you, but I won't need a lot of men. A couple of competent engineers with construction experience would be helpful, though." I hadn't told Tessia yet that my magical powers had been increased tenfold by the Goddess. I needed to go off into the mountains and try out the new powers, and the construction of the aqueduct would be an interesting challenge. Once I had a sense of my new powers, then I would tell her.

"How long will this aqueduct take to build?" Tessia asked.

"Not long, just a few months," I answered. "The beauty of Adamu's design is that it takes advantage of the existing terrain. We just have to quarry and move enough rock to alter the water flow in a few places, so the spring water will flow down the slope of the mountain instead of disappearing underground. We can have fresh water flowing into the city by winter."

"And what's the next problem we need to solve, Mage?" Tessia asked.

"There are a lot of children in the city and the refugee camps who are not getting enough to eat. There's plenty of food available in the kingdom, but much of it goes to waste." I answered.

"A lot of food goes to waste?" Tessia asked.

"Yes, a lot of food goes to fatten pigs and chickens. Also, food rots in storage because people can't afford to buy it."

“People need to eat meat, though, don’t they?” Alaric asked.

“No, actually, speaking as the queen’s Healer-in-Chief, I have to say that people would be much healthier if they ate more fruits and vegetables and less meat, or no meat at all. I’m hoping that since the queen has now given up meat, her example will inspire her subjects to improve their diets. Farmers should move away from raising animals and start growing vegetables,” I said.

Alaric nodded his head, sensing there were changes coming to the kingdom in the ways people lived. I knew he would adapt easily, but I wondered what the reaction would be among most of the citizens… but these changes were necessary. We could no longer continue as we had.

Tessia looked at Kana, Femke and Idella standing in the orchard. They were talking softly and looking into each other’s faces intensely. “I know who should lead that initiative,” Tessia said.

“Kana?” I asked.

“All three of them – Kana, Idella and Femke. I feel sorry for any man who tries to stop them from feeding hungry children,” Tessia answered ruefully.

Kana suddenly turned and looked at us as if she’d heard Tessia, but the three women were too far away to have heard us unless, of course, they, like Tyrmiss, could hear the thoughts of people experiencing strong feelings. I’d learned it is a mistake to underestimate women who’ve grown into their wisdom. Crones have quiet powers men can only guess at.

The three women started walking toward us. I could tell from Idella’s face she was aware that Tessia, Alaric and I were making plans, and she wanted to be part of them. I knew my wife was a powerful idealistic woman who would emerge as a leader of reform in the city. Tessia and I would be counting on her.

This evening, Tessia and I would begin telling Idella and our friends everything that had happened during our quest.

Strumming my lyre, I would sing of the war between men and dragons, of the death of Ena, of Adamu's decision to stay in Hoclav City, and of the Blessed Isle where Zygmunt and Wessel were spending their final years. The whole story would come spilling out over the coming weeks. We'd tell our loved ones about visiting the underworld where Ena neither remembered us nor her previous life, but she was radiant and happy, and how Lord Death welcomed Tessia and me as his honored guests. We would describe the dining table where bloody cuts of meat from every person or animal we'd ever killed lay before us in horrible excess. I would recount my journey to the archipelago with Tyrmiss, and how my magical powers had increased, and how Tyrmiss had been given two dragon eggs that carried the potential to save her kind from extinction. But most importantly, I would tell my wise and beautiful wife what I had learned about the presence of the Goddess in our lives.

This orchard, this marriage, this life. *This* Blessed Isle.

The author would like to thank Kim Davis, Jacqui Davis, Liz Evans, Cat Smith, Benny Fife and Andrew Dunn for their brilliant and tireless attention to the publication of this novel.

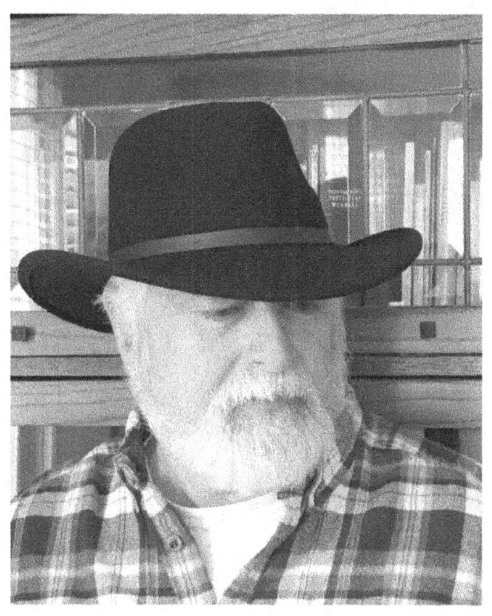

About the Author

Born and raised in Texas, Michael Simms has worked as a squire and armorer to a Hungarian fencing master, stable hand, gardener, forager, estate agent, college teacher, editor, publisher, technical writer, lexicographer, political organizer, and literary impresario. He is the author of seven collections of poetry and a textbook about poetry. In 2011 Simms was recognized by the Pennsylvania State Legislature for his contribution to the arts. Simms and his wife Eva live in the Pittsburgh neighborhood of Mount Washington overlooking the confluence of the Allegheny and Monongahela Rivers.

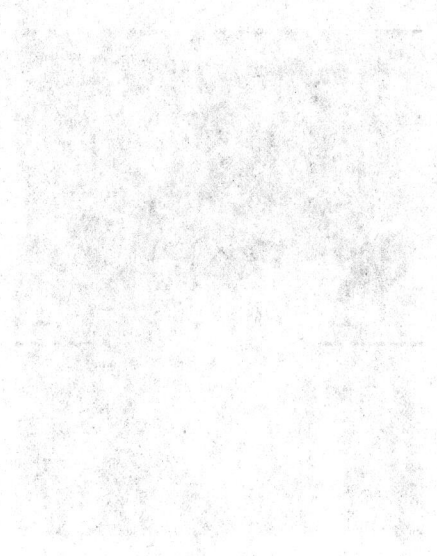

About the Author

[illegible]

www.ingramcontent.com/pod-product-compliance
Lightning Source LLC
Chambersburg PA
CBHW011644010726
47495CB00011B/2897

* 9 7 8 1 9 6 3 6 9 5 0 9 0 *